Heartward

"Whoooo. This one hits you right in the feels. Man."
—Love Bytes

"I really enjoyed this emotional and well written full length story."
—Long and Short Reviews

Pulling Strings

"I don't have any problem recommending Pulling Strings. It's a good, solid mystery/romance, and if that's up your alley, you should definitely pick this one up."
—Joyfully Jay

"I love it when a story can cause me to keep guessing until end and make it plausible at the same time. Very well done."
—Gay Book Reviews

Twice Baked

"This a great second chance romance novel... There is loads of charm and romance."
—MM Good Book Reviews

"A fun and flirty story I enjoyed and I believe you will, too."
—Bayou Book Junkie

By ANDREW GREY

Published by DREAMSPINNER PRESS
www.dreamspinnerpress.com

By Andrew Grey

Published by DREAMSPINNER PRESS
www.dreamspinnerpress.com

By ANDREW GREY

Published by DREAMSPINNER PRESS
www.dreamspinnerpress.com

andrew grey

Catch

of a Lifetime

REAMSPINNER
PRESS

Published by
DREAMSPINNER PRESS

5032 Capital Circle SW, Suite 2, PMB# 279,
Tallahassee, FL 32305-7886 USA
www.dreamspinnerpress.com

This is a work of fiction. Names, characters, places, and incidents either are the product of author imagination or are used fictitiously, and any resemblance to actual persons, living or dead, business establishments, events, or locales is entirely coincidental.

Catch of a Lifetime
© 2020 Andrew Grey

Cover Art
© 2020 Kanaxa
Cover content is for illustrative purposes only and any person depicted on the cover is a model.

Mass Market Paperback ISBN: 978-1-64108-223-5
Trade Paperback ISBN: 978-1-64405-663-9
Digital ISBN: 978-1-64405-662-2
Library of Congress Control Number: 2019953339
Mass Market Paperback published July 2020
v. 1.0

Printed in the United States of America
∞
This paper meets the requirements of
ANSI/NISO Z39.48-1992 (Permanence of Paper).

To Lynn for her story help, to Mike G for the fishing expertise, and to the tour boat captain off Longboat Key who inspired the story in the first place. And a special thank-you to Karen Rose and Mr. R for the amazing day that started it all.

Chapter 1

"Is THERE any news on the sneaker commercial?" Ryan asked as he strode into the tiny living room, closing his bedroom door behind him. "You were talking about it like it was a sure thing three days ago."

Robert Todd Reynolds—aka Arty—sighed softly. "I was, and I thought I had nailed it. Even Margaret thought I had a real chance." He pulled on his shoes for work and then checked himself in the mirror behind the single closet door. He and Ryan had to share a lot of things in this tiny place. It was little more than two rooms with a walk-in closet. Ryan, a working clothes designer, paid more of the rent than Arty, a currently out-of-work actor, so he slept in the bedroom while Arty used the converted closet, which barely held his bed. But with the prices of apartments in New York, it was all he could afford on the salary he brought in from his multiple day jobs.

"But they gave it to someone else?" Ryan asked, sitting down on the futon, which creaked under his weight. The piece of furniture had come with the fourth-floor walk-up apartment, and Ryan had reworked the cover. It sounded like Arty needed to tighten up the frame again. He hoped the thing held together for a little longer.

"Yeah." Arty shook his head. "Margaret messaged me that they decided to give it to a fresh face." He turned to the mirror once again. "I never realized that I had an old face." He pulled at his cheeks and neck as though he were giving himself a face-lift.

"You don't and you know it," Ryan told him. "That's just silly. You did those two commercials last year, and you've booked other jobs regularly. That's more than most other people do." Ryan sat back. "What we do is fucking hard to break into. You want to get noticed by agents, scouts, and producers.... Me, I'd be thrilled if I could get anyone to look at my fashion designs."

"But at least you're working in your industry," Arty said. In the back of his mind, the idea nagged at him that the limited success he'd had was all there would be, and that he was never going to truly make it. "And it's just a matter of time before someone notices the work you're doing. After all, you're a walking business card." That was another reason Ryan had the larger room—so he could have a place to sew and create. He made all his own clothes and was the best-dressed person Arty knew. He had even made a few things for Arty.

"And you will too. It takes time." Ryan was right and wrong at the same time. Ryan knew there were no guarantees in this business. Yes, Arty needed to put in his time and always give his best, but he'd been doing that for five years. And after the commercials, he thought he'd broken through, especially after two more had followed in fairly rapid succession.

"Well, time is the one thing I don't have right now. I need to get to work." Arty grabbed his coat out of the closet and closed the door. "I'll be home really late."

Ryan nodded. "I have a date with Kirk tonight, so I don't know how late I'll be or if I'll be home at all." He grinned, and Arty groaned. Ryan was so danged lucky when it came to guys. He had been dating Kirk for nearly six months, and they were getting pretty serious. Arty was a little jealous of him, especially after his own prolonged dry spell. His own relationships rarely lasted longer than a few weeks, and then he'd have to break a date because of a work schedule change at one of his jobs, or he'd have an audition. His schedule and time were rarely his own, and Arty was constantly juggling his priorities. Still, it was better than being a fisherman on Florida's Gulf Coast, like his dad.

"Be safe," Arty reminded him and hugged Ryan before putting on his long coat and hurrying out the door and down the stairs. Thankfully, he worked at Squires Steak House, just a block away from his building, so he didn't have to spend much time in the wind and snow. The only thing he didn't like about New York was the cold winters.

Growing up in Florida, he suffered from thin blood, as his mother would say, and the cold went right through him. New York summers were a walk in the park for him when everyone else was sweltering, but these frigid temperatures, and all the snow... they were almost more than he could stand. Arty pulled his coat closer around him as soon as he stepped out of the building, turning into the wind and sloshing through the slushy sidewalk with its hidden patches of ice that he knew were there, even if he couldn't see them.

He hurried on down the sidewalk as quickly as he dared, passing curtained apartment windows that spilled light out onto the street, adding to the glow that was the city after dark, so different from the dots of light and darkness over the water that he'd grown up with. New York was about as far as he could imagine from what had been his home for most of his life, up until the last four years. Still, the city was his home of choice now, and he was happy here.

"Hey, Arty," Clark said as he approached the other direction on his way home. "You'd better hurry or you're going to be late, and Monty is in a real mood. He's feeling particularly imperial tonight." He grinned, and Arty rolled his eyes.

"I'll hurry, and watch out for him." Arty waved and hustled on so he wouldn't be late. When Monty was in a bad mood, he could be as demanding as a drill sergeant. And since he was the person who managed all the servers and set up the various stations, Arty didn't want to get on his bad side. Arty burst through the side entrance and into the kitchen area of the restaurant, hung up his coat in the employee area, and checked that he was presentable. Then he clocked in and found Monty to start his shift.

It was a "run Arty off his feet" kind of night, or at least it seemed to be. Not that Arty didn't always work hard and do his best to stay on task, but tonight, things just seemed off for some reason. His usual efficiency wasn't in tune with his diners, and he ended up making a lot of extra trips. His phone vibrated in his pocket while he was at a table, but he ignored it, taking a customer order even as his heart beat a little faster in anticipation. His agent, Margaret, worked weird hours and caught up on phone calls at unexpected times, so he never knew when he'd get important news.

"Yes, ma'am, the beef is properly aged. It's the only way we prepare it," Arty answered the diner's question. The vibrating stopped, and he finished taking the order for his table, answering questions he'd been asked a million times and somehow finding patience. "Thank you," he said when they finally finished. Then he hurried to the server station to put the order in to the kitchen, then moved on to the prep area to arrange for their salads and bread.

He peered around him and hazarded a look at his phone. It wasn't a number he recognized, but the area code indicated it was from Florida, where his father still lived. Arty stepped into the kitchen and to the break area. If he was lucky, Monty wouldn't see him. He pressed the button to return the call and waited.

"Arty," a familiar voice answered, but he had trouble putting a name to it at first. "Thank goodness you called back. I was going to keep trying. Sorry, this is Evelyn Marshall."

His back straightened until he remembered he wasn't once again sitting at her piano, with her giving him instructions on the proper way to sit and approach the keys. "It's good to hear your voice. What can I help you with, ma'am?" Manners had been drilled into him by his mother before she passed away.

"I'm calling because of your father." She whispered now, and he knew the signal. He may not have been there, but she had some "secret" information to impart. "He fell on the boat the last time he was out. His boot got caught in one of the lines, and there was a goliath grouper on the other end. It went up and cut his leg pretty badly. Not only that, but he broke his other leg when he fell on the deck. The cut got infected." She fluttered and huffed for breath. Mrs. Marshall always did that when she got excited.

Arty waited, glancing around, knowing he had to get back out front. "I only have a few seconds. I'm at work right now."

"Oh, of course, dear," she breathed.

"I get a break in a few hours. Can I call you then or is that too late?" He was concerned about her, his dad, and the fact that he was going to get his ass handed to him if he didn't get back out to his tables.

"I'm old—we never sleep. Call as soon as you can." She hung up, and Arty put his phone back in his pocket and returned to the prep area, grabbed what he needed from the station, and headed out to his tables, double-time, serving salads and bread, refilling waters and drinks, and getting extra butter, salad dressing—everything his patrons needed.

Finally he got a few minutes and went in the back, sat down, and slipped off his shoes so his feet could breathe a minute. He should try to eat something, but instead, he called Mrs. Marshall's number, and once again she answered as though she'd just run a race.

"Arty, sweetheart," she said as soon as she picked up the phone. "Your father would hate me for saying anything, but I thought you needed to know."

"You said Dad got hurt?" Arty asked. His dad was tough as nails and came through everything just fine. He always had.

"Yes. And he hasn't been able to take the boat out. His crew has signed on to other boats because they need the work, and your father is sitting at home. I bring him food, so he isn't starving, but…." She paused, and the whisper started. "I was there and saw a letter from the bank. He tried to hide it, but this old biddy can read fast." She chuckled. "The loan on his boat is due, and…."

Arty closed his eyes and his head pounded. He was well aware of the perils of what his father did for a living. "Jesus, Dad," he groaned under his breath. Ruin was always just around the corner, waiting to snatch away everything a person had, just like that. "He'd never ask for help, even though everyone there would pitch in, if he asked." Arty's father was as stubborn as a mule and sometimes twice as thick.

She didn't argue. "Be that as it may, your dad needs you, and you know he'll never ask." "I'll call him as soon as I can."

"You can't, dear. They turned off his phone," she said. "He's in real trouble." While Mrs. Marshall might be dramatic, she wasn't prone to exaggeration. "You need to come down here and help him, Arty. You're the only one who can. He isn't letting the rest of us in. Please. I worry about him." She started to sniffle, and that caught Arty's attention.

"I'll see what I can do, I promise. I'll call you tomorrow." He had saved most of the money he had earned from his commercials and other small acting parts because his expenses were low enough that he was able to support himself on his other jobs. So maybe he could send his dad enough to get him through until he could get back to work.

"Just tell me when your plane gets in and I'll come meet you." She sniffed again, and Arty slipped on his shoes, getting ready to face more hungry diners. Mrs. Marshall was right. There was no way Arty could leave his father hanging out on the Gulf winds. He'd have to go home, whether he wanted to or not.

Chapter 2

IT TOOK a few days to arrange things and find a flight that wasn't going to cost him an arm and a leg, but before he knew it, he was stepping out of the Tampa airport and into January Florida sun. God, it felt good to be back in the warmth. Arty took a deep breath of the slightly salty air that told him he was home. He tried to push aside his nervousness about what he was going to do and find when he got to his father's place. He had sent his dad an email, but he doubted his father looked at it. Mrs. Marshall had promised to tell his father that he was coming, but Arty wasn't even sure of the reception he was going to get when he arrived, given that his father hadn't called himself. He and his father had never seen eye to eye, and there was no reason for that to have changed. He sent a message to Mrs. Marshall to let her know that he had arrived and did the same with Ryan.

His phone immediately rang. "You going to be okay?" Ryan asked. "You got out just in time. It started to snow an hour ago. God, I wish I could have gone with you."

"Me too." He didn't say anything about the fact that Ryan, with his fine clothes and cosmopolitan thinking, would be as out of place in his small fishing town as a red snapper at a chicken-eating contest. "I'm waiting for my ride, but I think they just showed up."

"Then call me later and let me know if it's as bad as you think and if there's anything I can do. I'm gonna miss you. I've gotten used to having you around." He and Ryan had always gotten along pretty well since they'd been sort of thrown together as roommates years ago. Over that time, they had become real and close friends.

"I'm going to miss you too. But I have to do this." Still, Arty wished he were back in the city, living the life he'd built for himself. Instead, he'd come home, and would likely be stepping back into the way things had been. Life here seemed backward, stuck in a time that had passed by everywhere else. Arty had wanted a future where he didn't have to spend his life and livelihood wondering whether the fish were biting. "I'll talk to you later," he said, pushing the End button on the phone as Mrs. Marshall pulled up in one of her pickup trucks. The Ford was huge and probably about five years old. Arty pulled open the passenger door and flipped open the side super cab door, hefting his luggage into the back. Then he closed it up and climbed inside.

"Thank you for doing this," Arty told Mrs. Marshall, pulling the passenger door closed. She nodded, then took off. They made their way out of the airport, heading south. Arty did his best not to grab the "oh shit" handle as Mrs. Marshall got on the freeway, but then she settled down and the ride got smoother. Thank God. "How is Dad?"

"The doctor is worried about the infection. He refused to take his pills at first, but I've gone over to make sure he gets them down. He growls at me, but at least he takes his medication now and the leg is showing signs of healing. The problem is that he won't stay still. He says he has to get to work, but he can't do that with the broken leg, and the wound on his leg can't heal if the infection doesn't clear up." She shook her head. "He needs to take it easy and rest, but he doesn't want to and keeps wheeling himself down to the docks. The break is bad enough that he can't walk yet, but…." She sped up, as though his father was going to get into trouble if she was gone too long.

"I don't know what I can do for him now that I'm here other than…." Arty's words trailed off as they crossed the Sunshine Skyway Bridge. The view always took his breath away, and as he turned to look out toward the Gulf, some part of his soul stirred slightly. It had been a long time since he'd seen the place that had been his home for the majority of his life.

Once across the bridge, Mrs. Marshall continued south, and after the bridges were behind them, she pulled off and into a parking lot, leaving the engine running. "Arty." Her usual casual joviality was gone in an instant.

"What aren't you telling me?" he asked.

"You have to do something for your father. He's
going to lose the boat, the house, everything. He has
enough debts that they'll take it all, including his IFQ—
the allocation that made up his fishing quota. When that
happens, there'll be no way for him to make a living.
You know that. He'll have nothing at all." She wiped
her eyes with the back of her hand. "And it's going to
be at least another six weeks before he's up and about
again."

"I see," Arty said softly. "Then I'd appreciate it if
you'd get me there quickly so I can talk to Dad and see
how bad things really are." Fishing, any kind of fishing,
was a hard job that paid very little. Arty had learned
that risk and reward usually went hand in hand—the
higher the risk, the greater the reward. Not in fishing.
The risks were huge and the rewards sucked. People
who fished did it because it was the only way of life
they knew, and most barely managed to make a living.

"Do you need to eat?" she asked as she put the
truck in gear.

"No, thanks. Since we're almost there, let me get
home so I can figure some things out." The sooner Arty
got to the bottom of what was happening and came up
with a plan, the sooner he could get back on a plane
home. This wasn't his life any longer. He'd worked
like hell, keeping two jobs most of the time and putting
himself in front of every casting agent he could with
only one goal in mind—never returning to the life he'd
left behind.

MRS. MARSHALL pulled up in front of the small
house he'd grown up in, the paint cracking in the Florida heat, but the yard was cared for the way it always

had been. Arty's mother had loved her garden, and his dad kept it up in her memory. "Thank you for everything," Arty said as he got out and pulled his bags out of the back. He reached across and took her hand. "I appreciate it."

"It's a pleasure, sweetheart. I'll bring over some dinner for the two of you tonight." She smiled and waved, and Arty closed the door, then turned toward the house and took a deep breath before going inside.

"Dad!"

He entered the kitchen. Nothing had changed. The old Formica table stood where it always had. The yellow-painted cabinets, now faded with age, were the color his mother had chosen. Arty could see into the small living room, the furniture the same, his dad's recliner, maybe a little more worn than it had been when he left, but still the same. The house was a time capsule.

"You came, huh, boy?" his dad said as he slowly wheeled himself in and went to the refrigerator to grab a beer. Arty would have expected to see his father using crutches, so the injury had to be worse than Arty had imagined. His dad set the beer on the table, then got another and handed it to Arty. As his dad took a gulp, Arty twisted off the top and tossed it in the trash, then took a seat. He looked at his dad, who had wheeled over to turn on the television and then settled himself in his chair, staring at the somewhat fuzzy picture on the screen.

Arty waited, wondering if his dad was going to say anything at all. Not that Arty was surprised; his dad never said a great deal to anyone. When Arty had been growing up, his dad had worked and was gone for weeks at a time on the boat. It had been Arty's mother who had done most of the job of raising him. He

finished his beer and put the bottle in the recycling before grabbing his bags and taking them to his room. After he'd unpacked, he went back out to the living room.
His dad hadn't moved, and Arty wasn't sure how to get
the information out of him that he needed. Experience
told him that his dad wasn't going to just open up. "I'm
going to go out and look around."

His dad nodded and continued watching television.
The nod may have been reflex and his dad could have
been asleep—Arty wasn't sure. But he left the house,
stepping out into the sunshine, walking toward the water a block and a half away.

The scent of salt water and fish tickled his nose
the closer he got to the docks. The White Pelican sat
at the edge of the docks where it had been since Arty's
first memory of the place, when his mom had brought
him there and told him to stay at the table in the corner while she worked her shift as a server. It hadn't
changed in all that time.

"Arty, how's your dad?" Milton asked from behind the bar. Arty went over, shaking his hand, and then
shrugged.

"Yeah, he's come in a few times, sits at one of the
tables with a beer and watches the water. Doesn't say
much," Milton said. The bartender used to help watch
him while his mother worked.

"Yup," Arty agreed. That was his dad. Never the
talker.

"Word is that he's in trouble," Milton added quietly and then offered a beer. Arty sighed and nodded,
thanking his friend.

"I don't know what to do," Arty said.

Milton leaned over the bar. "I wish I could tell you.
I know things aren't good. The run he was on when he

got hurt was cut way short because of his injury, so it was pretty much a total loss from what I heard." Milton heard just about everything that went on.

Arty nodded and turned to look out at the bay. He had grown up here and had fished the waters off the coast since he was old enough to bait the leaders. "Hopefully Dad will open up and I can figure out exactly where things stand."

"Don't count on it," Milton said and handed Arty a menu. Arty ordered the shrimp and settled on the stool. He and Milton talked about things as he served, and people Arty had known since childhood came up to say hello and tell him they hoped his dad got better real soon.

After he'd eaten and talked for a while, Arty walked back to the house. The television was off, and his dad was asleep in his recliner with his legs up, the wheelchair close at hand. Arty remained quiet and returned to his room. That had changed. It looked as if his dad was using it as an office of sorts—there was a small desk against the wall. The bed was the same one Arty had grown up sleeping in, and the curtains were the ones his mom had made. He pulled out the chair at the cluttered desk and started going through some of the papers.

What he found was ugly, really ugly. The bills were piling up, and his dad was in debt to the fishery to the tune of thousands of dollars. And Arty knew that in order to go out again, his dad would have to take on more debt.

Most fishermen lived close to the edge and needed what they made on an outing to make the bill. So they borrowed to outfit the boat—with fuel, food, and things for each trip—then paid it back when they returned, hopefully with their fish lockers nearly overflowing. He remembered that his father was usually at least five thousand dollars in debt at the start of a run.

The amount of money his father owed would wipe out at least one fishing run completely, and probably two, before his dad could even hope to make a dime to start in on the personal bills. This was pretty bad, and Arty knew it was only part of the picture. He had no idea if the mortgage was up to date. Mrs. Marshall had said the phone was shut off, so Arty got on his phone, gave them a credit card, and got the service reestablished. A few minutes after he hung up, the house phone rang, and his dad groaned and answered it.

"Boy, what did you do?" his dad called down the hall and then grew quiet. Arty didn't answer because it was pretty obvious. Leaving the bedroom, he found his dad still in his chair, now watching television.

"How bad is it, Dad?" he asked, cutting to the chase.

"Nothing I can't handle, boy," his dad grumbled. "You just do whatever it is you do. I'll be just fine once I can walk again. You ain't got to worry about nothin'." He lowered his legs and sat up. "I don't even know why you came. I been fine for years without you." He sat back, putting his feet up again.

"You can't walk, your leg is infected, they turned off your phone because you couldn't pay the bill…."

"I didn't want to talk into that damn thing anymore. They can take it for all I care." Of course, *that* was the one thing he chose to argue about.

"What about the boat? Who's looking after it? How are you going to go out with your leg like that?" Arty tried not to sound too demanding, but it was hard. Burying his head in the sand wasn't going to help anyone.

"Evelyn sure has a big mouth," his dad groused, half under his breath.

"Don't you say anything against Mrs. Marshall. She cares about you," Arty snapped back.

"Which is more than I can say about you." His dad groaned and sat up. "I'm going to go to bed for a while." He muscled himself toward his chair, and Arty tried to help him, but his dad batted him away. Once his dad was in his chair after nearly toppling it, he wheeled himself to his room and closed the door.

The house was quiet, and Arty didn't know what else to do. Outside, the sun had set. He was about to leave again when Mrs. Marshall knocked on the door. He opened it and let her inside.

"Where is Byron?" she asked, setting down a dish of pasta and sauce that any New Yorker would drool over. Mrs. Marshall was an amazing cook, and Arty's stomach rumbled.

"He was tired and went to lie down." Arty wasn't going to argue with his father, so he simply put the dish in the refrigerator. "I'll make sure he gets some when he gets up. Thank you."

She nodded and patted Arty on the shoulder. "You're a good boy for doing this." She smiled and stepped outside.

"Would you like something to drink?"

"No, sweetheart. I need to get back home, but thank you. You have a good night." She stepped out in the darkness, walking down the street toward her house. Arty watched her go, standing in the doorway, breathing sea air with a slight chill around the edge. He didn't quite know what to do and stepped outside.

A lone figure walked slowly down the street. Arty leaned against the house, watching the well-built young man as he ambled toward the water. He should simply look away and go back to figuring out what he was going to do, but he couldn't seem to look away. The man had wide shoulders and narrow hips, and when he passed under the streetlight, Arty got a good enough look that he almost whistled. Wavy brown hair, a butt encased in jeans that molded to him—this wasn't someone he'd ever seen around here before. The guy stopped and turned and looked both ways, facing Arty for only a few seconds. Their gazes met and a flutter of instant attraction bubbled in Arty's belly. He actually gasped at how strong it hit him. Arty watched the guy as he stopped and pulled something out of his pocket. It looked like a few bills, but he couldn't be sure. He counted, then folded them and put the bills back in his pocket. The man's shoulders rose and fell, and then he turned around, treating Arty to an amazing view of his chest and a glimpse of his young but beautiful face. *Wow, what is this guy doing here?* Arty blinked to make sure the man wasn't some sort of imagining his lonely mind had cooked up. But no, he was real and looking back at him.

Arty saw beautiful people all the time. It was part of the business he was in, but this guy went beyond that. Arty even thought of taking the few steps through the yard to talk to him. If nothing else, he could find out what a guy like him was doing here, maybe see why he seemed so intent on counting a few bills. Shrugging, Arty needed a second to screw up his courage, then took a step forward. A dull thud from inside the house drew his attention, and he peeked inside to see what it was. When Arty turned back, the guy had gone back the way he'd come, his shoulders a little hunched and his stride less sure. The vision in tight denim passed behind the hedge, and Arty lost sight of him.

Arty ended up wandering down to the docks and out to where his dad's boat sat bobbing in the surf. He climbed aboard and looked around. It needed some cleanup after the rains, but was otherwise in good shape. One thing his dad understood was that he needed to take good care of his equipment.

"Who's on board?" a rough, deep voice called.

"It's me, Reginald," Arty said as he turned around from the door to the pilothouse. "I was just checking on the boat for my father." Arty couldn't remember a time when he hadn't known Reginald. He and his father used to fish together before Reginald ostensibly retired a few years ago.

"Arty?" he said, his weathered face breaking into a grin. "Boy, it's so good to see you." Arty stepped forward and was engulfed in a hug, the kind that he might have wished to receive from his father, but knew better than to hope for. "It's been a while since I've seen you." He took a step back to look Arty over. "You look like you're doing good."

"Things are okay." Arty smiled. It was good to see the old family friend. "I did a few commercials and things when I was in New York. I like it there." Or at least he did most of the time.

"What are you doing here?"

Arty smiled as Reginald stepped back. "I'm here to see to Dad and…." He didn't want to talk about his father's business. But then, Reginald was sure to know what was going on. "I'm here to see how bad things are."

Reginald hesitated and then just seemed to come out with it. "They're bad. And I don't think he's going to make it this time. The last two trips out haven't been good. He had a run going and then got hurt, and you know it may be the twenty-first century, but we're still people of the sea and very suspicious. Your dad's crew has already moved on, and you can't blame them. They need to make a living, and they can't sitting on shore."

Arty knew that was true. "So what the hell do I do?" Arty stepped toward the dock. Reginald had been around long enough that Arty knew he could ask his advice and get something solid.

"Take the boat out and fish like the devil is after you."

"How in the hell can I do that?" Arty asked.

"You'll have to find a way to equip the boat. Your dad has a quota that he hasn't fulfilled, so go out and make a dent in it. There is the potential to help pay down the debt with a few good runs. If your dad was in this position and had fulfilled his quota, then he'd be done for. But as it is, there's still a chance to make it up. I'll come with you, and my son-in-law, Beck, might too. He fished before he got a job in Tampa. He's laid off this month and is looking to pick up some extra money. I'll see if he'll come. Then all we need is one more man."

"Why don't you take out the boat?" Arty asked.

"Because you're his son, you can use your father's quota. I can't, and we can't grouper fish without a quota."

Right. Arty had forgotten that. The IFQ was his father's most valuable asset, even more valuable than the boat. But it was attached to his father and not the boat. As his son, Arty could use his father's quota, but nobody else could. And it was the only way they might make enough money to save his dad.

"So, just find another man to go and then work on equipping the boat. We'll go out in two days. It will be tough, and you're going to have to find the money to equip the boat yourself because the fishery isn't going to loan you any money...." His voice trailed off as Arty's leg began to shake. He hadn't come down here to take his father's boat out and spend the entire time fishing. This was exactly why he had left in the first place. He hadn't wanted to spend his life near the bay putting lines in the water and praying that he actually caught something worthwhile.

"I'll have to think about it." And he had plenty to think about. He didn't know Beck and for a second wondered if he'd have a problem working with a gay man. Not that it mattered all that much. Arty needed to help his dad. That was what mattered.

"Of course," Reginald said. "Call me in the morning with your decision so I can make arrangements at home if you want me to go out with you." If Arty did decide to take the boat out, he couldn't think of anyone he'd rather have on his crew than Reginald. The older man patted Arty on the shoulder and stepped off the boat. Arty followed him, intending to walk down the dock and back to the house. Then he looked up to the night sky with its curtain of stars. Without thinking, Arty lay down on the dock, staring upward as the waves lapped at the shore and a lonely bell tolled softly in the distance. The sounds, and even the strong, pungent aroma of the fishery, were familiar. Arty was thankful for the breeze that kept the worst of the smell away. But regardless, all of it reminded him of New York, and he let it lull him into a sort of daze.

Arty sighed and continued staring, wishing the answers would come to him. His dad didn't want him here. He'd said so. And it would be so easy to turn around and go home. It was what Arty wanted to do... go back to New York and his life. But Arty couldn't leave his dad with the way things were. He banged the wood slats with his fist and clenched his teeth. Hell, he wanted to shout at the sky, but he didn't need to create a spectacle of himself.

"I figured I'd find you here," a female voice said, and Arty sat up.

"Rosie." He stood and smiled, coming to her, both of them falling into a deep hug. "It's so good to see you." He stepped back. "How are you?"

"I'm fine." She rubbed her prodigious belly. "Carter is about to bust a gut, he's so happy we're having a boy." She grinned and then it faded. "I stopped at the house, but it was dark and I figured your dad was resting. So I took a chance." He and Rosie had gone to high school together and hung out quite a bit when they were younger. He should have expected that he'd run into everyone sooner or later. It was a small community.

"You hungry?" Arty asked.

"Lord, I look like I swallowed a basketball. Of course I'm hungry," Rosie answered sarcastically, and Arty smiled. Some things never changed. And maybe that wasn't such a bad thing.

"Then let's go back to the house. I have Evelyn Marshall's pasta there." That was enough to entice just about anybody.

"Okay." She turned, and they slowly made their way back to the house. "I heard about your dad. It's pretty much all over town. What are you going to do?"

Arty had hoped for some time to ruminate on the options open to him. "Reginald says I should take Dad's boat out. He said he'd go with me, and his son-in-law might too." The thought had Arty's stomach in knots. "I haven't been out fishing in years, and I was never the captain. Dad was always in command, and I was only one of the hands. He made the decisions and knew what he was doing. What if I get out there and can't find any fish?" He sighed softly. "I want to help Dad, but what if I can't do it and end up making things worse?" Arty slowed his pace when he began to pull ahead. "Dad is the one who knows these waters."

"And so does Reginald. You know that. He knows almost as much as your father." Rosie took his hand, and they walked quietly for a little bit.

"I could write him a check to cover everything," he offered. "Not that Dad would take it."

Rosie stopped. "Do you have that kind of money?" She hummed. "Rich star that you are."

"It would take most of what I've saved." And it didn't look like there would be more of that kind of money coming in soon. Arty liked knowing the cash was there if he needed it. He hated living hand to mouth. Arty knew what that was like all too well. His dad and mom both worked hard and long to put food on the table. Hell, his mother had worked almost until the day she died. And they never seemed to get ahead. Even after all these years, his dad still pretty much lived on the edge. Arty had wanted more from his life. He wanted the chance to be more and have more. Arty wanted his version of the American dream, and he wasn't going to find it here.

"You could try, but your dad would never cash the check. He's too proud, and…." She turned to him. "He would never mortgage your future for his troubles. You dad is proud of you."

Arty scoffed. He certainly had never heard it.

"He is. It's clear when he talks about you." She tugged at his arm. "But be that as it may, you have to do what's best for you."

Arty wasn't sure if that was true. "I almost never saw my dad when I was growing up. He was out to sea or working in the fishery… or off somewhere. I barely know him." He swallowed hard. "I bet I've spent less than… I don't know, a week or so, all told, with him, in all those years, that wasn't working on a boat." The thing was that Arty was getting a pretty clear picture of what he should do. He just didn't want to do it. Spending days at sea was not his idea of fun. He sighed. "I spent my entire life trying to get away from this so I could have a chance at a different life. So I could maybe make something of myself that didn't leave me smelling like fish, or covered in a saltwater crust."

She nodded as they stood in the glow of one of the streetlights. "Life isn't fair."

"It sure as fuck isn't," Arty muttered. "I told Reginald that I'd think about it and tell him in the morning." He motioned her forward, and they continued to the house.

A light was on in the living room, and Arty held the door for Rosie. His father was on the phone and hung up as soon as Arty came inside. "Why'd you have that damn thing reconnected? The thing rang nonstop." He smacked the top of the table, and Arty could just imagine the kind of calls that were coming in.

Arty shared a knowing look with Rosie and did his best to ignore his father's frustration. "Come on. I'll heat up some of the pasta, and we can have something to eat." She sat at the table, and Arty got out the pasta, then filled some plates. "Dad, are you hungry?"

"No." Arty heard him mumbling and grousing, and then his chair rolled down the hall and into his room. The door closed with a bang, and Arty shook his head. He tried to understand what his dad was feeling about the situation he found himself in, then shivered, nearly dropping the plate before slipping it into the microwave. "I don't know what he expects." Rosie just looked at him, apparently at a loss as well. But one thing was clear—something needed to be done, or his father was going to find himself out in the warm Florida sun without a roof over his head.

Chapter 3

"ALL RIGHT, let's do it," Arty told Reginald the following morning. "This isn't the kind of thing I expected to be doing, but it looks like I don't have much choice." He sighed as they sat across from each other at one of the White Pelican's scarred tables, the real version of the restaurant's namesake perched a few feet away on the pilings. Reginald nodded. "I can get us outfitted," Arty added. "I have enough to get started, so at least we aren't going to need the processing plant to front the cost." Usually the processing plant would loan them the money to go out, with the stipulation that their catch be sold back to them. Arty suspected that often the fishermen didn't get the best price out of this arrangement, but he didn't have proof of that.

"Excellent, because there was no way they were going to do that." Reginald leaned over the table. "That also means you can sell your catch wherever you want." He glanced around, but no one was listening. "It can be riskier, but grouper prices have been real good, so maybe you can squeeze some extra cash out of the catch." There had always been an uneasy relationship between the fish processors and the fishermen. They needed each other, but the tension around price, and the fact that they tended to keep the fishermen on a leash by lending them the money to go out, chafed. It was the way things were done, but it didn't change the fact that a yoke was still a yoke.

And speak of the devil... Gerald Price, the grandson of the plant owner, strode up to where they were sitting, joining their table as though he had a right. He wore a light shirt and jacket, and acted as if he thought he was above everyone else. "I hear you're thinking of taking the boat out." Gerald turned to where Arty's dad's boat was moored. Arty didn't shift his gaze away from the weasel he remembered from high school. He'd hoped Gerald had grown up. It didn't look like it.

"That's the plan. I need to help Dad." Arty figured it was best if he didn't antagonize Gerald. But he wasn't going to back down either.

Gerald motioned toward the counter, and a cup of coffee was brought over and placed in front of him. Man, he was playing the king. The shit. "You know the plant can't loan you any more money." He sipped his coffee, the undertone that things were very dire sitting in the air like thick morning fog.

"I'm aware of that," Arty said. "It isn't an issue. The purpose of my trip is to get my family out of trouble, not in deeper." He held Gerald's gaze, staring until

Gerald broke eye contact. "I'd also like a detailed accounting of what Dad owes, and what for, so I can go over all of it."

Gerald stood quickly, nearly toppling his chair. "How dare you…," Gerald growled.

Arty stayed still even as Reginald shifted uncomfortably. Something was rotten in the state of Denmark, and Arty seemed to have pressed just the right buttons. "I just want to see what I'm dealing with. It's that simple." Only it wasn't and Arty knew it. Even as a kid, he had remembered asking his dad why their fuel cost more than at other places. But his dad had waved it away. Other supplies cost more, as well, but Arty had always been told to mind his own business. Now the company-store-type picture started coming into focus. But he needed to play it down. "Are you drinking too much coffee? You're jumpy."

Gerald cleared his throat and sat back down. "So, you're doing this on your own."

"Yup." He turned to Reginald, who went back to his breakfast. Arty did the same.

"You know very little changes around here," Gerald said softly, his gaze sweeping over the docks and even the restaurant, which were primarily on property his family owned. Gerald's own little fiefdom. Too bad it stank to high heaven most of the time.

"Tell me about it," Arty said, trying to add some lightness to his voice. "I suppose everyone still goes to the games on Friday night, sitting on those bleachers, watching the Manatees play." He grinned. "And mostly lose."

"Yeah. Things don't change much," Gerald said with a slight sneer and got to his feet once again. "Come to the office this afternoon and I'll have the papers you asked for."

"Thanks, Gerald. I appreciate it." Arty grinned. "And be sure to say hello to your mom for me. Tell her that maybe if I have a chance, I'll try to stop by." Gerald paled, just as Arty expected. He said nothing more, and Gerald stalked away with a little less cock-of-the-walk in his step. Gerald's mother was a grand lady, and they both knew that she wouldn't stand for any games or shady dealings. She was his kryptonite.

"Boy, what are you thinking, poking the bear like that?" Reginald grunted once Gerald was out of ear-shot. "We gotta sell our catch somewhere, and—"

Arty didn't look away. "He'll buy our catch… if we decide to sell to him." Arty turned his attention to his breakfast, his appetite suddenly returning. "I'll arrange for the supplies and get the boat stocked."

"I made a list of what I thought we would need," Reginald said absently. "And you'll need to get some notices up for our open position."

"Thanks." Arty took the list and shoved it into his pocket. "Listen, would you mind talking to Dad? Get his numbers and any information you think he'll share. You'll have a better shot at convincing the stubborn ass that this is for his own good. Dad guards that information as if it's gold. You're about the only man alive he'll trust with his treasured fishing spots."

"Won't he give them to you?" Reginald asked. "You're his son."

Arty shrugged. "Dad hasn't said more than two sentences to me since I got here, unless it's to yell about something." Arty wished, once again, that he and his father had developed a way to speak with one another. "It's his way." At least, that's the way it was with Arty.

"And what if he doesn't want to talk to me?" Reginald asked.

"Then I'll put myself in the line of fire." There was little else he could do.

JAMIE WAS about to give up. He had been looking for a job of some sort for days and was getting nowhere. Fear stabbed at him. If he didn't find something soon.... Failure was looking him right in the face. All he had wanted was a chance to try to build a life away from the farm and his father. And maybe find an ounce of independence. Instead, Jamie was down to his last few dollars and ounces of hope. He had been eating cheap noodles for days. His aunt was nice and probably would have given him some money if he'd asked for it, but Jamie didn't want to. Jamie's aunt barely had enough to take care of herself, and Jamie was determined to build his own life. Besides, his aunt would encourage him to go home. And returning home to his father and living the life his father wanted for him was the last thing he wanted to do. He'd be damned if he'd go crawling back to Iowa and live under his father's thumb. Jamie wanted to make his own way and have his own dreams, and they didn't include spending the rest of his life on his father's farm.

Jamie walked toward the dock and stopped when he saw a man—the one he'd seen watching him the other night—tack a piece of paper up on one of the telephone poles.

Wow, he was handsome in the daylight, with hair that shone in the sun and clothes a lot nicer than the ones Jamie was wearing. Jamie found himself heading over as the other man walked closer to the docks. He was stunning—sort of like the people you saw on television and wondered if they were real or not. This guy looked like one of those people. Tall, but not huge, and as his shape retreated, Jamie caught his wide shoulders and narrow waist.

Hurrying to see what the guy had posted, Jamie grabbed and read the flier. It was for a job, thank God. Maybe this was his chance! Jamie looked around and pulled down the paper, folded it, and put it in his pocket. Then he followed the man, telling himself he wanted to ask him about the job. But really, he just wanted to see him one more time.

Jamie had been to the White Pelican before and figured that was where the guy was heading. He put up another flier and continued on, walking around toward the front of the restaurant. Jamie checked the money in his pocket—he had enough for a hamburger. He'd been down to his last few dollars but had managed to get a day job spreading mulch for a lady down the street from his aunt, and she had been generous.

The tables were full, with only an empty stool at the tiny bar area. He sat down, looking over the people having lunch, their conversations overlapping one another, and watching as pelicans darted around, swooping over the water to land on the pilings.

"Gerald," the guy said in a rather sultry voice that sent a ripple through him. God, even his voice was stunning. "Is it okay if I put up a few fliers? I need a crew member." He leaned right next to Jamie, and as he inhaled, the scent of his subtle cologne, combined with manly musk, tickled the back of Jamie's nose.

"Sure, Arty, go ahead. I don't know how much luck you're going to have, but you're more than welcome."

He smiled and Jamie glanced around. As soon as he did, he found Arty looking back at him.

Jamie was a little stunned and stared back until he realized he was being rude and lowered his gaze.

"Arty," Gerald said, turning away. "Was there something else you wanted?" Gerald tapped the top of the bar. "I am a little busy here." There was no heat in his voice.

"Sorry. Thanks, I appreciate it." Arty moved away, and Jamie picked up a menu and watched him go from around the side.

"What can I get you?" Gerald asked him, and Jamie put in his order, wishing he'd had the courage to actually say something to Arty. But even now, he wasn't sure the guy could possibly be real.

ARTY SPENT the next day getting the supplies they needed and the boat ready to go. He found the GPS and backup GPS equipment along with the primary and backup bottom sonar. Both were essential systems, and the complete failure of either would leave them in the dark, so backups were essential. The boat was fueled and the water tanks filled. Arty also tested out all the boat's systems, including its ability to make ice—another point of failure that could spell doom and send them back to port. By the end of the day, Arty was exhausted, but he was on track to be finished the following day, when he'd talk to people about a fourth on their expedition.

Tired and nearly worn out, he returned to the house, where he was met by his father. "What do you think you're doing, boy?"

"I'm equipping the boat to take it out. You can't do it, and if we're going to eat, we have to work." He threw one of his father's sayings back at him. "Did Reginald talk to you?"

"Yes." The glare was enough to freeze water in an instant.

"Did you give him your numbers? We're going to need them." Those were the coordinates that his father used to place his lines. They were a distillation of his years of fishing and should get them in the ballpark of good locations.

"You should know better than that." He turned, gliding away. "What are you, dumb? You never give your numbers to nobody."

"Then give them to me. And I need you to sign this." Arty handed his father a sheet of paper. "It's authorization for me to use your IFQ." It would allow him, as a family member, to fish in his father's place.

His dad batted Arty's hand away. "What makes you think I'm going to let you go out on your own? You ain't been here in years, and you don't know nothing about being captain."

"Maybe. But I know enough. And I have to go out so you don't lose your house and the boat and everything else, you stubborn mule." Arty was his father's son, after all. Part of him came from the same damned animal.

"I ain't going to sign it." His dad wheeled himself down the hall.

"Then you're a fool. A complete and total fool. I have the boat stocked and loaded. All I need is one more man and I'll be ready to go." Arty strode down the hall.

"I didn't ask you to do none of it." His dad glared with all the angry fires of hell.

"Give it a rest. I'm doing this for you. A couple of runs and you'll be square again, your leg healed, and ready to go. You can go back to being the most pig-headed man in the state of Florida if you want. But you aren't going to get that chance if I don't take the boat out and catch some damn fish."

His father sat still, his hands clenching and un-clenching. "I don't ask for shit." He went into his room and closed the door. Arty sighed and opened the refrig-erator to get a beer. It was growing dark outside, and Arty stepped into the night air. He didn't know how he was going to convince his dad to give him the bearings he needed.

His phone rang, and he answered it. "You still alive?" Ryan asked.

"Yeah. I'm going to take the boat out, so I'm not going to have cell service for a while." Arty was deter-mined to do this, somehow. "I'll still be on land tomor-row, but after that I'll be leaving." At least that was the plan. "How is everything in New York?"

"Cold and snowy. We're all gearing up for a real blizzard tonight." Ryan even sounded cold.

Arty lifted his gaze to the night sky, taking note of the chill in the air. "It's really nice here."

"Bitch," Ryan teased. "You don't need to rub it in." He chuckled. "How are things otherwise? Do you have any idea how long you're going to be there? Is there any interesting eye candy?"

God, Ryan's mind went in a million directions at once. "Maybe a month. I'm hoping two fishing runs will get Dad off the precipice. By then he should be better, and I can come back." Arty wished it could be sooner, but it was what it was. "I still need one more man. And my dad is being stubborn about giving me the information I need."

"Why?" Ryan asked. "You're doing all this for him. If he doesn't want you there, then get on the next plane and come home. It may be frigid here, but we miss you."

"I think he's proud. Dad has never had to take help from anyone else before, and he certainly never wanted anything from me. But I can't do anything about it if he won't talk to me."

"You are two peas in a pod, then. You insist on taking care of everything yourself and feel it's some kind of personal failure when you can't." Ryan had this ability to see to the heart of things. "Imagine how it must be for a guy like your dad to feel helpless, because that's pretty much what he has to be feeling. You come in, and yeah, you're trying to help, but to him, it looks like you're taking over." Ryan sighed. "If I were to give you advice…. But I won't, because advice is like cheap toilet paper. It does no good and leaves you with crap on your hands."

"Thanks for that image," Arty groaned.

"Give your dad some time." Arty wasn't sure what that was going to get him. His father wasn't exactly known for changing his mind. If that was the case, then Arty needed to figure out another way.

"Now the important question, the eye candy? Everyone is so bundled up here. You have to give me something to keep me warm."

Arty laughed and it felt good. "It's winter here, so guys aren't exactly running around in bathing suits. But…."

"Oh, I love a good butt," Ryan teased, and Arty rolled his eyes.

"Very punny," Arty said with a slight smile. "Seriously, there is this guy I keep seeing around. First just walking, and then hanging around the dock today. Man…." That afternoon while he was loading supplies, he'd seen the guy from the other night, and in the light of day, he was even more good-looking. "He's muscular, not too tall, great eyes, and has this wavy hair."

"Have you taken him to watch the submarine races?" Ryan deadpanned.

"God. I've seen him around a few times. And he's gorgeous, with these eyes that seem to have… I don't know. It's hard to say what's going on." Arty stammered as the intensity, and maybe fear, in the guy's eyes filled Arty's mind. It was hard for him to let that haunted expression go. He kept pondering it. How a stranger he had only seen but never spoken to could get to him that way was beyond him.

"Dude…." Ryan drew out the word, and Arty knew exactly what he meant. It was weird that a guy who was a complete stranger could so completely get under his skin.

THE FOLLOWING morning, Arty got up and went into the kitchen to have something to drink before heading out to the White Pelican to see if anyone had answered his fliers. His father wasn't up yet. Arty wouldn't have even been sure he *had* come out of his room at all—if it hadn't been for the signed paper on the table giving him permission to use the IFQ, and a list of GPS coordinates. There was nothing else, and Arty wasn't going to try to figure out what had changed in his father's mind. Maybe he'd gotten drunk and written out what Arty wanted. Who knew? He took the pages and placed them in a file he needed to take on board.

He went down to his father's room, but the door was closed. Arty thought of knocking, but stopped, listening instead. He heard nothing at all. He sighed and turned away, heading out to take care of business.

Ten minutes later, Arty once again sat at the White Pelican, wearing sunglasses because the sky and water were so bright, the glare was nearly blinding. He had put up notices all over the area, and he hoped he'd caught someone's interest.

"Looks like you got a live one," Milton said, tilting his head toward a man who rolled and crushed a ball cap in his hand.

"You have to be kidding," Arty said. "That kid looks to be about twelve." He was exaggerating, of course, but he had to say something. This was the guy he had been seeing around for the past few days, the one he also kept seeing when he closed his eyes at night. Jesus. He wanted to fan himself—this was almost like a fantasy come to life. Arty licked his lips and took a second to calm down. He had a job to do, and that was where he needed to keep his attention, not on the hottie who was already on his way over.

"Maybe, but he's big enough to do the job." Milton stepped away and went over to speak to the man before leading him to the table. Arty had a few seconds to clear his head before standing and introducing himself.

"Jamie Wilson." The younger man held Arty's hand firmly and met his gaze. That, at least, said something about him, as did the way he didn't look away. Many people would have. "I saw your advertisement and I'm looking for work." His voice was as warm as melted butter.

"Have you ever worked on a boat before?" Arty asked.

"No. But I spent a lot of years shoveling shit out of barns and hauling everything you can think of on my dad's farm. I can do whatever work you need." He was obviously strong, and damned good to look at. Not that it mattered. Arty pushed that notion out of his mind. He wasn't here to make friends or meet people. He had a job to do that would help get his dad back on his feet, both literally and figuratively. Then he could go home. No detours.

"Is farming the only thing you've done?" Arty was curious, but figured if the guy had spent his life on the farm, he wasn't afraid of hard work, or smelling bad. That was one point in his favor.

"I guess. But I did just about everything on the farm—from planting, harvesting, and breeding the animals." Jamie blushed beet red, and Arty wondered how green and innocent this guy was. "That didn't sound right." A little additional color rose in his cheeks.

"Are you squeamish about cutting fish and baiting hooks? Because you'll be doing a lot of that," Arty said.

Jamie grinned. "Are you squeamish about birthing cows, horses, and pigs? I've seen them and had my hands inside a horse to help a foal." He cocked his eyebrows, and Arty was glad to see that the shy kid he'd thought had come to him was a misconception. Jamie may have been nervous, but he wasn't shy.

"Okay, then. You're obviously strong enough to be able to help us. We'll be out to sea for eight to fourteen days, and there will be four of us in close quarters. As pay, you'll get a 10 percent share of the proceeds of the catch. We work from sunup to sundown, with not much to do in between but prep, clean the boat, and sleep." Fishing was damned hard work.

"I understand" was all Jamie said.

"What else can you do?"

"I can fix any engine. I kept the tractor and cars running on the farm."

Arty nodded. This was almost too good to be true. "What are you doing here? You have skills that will put you in good stead a lot of places. Why this?"

Jamie shrugged. "I need the work and saw the ad." It was a simple answer, and Arty didn't need to know the man's life story to work with him. Still, the urgency and desperation in his voice called to him. He knew what it was like to be down to your last bit of luck. He'd been there once, and meeting Ryan, a stranger then, had been his salvation. Maybe he could pay that kindness forward and take a chance on Jamie. God, he hoped his gut was leading him in the right direction. He hoped it was his gut… and not the little head between his legs.

"Okay," Arty said. He wished he had time for some of the formalities. But it didn't look like there was anyone else on their way to come to his rescue. Thankfully, Reginald came in with Beck, and Arty introduced everyone to Jamie. They all settled at the table for breakfast, with Jamie and Beck talking easily, as if they were old friends. Reginald and Arty listened and shared a look. They needed the help, and experience or not, Jamie was the only one who had shown up, and he seemed more than capable. So, after filling their bellies, Reginald went over the way things worked so they were all in agreement, including everyone's share of the haul. Then they each signed the page that laid it all out so there would be no misunderstandings.

"Who sells the catch when we get back?" Jamie asked.

"That will be Arty's job as captain. And since we aren't borrowing money for this run, we can sell it wherever we get the best price," Reginald said, obviously tickled. Arty was pretty pleased about it as well.

"So, what's next?" Jamie asked eagerly. Arty liked his energy, even if he was a little unsure of his decision. Jamie seemed to have drive and was motivated. That could go a long way in the job ahead. But spending two weeks on a small boat wasn't the same as being on a farm with wide-open spaces. Granted, at sea there was plenty of space, but all of it was out of your immediate reach.

"Be here on the dock at 3:00 a.m. the day after tomorrow. I want to get loaded, then head out and be on the Gulf as quickly as we can. I got Dad's numbers, and I'll make a plan to get us there as fast as we can." Arty still needed to figure out the best way to go about making the spots that his dad used, and he figured he and Reginald would sit down and plan it out. "Tomorrow we'll firm everything up, and then we'll leave well before sunrise the next day. Be ready to work, and feel free to bring something special for food if you want."

"But no bananas," Reginald cautioned. "They're bad luck. And remember—we throw nothing overboard, so don't pack anything that is going to make huge amounts of trash, because we have to store it."

"Bananas are bad luck?" Jamie asked and then snickered. "Okay. No bananas." He leaned over the table. "But you should see what I can do with a banana. No splits, then." Beck and Reginald were already talking food, so they didn't seem to hear, but Arty nearly swallowed his tongue, wondering if Jamie even realized how that sounded. "What else?"

Arty got his mind out of the gutter and off Jamie's full lips and the twinkle of mischief in his eyes. "Nothing that I can think of."

Jamie nodded. "So, I have the job, like, officially?" he asked, hope springing into his expression.

"Well, you'll be part of the team, yes," Arty explained. "Look, you need to know. This isn't pay by the hour. If we don't find any fish, then none of us makes a dime." And the thought chilled him to the bone. "Fishing is risky; it always has been." He drummed his fingers on the table. "Sometimes I wonder why anyone does it at all."

"Because it's our life," Reginald supplied and turned toward the water. "I don't think I could imagine a life where I didn't spend part of it out there on the water in the sun and salt air." He sighed, and Arty followed his gaze. So did Jamie.

"What are we looking for?" Jamie asked.

Arty snickered. "I think the meaning of life is supposed to be out there somewhere. But I never found it." Not on the sea, or land, as far as that went. He turned to Jamie. "Maybe you will."

Reginald stood, and Beck did the same. "We'll be ready to shove off on time," Reginald said.

"Good. We can meet tomorrow to go over the route plan."

Reginald shook his head. "That isn't my expertise. Your father was always the one who had the gift for finding the fish. That was his real talent. You get whatever you can from him, and then we'll go from there." Reginald and Beck extended their hands, and Arty shook them. Then they left the restaurant, and Arty sat back down.

"You really want to do this?" he asked Jamie, and for the first time, saw doubt flash in his eyes.

"They seem like good people, and I asked around about you after I saw the flier." The corners of his lips turned upward. "They said you were doing this to help your dad. That this wasn't your life. Everyone talked about you as though you were a saint or something."

Arty scoffed. "Nope. God knows I'm no saint."

"Me either," Jamie said. "But I'd never do for my dad what you're doing for yours." His gaze shifted slightly, looking out over Arty's shoulder. "I need to make some money, and I want to see what it's like out there."

A notion occurred to Arty. "Have you ever been on a boat?" God, he should have asked that before. What if Jamie got seasick? Good Lord, just what he needed—a landlubber who spent the entire trip puking over the side.

"Yes. On Lake Michigan with my uncle a few times. But that's not the same as it is down here. I like being outdoors. I tried working in a restaurant for a while, but got stir-crazy always being inside. Hot or cold, even when it rains, it's best to be outside where you can see it coming." There was something so serious in Jamie's voice that it made Arty wonder just what he was saying. It was as if Jamie didn't have anyone to watch his back, and that maybe the threat was coming from close to home.

"Okay, then," Arty said, watching Jamie's faraway expression. There was more to this man than muscles and a baby face. There was pain behind those eyes, tinged with desperation, both of which Arty was well acquainted with.

"Is there anything else?" Jamie asked, and Arty shook his head. Jamie thanked him and stood to leave the covered seating area of the restaurant. Arty found he couldn't look away as Jamie strode across the parking area before disappearing behind a stand of palm trees.

Arty realized his heart beat faster and he was sweating under his T-shirt, though it wasn't that warm. Good God, those eyes were nearly as blue as the clear sky. He had a type, Arty knew that, and Jamie ticked every single one of the boxes. Of course, he had no idea if Jamie was gay or even interested, but that banana joke had sure as hell been suggestive. Arty finished his coffee. He needed to get his mind away from that subject and keep it on what was important. He was here to help his dad, not get involved with guys or form any ties. His life was back in New York, and once this little adventure was over, he was returning back to his life and career... such as they were.

"Something... or someone interesting?" Milton asked as he began clearing the table. When Arty lifted his gaze, Milton winked. "I've seen him around a few times, and he's a real nice guy. I think you did a good thing. And who knows? Sometimes nice guys do get rewarded."

Arty didn't quite know what to make of that, but he nodded and paid the bill. He had work to do, and he needed to get the last of what he needed from his father. Then he needed rest, because once they set sail, it was going to be all work. At least that was his intention. But his mind niggled him, and he knew that if he ignored the warning bells going off in his head, he could definitely have some fun with Jamie.

Chapter 4

IT WAS still very dark, with few people around, as Jamie walked down the street toward the docks, following the sounds of the water and boats. There was just enough light that he managed to miss the puddle of brackish water in front of him and make it to the dock with his shoes and bag dry. He followed Arty's voice to the boat. "Permission to come aboard?" he asked like they did in the movies, and Arty smiled. Jamie took his first steps onto the deck and into what he hoped would be the beginning of true independence.

"Come on and go below. Beck will show you your berth and where to stow your gear." Arty motioned, and Jamie surveyed what was going to be his home for the next two weeks. To say he was a *little* nervous would be a lie. Arty opened the hatch, and Jamie went below into the cabin area, which barely had enough room for him and Beck, let alone the others.

"I don't have a lot of space, as you can see, but put your things in here." Beck opened a hatch under one of the seat cushions, and Jamie put his bag inside. "Did you bring anything else?"

"Just this. I thought I'd contribute some food." Jamie held up the reusable grocery bag, and Beck got to putting things away.

"Almost everything in here performs double duty," Beck explained. "The table will fold down into a bed for me, and the storage bench with your stuff is your bed. The two up front will be for Dad and Arty."

Jamie looked around. "There's more room on the bench. Doesn't Reginald want it?" Jamie had learned to sleep just about anywhere. Not that he was particularly proud of that fact, because it made him seem desperate.

"You don't mind?" Beck asked. "We assigned them by lot, well, except for Arty. He's the captain, so that's his bed." Beck began moving around his bag and another, and soon Jamie's things were up front. Hopefully he had made a friend, or two.

"You ready?" Arty called down, and he and Beck answered that they were. Reginald cast off the lines, and Arty glided them out of the berth and onto the dark water. Jamie went on deck and sat off to the side.

"What do we do?" Jamie asked.

"My suggestion is that everyone rest. We're going to be hours going out to the first location. I have the wheel and the numbers." Everyone gathered as they passed under the bridge and moved into the open Gulf. Once out into open water, Arty opened up the engines, and Jamie sat on a bench under the protection of the cabin as they skimmed over the waves, leaving the lights of Longboat Key behind them.

Beck and Reginald were below, and Arty dimmed the lights, checking his screens. Jamie watched him. "What are the screens?"

"This one is a GPS. I plotted a course to our first location, and it's guiding me there. It's going to take three or four hours, providing we can find good bottom, which is what that does," Arty said, indicating the other instrument. "It's off right now because we don't need it at the moment." Arty yawned, and Jamie leaned back in the seat.

"Have you been doing this a long time?" He tried to stifle his own yawn and failed.

"I used to go out with my dad all the time, but for the last few years, I've been in New York. Dad got hurt and needed some help, so here I am." Arty didn't sound too thrilled and turned back to his instruments. "If you want to rest, I suggest you go below. Sometimes water will splash up, and you don't want to get wet. I have things here for a while, and we can't do much until daybreak."

Jamie thought about it, but sat back and closed his eyes, the rocking of the boat and the hum of the engine lulling him easily to sleep. When he woke, it was to near silence. The engines were much quieter, and Arty was nowhere to be seen. He blinked and sat upright, wondering if something was wrong. Arty came up from below and revved the engines once again. "We'll be at our first stop in about two hours. Go get something to eat if you want, and then Reginald will get you started and give you an orientation of what you can expect."

"Thanks." Jamie really hoped he did a good job. He had no doubt he would work hard. That had been drilled into him since he could walk. It was a matter of actually doing the work so others wouldn't need to pick up the slack.

"Don't worry, you'll be fine." Arty gave him a smile, and Jamie went below.

Beck had set out a cold breakfast with some bread, cheese, fruit, and meat. The amount was a little startling. "Eat plenty. You're going to work it off." Beck passed him a full plate, and he took a second one up top for Arty.

"Thanks." Arty dug right in, and Jamie sat in the other seat, facing forward, looking out through the front windows, seeing nothing but water sparkling in the sun.

"It's humbling and I suppose dangerous. My dad always said to respect the land and the animals. I suppose that goes out here too, for the sea." Jamie was just talking, probably because he was a little nervous.

"It does, indeed. The water, the fish, the equipment, all of it needs to be respected. The water will drown you, the fish can bite or cut you, the equipment can get tangled either in itself or in you. Out here, everything seems to be able to hurt you, and we can be many hours, or even days, away from shore. So yes, respect the water, but don't fear it. And if you need help, be sure to ask. We all have plenty of experience, and we've all been injured, so we know what to do."

Jamie sighed. "I know. I'd hate to be the reason this enterprise fails." God, he knew that feeling far too well. Maybe this wasn't such a good idea, but he was here and it was too late to turn back. All he could do now was make the very most of it. Jamie was no stranger to hard work, and he figured that any of his shortcomings could be rectified if he more than pulled his weight.

"You won't be. The only way we'll fail is if we don't find the fish, and that's on me." Arty patted the second device on his dashboard.

Jamie nodded and leaned closer. "Sounds like maybe we're both a little worried."

Arty turned to him with a nervous smile. "You can say that again." He turned back to his instruments, and Jamie returned to eating his breakfast. Arty ate when he had the chance, and when they were done, Jamie took the plates down to the kitchen and washed the dishes in the sink. Beck showed him where to put them away, and after he was finished, Jamie joined everyone on deck.

"We're about an hour out. Let's get the equipment set up, and then I'll start looking for some good bottom. I thought we would put in two lines, one on each side of the boat to start with. If the spot proves good, we can add buoy lines and then circle around to pick them up."

Jamie wasn't sure what Arty meant, but Reginald got him busy, helping him set up lines and then showing him how to cut bait. "Pieces about that big with skin. It helps keep the bait on the line. We're going to need plenty, but don't waste it." Reginald checked Jamie's work and then patted him on the shoulder. "That's real good. Just keep that up."

The lines were on large reels, like small winches with short poles. One was anchored to the back corner of the boat, and another was set up on the other side of the boat, partway up. Jamie figured that was to put as much space between them as possible.

"Mine looks good," Beck said.

"So does mine," Reginald agreed. "We have to be careful not to get them crossed or tangled." Jamie turned around just as a pair of gloves hit him in the chest.

"Wear those if you're working with the lines or hooks. The lines will cut your hands quicker than anything. And be careful of the hooks." There was no heat in Reginald's admonition. "As well, watch out for the fins. They can be like razors." Jamie washed his hands, put on the gloves, and went back to work, grateful to be in the center of the boat and under cover.

The guys worked as Arty maneuvered the boat in weird patterns. "Okay, let's get some lines down," Arty called. Reginald and Beck got to work on what they called a bandit, which seemed to be the oversized fishing reel.

"Grouper are deepwater fish. We'll bait the hooks, two to three on a leader for each line, give the fish a chance to react, and then haul up the line to check our luck," Beck explained, and he and Reginald began baiting the mounted reels and lowering them in the water. "These lines are on automatic sensors. It will keep the bait near the bottom and haul up the line automatically when a fish bites. We have two of them. The rest of the lines are done by hand."

"Damn, there's a lot to learn."

Arty came up behind him as the boat bobbed on the gentle waves. "You're going to do fine." He was so close that Jamie could feel the heat from his body. He may have shivered at the zing of attraction.

Jamie had developed pretty good instincts over the years, and judging by the way he had seen Arty looking at him a few times, even with his sunglasses on, he was pretty sure that Arty was gay too. But Beck and Reginald seemed like down-to-earth guys, and he had learned through bitter experience to be wary. "Thanks."

"We all have to do our part." One of the lines clicked, and the reel brought it up. "Snapper," Arty said when the fish appeared. Reginald got it out of the water, jabbed it with a syringe, and then in a quick movement, pulled the plunger and tossed the sizable fish back.

"Why'd he do that?" Jamie asked.

"We have to throw the snapper back, but if we didn't remove the air from their internal bladder first, they'd die. Respect the fish and do as little harm as possible. That same fish could be caught by someone like us during red snapper reason," Arty explained as Beck rebaited the line and sent it to the bottom, grabbed another, and brought it up.

The process was repeated until the lines went quiet, and then Reginald and Beck hauled them all up and Arty moved them to another location. The guys baited hooks and had them ready while they moved. They ate during the breaks and had lines in the water almost as soon as the boat stopped. Jamie kept an eye on the bait, making sure there was some ready at all times.

"Is it usually like this?" he asked. They had already brought up a number of fish and even a few sharks, but not a single grouper.

"Sometimes," Arty told him. "This can be a tough, shitty business," he complained and turned to the others. "Have you ever wondered why we even bother?" Man, Arty seemed down, and as the hours passed, they only caught two keep-size grouper, which they put on ice in one of the many cooler boxes built into the boat. Each cooler wasn't very big, but put together, it was pretty clear that they could hold a lot of fish.

"Let's move. This was a location Dad had as a maybe, but it feels like a bust." All the lines were pulled up and secured, and then Arty revved the engine and they were off.

"Kɪᴅ, ʏᴏᴜ have to be patient," Reginald told Arty, and Jamie did his best not to listen in. "I know it's hard."

"Yeah, but what if we don't find anything?" Arty asked.

"It's only the first day," Reginald explained, then patted Arty's shoulder, and went back to work.

Jamie felt the same anxiety. He hadn't been sure about what he'd expected, but it hadn't been catching fish after fish, only to have to throw them back. They seemed to get everything except what they were after, and he had signed on to try to make some money. At this rate, they were going to be out here until dooms-day and come back with just enough to make sure they all got nothing. Patience, he told himself. He needed to have patience. Nothing ever came easily to him. He'd have to work at it.

The breeze was cool off the water, and Jamie need-ed his jacket. He was going to have to figure out how to clean the fish guts off of it when he was done for the day, because it was covered. In the afternoon, the sun warmed things enough that he could take the jacket off, but as the sun began to set, he pulled his jacket on again.

"Well, guys, that's it for today," Arty said, calling an end to their first day. The lines were hauled in and stowed, and Beck showed Jamie how to clean the deck.

"We pump seawater for that. Don't use the fresh or we'll run out." He left Jamie to it, and he worked, trying to tamp down his disappointment. But what had he expected? For the fish to just jump into the boat?

"Some days are like this, and tomorrow will be better," Arty said. He went to the back and tossed the anchor into the water, then cut the engines. "The bat-teries are well charged and will hold us for the night. We just have to be careful of usage. They'll recharge tomorrow."

"What's the weather look like?" Reginald asked once everyone was below.

"It's supposed to be cloudy tomorrow, with the chance of showers, but the winds are supposed to remain light, which will keep us riding smoothly. We can fish in the rain and fog. Who knows? Maybe it will change our luck." Arty slid into the seat, and Beck set to making a simple but hearty dinner of warm sandwiches and half a gallon of pasta salad that he pulled out of a cooler.

AFTER EATING more than he thought possible, Jamie wandered up onto the deck. The running lights were on, and a small amount of light leaked out from the cabin, but otherwise it was pitch-black, and the sky was lit with a billion stars. "I used to go out at night away from the farm and watch these same stars," he said as Arty closed the cabin door. Jamie sat on one of the benches and then lay down, looking upward.

"Me too. I've seen these stars many times from out here." The water lapped the side of the boat, the sound incredibly soothing.

"You came with your dad, right?" Jamie asked.

"Yeah. Dad was always happiest when he was on the water. I used to go out with him when I was out of school." Arty sighed.

"Was it something special the two of you did?" Jamie asked, more than curious about Arty, though a little nervous because of the way his belly kept fluttering when they were together. Jamie wasn't quite sure how to handle it. He reminded himself that this was a job and that he needed to keep his head and thoughts where they belonged. He didn't want to get into trouble.

"Oh God, no. Being out here with my father was sheer hell. I could never do anything right, and he worked me harder than he worked anyone else because I was his son. I came with him the first time when I was fourteen, and I baited hooks all day and then had to make dinner and clean up. The other men played cards after dark, but once I was done with the dishes, Dad had me clean the deck. He never let up over the years. Once, I was so tired, I fell asleep right where you are now. Dad woke me with a bucket of water." The touch of ice in Arty's voice was unmistakable.

"Why? You were a kid." Jamie was aghast.

"Yeah, well, Dad had decided he wanted me to toughen up. I was sixteen when that happened and woke up sputtering. He had no good reason to do it, because I had finished my work. But what the hell could I do? He was my dad and the captain. I wish now that I had stood up to him. That was probably what he was trying to get me to do. But I went back to work. I don't know to this day what he was thinking. Dad never talks about very much, and it's always a matter of looking at the clues and trying to figure out what he means."

At least Jamie never had that problem. "My dad yells. No doubt about what he's feeling. I lived at home and wanted to eat, so I worked. There wasn't a lot to do with any spare time. I asked Dad for a horse, but he wasn't going to have any 'hayburners' on his farm." Jamie smiled. "When I was sixteen, I was working after school and on weekends. I told my dad that I should be paid for what I did, and you'd have thought I'd crapped in his best shoes." Jamie remembered that day very clearly. "So I went on strike. I had a friend, and I arranged to stay at his house for a few weeks. I had some money, so I was able to pay my own way. His mom and dad were supportive."

Arty chuckled softly. "Wow. What happened?"

"Dad came over, demanding that I come home or he was going to call the police. My friend's mom told him that was fine with her. She'd wait until the police got there, and then she'd explain to them that I would be in danger if I went back there." Jamie grinned in the darkness. "She was a little over five feet, and my dad is about six-three. She stared him down and said that as long as he thought his children were indentured servants, then he was in violation of the law, and that I deserved to be protected. So she was going to do it, since he wouldn't." Jamie laughed outright. "That was one of the few times I ever saw my dad bested."

"Damn…," Arty breathed. "Did he come around?"

"Yeah, he did. He paid me so much every week for what I worked after that. I had to buy my own clothes and things, but in the end, we were all better off." Jamie turned his head to the side, but couldn't see very much more than an outline in the darkness.

"My dad paid me for my work," Arty said. "He never stiffed me that way. I got a share of the haul from each trip I went on, just like any of the other hands. That wasn't the issue. My dad and I were out here like this, all the time, and still I know nothing about him. I've talked to you more tonight than I did with my dad on all those trips combined." The boat rocked on a larger wave, settling into the trough, and the motion dissipated. "My mom died when I was thirteen, and that made for some very lonely teenage years. Friends told me that he changed after she died. I think that's true."

Jamie could understand grief, especially for someone so close. But he still shouldn't have ignored his son. That made little sense to him. But then, after his own father's behavior, nothing should surprise him at all.

"Morning is going to come very early, and we should get some rest." Arty got up, stretching. "I have to be up first because I'm going to try to move us before it gets light so we can have as much of the day to fish as possible." Arty said good night, and Jamie followed him into the cabin. He got out his kit and did a quick cleanup. Then he felt his way into his bed and closed his eyes, barely hearing Beck and Reginald snoring, though he was acutely cognizant of the fact that Arty was just a foot or so away. And that only added to the heat that was already building in the cabin.

IT WAS still dark when Jamie woke. The boat rocked vigorously from side to side. He somehow found his legs by holding the side of the cabin until he could locate his kit. Jamie washed a pill down with a glass of water and then headed topside and found Arty already about.

The sea had grown rough, and there was almost nothing he could see beyond what was visible in the running lights. "What a difference a day makes," Arty said as Jamie climbed on deck. "Go ahead and pull up the anchor. I want to get the engines started so we can move. That will dissipate some of the bobbing-cork feeling, and we can go to the next location."

Jamie hooked up the anchor line, tugging the heavy weight upward and then into its place. Arty pressed the button to start the engine, and it churned, but didn't turn over. Arty tried again, and Jamie turned to where he sat in his seat. He tried yet again, and the engines rolled and sent up black smoke out of the back of the boat before fully roaring to life. Jamie released the breath he'd been holding as Arty turned them around and started the boat forward.

"Are the others still in bed?" Jamie asked.

"Yes. And it's going to be a rough day." Spray shot up onto the front windows, so Arty started the wipers. "Go below if you like and sleep for another hour or two. There isn't going to be anything worth seeing, and you might as well rest while you can. If the others are up, tell them the same thing. I hope to be able to start fishing at dawn. Let's hope our luck improves even though the weather hasn't." He turned away, and Jamie did as he was told, watching as more spray hit the windows.

The random movement of the boat had settled, but the noise of the water rushing by the hull was something else. Beck and Reginald were stirring, and Jamie relayed Arty's message and then climbed back into bed, closing his eyes and trying to go back to sleep. But it wasn't going to happen. There was too much noise with the water slapping the hull right outside where he lay. He got back up, going past the others, who were both asleep. He went back topside and sat on one of the coverings in the center of the boat. Someone had made a pad for it, and with the fresh air and roll of the boat, he closed his eyes and dozed off.

He had meant to keep Arty company, but he must have needed the rest. It was daylight when he cracked his eyes open again, the clouds reaching the water at the horizon, which was much nearer than it had been the day before. "I'm sorry. I came back up to keep you company." Jamie rubbed his eyes, and Beck came up from below with crackers, cheese, and sausage, and set them on the small table under the cabin roof.

Jamie ate tentatively, unsure how the movement was going to affect his belly, but his appetite kicked in and he ate more heartily after a few bites. "Another half hour or so," Arty said, and Jamie finished eating, then got to work, so that by the time they were on-site, lines were ready to be baited and dropped. They went through the same process as the day before, made more difficult because of the rocking boat and the drift.

"Don't tangle the lines," Reginald told Beck. Somehow Arty seemed to find an area that looked good to him, and as soon as they stopped, they dropped the lines.

"Jamie, take that one," Reginald called as he hauled in a line.

Jamie hurried over and started reeling. The fish was putting up one hell of a fight, and one of the automatic reels clicked and started hauling in as well. "Well, look at this," he said with a grin, hauling a dark-colored fish out of the water. Beck raced over and got the hook out of its mouth.

"Damn, kid, that's got to be a forty-pound black grouper. Well done." He slid it into the box along with some ice. "Bait your hook and get the line down again." He hurried back and took another grouper off the line, put it in the box, and sent the baited line back down.

"We've hit the mother lode," Reginald said as he added another fish to the box. Already they had caught more grouper today than they had the entire day yesterday.

"Cut some more bait. We're going to need it," Reginald said as he hauled up yet another line, while Beck did the same. It seemed a little surreal as fish after fish emerged from the depths.

"Shark," Beck called, and Reginald hurried over with a small club. He stunned it, and they got the hook out before dropping it back in the water. The work was smooth—lines came up, grouper were taken off and either placed in the box or, if they were too small, had their bladders emptied and then were dropped back in the water. Snapper and other species were returned as well. This went on for what seemed like hours of frantic activity, and then it got quiet.

"Pull them up. I'm going to move," Arty called, and Jamie helped reel in the lines. The others rebaited any hooks that needed it as Arty moved the boat, and Jamie cut the bait. "Okay, I've got her steady—drop the lines."

They did, and fish hit immediately once again. "This must be a grouper hot spot," Jamie said.

"The bottom is perfect—limestone with plenty of areas to hide. And if you look over the side, there are tons of little fish, even at the surface. It must be teeming with feeders down there."

"Jesus," Beck called. "I've got a monster." The automatic reel he was using strained as it worked to bring in the line. Jamie wanted to go over and look, but one of the lines on his side hit, and he started to draw it in. Another beautiful black grouper came out, and he got it off the line the way Beck had shown him and into the locker, then added more ice just as Beck and Reginald whistled.

Three hooks on the line held fish, and damned if two of them didn't have amazing grouper. The third was a red snapper. Reginald got each off the line and iced down, then treated the snapper and put it back into the water.

Lunch was sandwiches, eaten quickly because the fish continued to favor them. Even Jamie, with his limited experience, knew that you made the most of good fortune when you got it.

"This box is full," Reginald declared as he added a thick layer of ice on top. "We'll start the second one and leave this closed. Don't open it except to add more ice each day, and it will be good until we get back to port."

"I wish we had full refrigeration," Arty said, but then shrugged. "Well, the faster we fill them all, the quicker we go back." He turned back to the wheel, and the three of them returned to the lines, hoping their luck held.

AFTER TWO more locations, not to mention a number of repositionings, Jamie was exhausted. His arms ached from the repetitive movements, but they had filled a second cooler box and had started a third. Arty, Reginald, and Beck were all thrilled and damned near celebrating by the time the light faded away and they were once again in darkness. The waves had thankfully diminished throughout the day, and now that night had fallen, the water was nearly calm once again.

"What's the plan for tomorrow?" Jamie asked as they sat around the table, Beck frying up a filleted fish that they had caught. It was simple and delicious, and they all tucked in. "Do we stay here?"

"No. We've taken a lot from this location, so we need to move on and let the fish move back in," Reginald explained. "Just like on land, the fish we took will create a gap that will get filled in by the surrounding areas, and the smaller fish will have a chance now at the food so they can get bigger. This is a good location and one we can come back to, but we need to give it a little time." Reginald lifted his gaze, and Arty nodded.

"I have the next location all planned, and it's only half an hour away." That meant that, hopefully, they could all sleep in. There were already bags under Arty's eyes, and Jamie worried that he was overdoing it. After dinner, Arty drank a beer and went topside for a few minutes, then returned and pulled the curtain to their bunk area. "I'll see you all in the morning."

Beck got a deck of cards and put out all the lights except the one at the table, then shuffled and dealt himself a game of solitaire. Jamie went into his things for a book and sat quietly reading. There wasn't a great deal to do other than be quiet. Reginald left the cabin to go up on deck, but returned a short while later, reporting that it had started to rain.

"I pulled all of the cushions and things into the cabin so they would stay dry, and battened everything down. We should be fine as long as it doesn't get too windy. Mostly it looks like a good rain, and the water is draining out of the boat the way it should." He closed the cabin door most of the way.

"Is this how things usually go?" Jamie asked, setting his book down.

"Yes and no. Most of the time, we would drink some and talk, maybe play cards or cribbage during the night. But Arty is getting up early so we have more fishing time, and that means we need to be quiet when he goes to bed early. If it wasn't raining, we'd play up on deck." Reginald grabbed the cards when Beck was done and dealt a hand for each of them, then pulled out a cribbage board. The two of them played in near silence, and Jamie returned to his reading, glancing at the curtain every now and again before finally closing the book and climbing into his bed.

The soft sound of card playing receded, and Jamie lay in bed as the boat rocked slowly back and forth.

"Not sleepy?" Arty asked really quietly, and Jamie rolled onto his side and found Arty looking at him.

"I should be," Jamie answered as Arty breathed deeply. It was warm, so they both lay in T-shirts and shorts on top of the covers. Jamie had hoped that with the sun going down, it would cool off, but he supposed they were fighting humidity more than anything else.

A breath of air reached them, filled with the scent of the ocean. One of the guys had probably opened the cabin door, because more fresh air washed over him. "Are you doing okay?"

"Yes." Jamie had heard of people going a little stir-crazy in the confined space, but he was all right. "I suppose it will get different in a few days."

"It always does," Arty explained. "Just keep your spirits up as best you can." He caught and held Jamie's gaze. God, Arty had amazing eyes and a long, sleek body. Jamie couldn't help wondering what it would be like to run his hands over him, to have free rein to explore. His skin grew warmer even as the cabin cooled a little. He licked his lips, and Arty did the same, sending the temperature even higher. Jamie stretched, his arms hanging over the edge of the bed, and Arty's fingers slid lightly along his palm.

The touch sent a ripple of excitement running through him, and Jamie lifted his head, not daring to move, in case something happened to break the spell he was under. Only a curtain separated them from the other two men, and he swallowed the moan that threatened, yet he couldn't pull away from the simple touch. Arty slid his fingers over Jamie's, and he wriggled them in return. He didn't dare move closer because he wasn't sure what would happen if he did. There was nothing they could do in the confined space with the others outside.

Jamie was on fire, his body in overdrive, and he didn't really know why. His belly fluttered, and he grew hotter by the second, even as the fresh air cooled the cabin. Finally, as the others moved through the cabin, Arty slowly pulled his hand back. The single light switched off, and everyone settled in to sleep.

Jamie watched Arty watch him for a while in their own private cocoon and he wished these moments would last, but then his eyelids grew heavy and he closed them, as the work and effort of the day caught up to him. Oh, but his dreams….

Chapter 5

THE CHILL from the night really settled over the entire boat. Arty slid out of bed as quietly as he could and dressed in the small triangle of space made by the beds and the curtain. Jamie was still asleep, his face relaxed in rest, and it was all Arty could do not to lean forward and taste his lips. He shook his head at the notion. A tingle-inducing touch in the darkness did not give him the right to something like that.

He pulled on warmer clothes and left the cabin. He grabbed a bottle of water from the cooler on deck and checked everything topside. The rain had continued for a while, and everything exposed was wet. Water had collected in a few spots, but starting the engine and getting the boat moving would force it all back and out of the boat.

He sipped the water and climbed into his captain's chair, chilled by the wind. "Okay, baby, now I need you to start and not give me trouble like you did yesterday." He made sure everything was set and then pressed the button. The engine rolled, but didn't start. Arty groaned and tried again. It turned over this time and rumbled before catching fully. Damn, he hated going through this every morning.

Arty was instantly aware of Jamie behind him, and a bubble of warmth built where he stood as Jamie came closer and stood next to his chair. "It's cold this morning."

Not that he felt the chill at the moment. Arty turned on the radio to the AM marine channel and got the forecast. "Cold, cloudy with patches of rain for much of the eastern Gulf."

"Looks like it's going to be a fun one today," Arty groused a little. "There's rain gear under that seat." Arty pointed. "You may as well get it out. We're going to need it at some point." He let Jamie get to work and went in back, pulling up the anchor. Then he returned to the cabin and got the boat moving forward.

"What do we do on a day like this?" Jamie asked.

"The same as any other day." Arty turned on the lights in the back in a feeble attempt to stave off the growing gloom. "We work pretty much whatever the weather is. Hopefully this won't last too much longer, and we can get into some sunny weather again. Still, it's going to be chilly." He yawned, and Jamie approached with the gear. Arty took his, and Jamie laid out the rest of the gear for the other guys.

"Will the weather affect the fishing?" Jamie asked.

"No. The grouper are deep enough that the weather up here has no effect, unless it's a hurricane or something strong enough to disrupt the water so far down." Arty pulled on the raincoat over his clothes and felt better. The chill was starting to get deeper into him.

"Arty... I...." Jamie drew closer, and Arty turned to meet his gaze. The intensity Arty found there threatened to bore a hole into him. Jamie placed a hand on his shoulder, and Arty leaned into the touch. It had been some time since he'd felt the gentle, caring caress of someone else, and he longed for it. He was afraid to move in case it ended and he was alone with his thoughts and worries once again. "Is this...?" Jamie asked but pulled away. Arty immediately missed the heat.

"God," Beck mumbled, and Jamie turned away, walking toward the back of the boat. Arty turned forward, looking out at nothing but water ahead. He needed a few minutes to clear his head and to think about something, anything other than Jamie. Sometimes other boats would appear on the horizon, and he prayed for something else to look at, something that would allow him to clear his head and think about anything other than Jamie. But no other vessel came close to them. So he found his thoughts constantly gravitating toward Jamie. He wanted this, but on a small boat with no privacy, it was out of the question. He needed to remember what he was here for.

"Dolphins," Jamie called, and Arty turned to look as a pod jumped and ran in their wake. He smiled as they skimmed along for a while.

"That's good luck," Beck said, and Arty smiled and nodded. He wasn't sure of that, but sometimes you could make your own luck, if you believed in it. Beck wandered back toward Jamie, and Arty wished he could go back as well, to watch the dolphins play. Hell, he was tempted to ask Beck to steer the boat so he could stand in the back with Jamie, maybe put his arm around him and just watch for a while.

Instead, he called out, "We should be ready in fifteen or twenty minutes."

"Reginald is getting the food together." Beck came over. "I don't think he's feeling very well. The cold is getting to him and he's stiff this morning." Arty nodded and didn't say anything more. Even he was feeling the cold. "He says he'll be okay in a little while. He just needs to warm up and get moving."

Beck got to work, and Jamie approached to peer out through the windows. "I think I'm plenty warm this morning," he whispered, and Arty shared a grin with him.

"Go get the bait ready." God, who knew that Jamie could be such a tease? Not that he minded. The last thing he'd expected on this trip was for Jamie to show interest in him. Arty glanced at Beck, who curled his upper lip for a second and then went back to getting the rods ready. For some reason, Arty hadn't pegged Beck as intolerant, but then again, he didn't know him that well. Still, it sent a chill up his back, and Arty remembered that on a boat this small, there was no room for discord. Everyone had to pull their weight and do their jobs, or they would all fail. Arty took a deep breath, reminding himself that he was the captain and needed to be the leader…. And that didn't include being interested in one of the men on his team.

Reginald came on deck with food. Arty ate while he maneuvered the boat and got them to their destination. "Let's get our lines in the water as quickly as we can." The weather really sucked, and the only thing that was going to improve the day was catching some fish and making progress on their goals, so they could all go back home.

"This has to be better than New York," Reginald said as he finished baiting one of the lines and got it in the water. "I don't know if I could stand snow."

"It took some getting used to," Arty said, glancing at Jamie and trying not to look like he was watching him too much. "The wind will go right through you sometimes."

"I hated New York. Everyone there was in such a hurry and they were rude—pushing, shoving, trying to get ahead of everyone else." Beck lowered his lines, barely turning back to the others.

"It was different. But I had some success there. I did some commercials and started to build a life." Arty liked New York. It was his kind of place.

Jamie gasped and then laughed. "Oh my God, that's where I've seen you before. You're the 'smooth as a baby's bottom' guy." Jamie grinned, and Arty rolled his eyes.

"Yes, that was one of the commercials I did. I'd hoped they'd want to do a follow-up, because it was really popular." Arty had kept his hopes up for the last year, but nothing had come of it. The ad had been great and ran for months. The razor company said it was their best campaign, but there had been nothing afterward. At least, not for him.

"Yeah, it was, and you looked really good. Did you guys see it?" Jamie asked as one of the lines clicked, and Beck hurried over, took off the fish, slid it into the box, and added ice. Then Jamie stood in the center of the boat, a wicked expression on his face, and pantomimed through the commercial, hitting each line spot-on and sending a wave of heat rushing through him. Damn, Arty was glad that Jamie hadn't shown up at the auditions—he'd probably have swiped the job out from under him.

"I think I might have. I don't tend to remember that sort of thing." Beck stiffened, and Arty kept the boat on spot, watching to make sure the others were safe. He didn't like the sneer in Beck's voice, but what could he do about it? Intolerance was something that took everyone by surprise at some time.

"Beck, watch your lines," Reginald snapped, and Beck paid attention to what he was supposed to be doing.

It started to rain as they moved to a new location. Arty found what appeared to be some real interesting bottom, and they got lines in the water as it started to pour. They all pulled their coats closer, heads down against the rain, and kept working. Arty was at least under cover, but the rain continued to build, coming down harder and harder. Arty was about to call it when Reginald and Beck brought in their lines at nearly the same time, each holding a huge, beautiful grouper. Jamie was under cover as well, rebaiting the hooks, and they dropped the lines, reeling in more.

The fish continued biting, so they kept fishing for the next half hour until the lines grew quiet. "That's enough. We're going to move, and everyone needs to get out of the rain," Arty called.

Jamie put the bait away and cleaned up the area in record time. Reginald got the lines brought up on his side, and Beck worked the other. "Holy shit," Beck called as the reel raced out. He locked the reel, but the automatic stop broke and the reel continued to spin. Beck held the reel, stopping the line, and slowly reeled it in. Arty watched, holding the boat steady. It was obvious that this was no grouper.

"Crap," Beck called, and Reginald raced over to help. The deck was wet, soaked from the rain, and Reginald didn't stop. He slid right into the side of the boat and tumbled overboard.

"Cut the line!" Arty cried, and Jamie grabbed the bait knife and snapped the fishing line. "Throw the ring. I'll bring the boat around." Beck tossed the ring from overhead into the water, pulling on the line.

"He's too heavy," Beck called, and Arty brought the boat in as tight a circle as he could. "He's got the ring," Beck added. "That's it, just a little to port. Perfect. He's right alongside." Arty cut the engine and hurried back, lowered the ladder, and helped Beck bring Reginald to it. The older man tossed up his raincoat and slowly tried to get out of the water.

"He can't climb out," Beck called. Jamie stopped at the cabin door and yanked off his boots, raincoat, and rain pants, his shirt hitting the deck as he dove into the water. Arty's level of anxiety spiked as soon as Jamie disappeared over the side. His entire body itched to help, but he had to keep the boat steady.

"Just hold on," Jamie yelled above the roar of the rain as the sky opened. One after the other, boots *thunk*ed up onto the deck, and then Reginald appeared over the back of the boat. He climbed onto the deck, and Beck got Reginald into the pilot area and out of the rain. Damn, Jamie was impressive. Arty was proud of how Jamie had taken action. Maybe he didn't have a right to feel that way, but he did anyway. Jamie was proving to be one hell of a man… and that was exciting and attractive as anything.

Wet clothes formed a pile, and once they were off, Beck got Reginald wrapped in a blanket and helped him down into the cabin. Jamie came up behind, gathering his sodden clothes, his jeans plastered to his body, water sluicing over him. He really did look like a drowned rat.

"Get your wet things off and go below to get dry and warm." Arty held the boat steady, and Beck returned to the deck. "How is he?"

"Wiped out. I have him resting and I'm going to get him fed." Beck pulled on his rain gear and went to the back, brought in the gear, and stowed it away. He got some ice to add to the lockers. "I guess that's pretty much it for the day."

"Unless the weather breaks."

"Do you want me to drop the anchor?" Beck seemed to look everywhere but at him. What did Beck think was going on? Whatever it was, Arty hated the distrust that was building, but he didn't know how to nip it in the bud without making it worse. Not that there was actually any reason for it in the first place.

"Yeah. The waves aren't too bad. It's just the rain. We'll hold here for a while and see if we can wait out this mess. Thank you."

Beck dropped the anchor, and Arty set the engines to idle. That would continue to provide power, but use a minimum of fuel. With that set and everything as closed up as they could get, Arty followed Beck down into the cabin. Reginald was in bed under the covers, drinking from a thermal mug. Jamie had changed and sat at the table reading, and Beck had gotten out of his wet gear.

"I shook out everything I could, and I'll hang the gear up on deck as soon as it stops pouring."

"Thanks." The entire place smelled like salt water, and there was little to take away the dampness. What they needed was for the rain to stop and the sun to come out. "Jamie, that was quick thinking."

Jamie sneezed and grabbed a tissue. "Man, that water was cold."

"I bet it was." Arty sat down across from him, and Beck handed him a mug of coffee. "You acted fast."

"The boots and rain gear were weighing me down," Reginald said. "I couldn't get them off."

"I'm glad everything turned out in the end," Jamie said, and Arty turned to Beck, who was busy making sandwiches and heating up some soup. That was what they all really needed—something hot in their bellies.

When it was done, Beck filled thermal mugs and passed them out. The tomato soup was canned, but the warmth hit the perfect spot. "We need to be more careful."

"Yes," Reginald said. "I feel like an idiot."

"No. I should have called it because of the weather before then. The deck was wet and slick, with the rain making it worse all the time." Arty sighed and drank some more, his heart rate finally returning to normal.

"None of us wanted to. We were catching fish, and when they're biting, we don't stop," Beck said as he sat down.

"What was that on the line?" Jamie asked.

"A goliath grouper. It's rare, but making a come-back, and they're protected. We couldn't have kept it, but it had to weigh a couple hundred pounds." He grew quiet, and Arty finished the soup and ate a sandwich before heading topside to see what was happening.

The rain had let up somewhat, but the clouds reached all the way to the water, and the fog threatened to surround them. Arty checked that the running lights were on and turned on others so they could be seen.

"This isn't something I expected," Jamie said as he stepped up on deck.

"Are you warmed up? That water will chill you to the bone." Arty checked over the deck as well as the engines.

"Yes, I'm fine. I'm dry and warm, if a little tired." Water slid down the front and side windows of the pilot enclosure. At least it wasn't raining quite as hard now.

"The radar shows that we should be coming out of the worst of it. Hopefully this weather will move on so that we can all dry out a little."

"Should we be fishing?" Jamie asked. "They aren't going to jump into the boat."

"No, they're not. But I think we can pick up where we left off in the morning. The weather will hopefully have improved by then." Arty sat in his seat, swiveling it around so he was looking back. A few moments of quiet with Jamie were just what he needed after all the excitement. "I never expected to be here once again. When I left for New York, I thought I had left this life behind."

"I bet you can't wait to get back." Jamie smiled with genuine warmth. "I hear it's pretty amazing."

"I like it. There's an energy there that seems to run through the entire city. Here, it feels quiet, almost sleepy." Arty sighed. "I'm not saying it's a bad thing, just different. Here I can breathe and think, maybe take a rest. There, it's like everyone is trying to catch you, so you have to run as fast as you can, all the time." Arty shook his head. "I suppose they both have their place."

"I think I'd like to go to New York. I want to be on the stage there." Jamie leaned against the dashboard. "I went to the theater in Iowa when I was a kid, and I always wanted to be one of those people. In high school, I tried out for the plays, but my dad would keep me too busy to rehearse. So I lied and said I had to stay after school and did it anyway. I played Will in *Oklahoma!* and I even learned to dance." He did a few steps and sang a little. Arty didn't want to laugh, but it struck him as funny. Not that Jamie could sing and dance— because he definitely could—but that he was doing it on a boat in the middle of the Gulf. "I was really good. But my favorite part was playing Stanley in *A Streetcar Named Desire*. It was so intense, and I lived that part for weeks." The fire in Jamie's eyes was something Arty could get used to. "That was in the winter, and Dad didn't mind as much."

"Why'd you come here?"

Jamie shrugged. "I had an aunt who lives in Sarasota, and I wrote and asked if I could stay. She was my mom's sister and a really good person. I bought the tickets and told my dad goodbye. That I wanted something different." He turned away, looking out into the rain, avoiding the drips off the roof. "I was done with school and wanted something more. I hoped I'd find it there. But I didn't. My aunt has three kids of her own, but she let me stay in the room over the garage. It's small, but nice. But I didn't realize that I'd be so far away from everything, and it's been hard to find a job."

"I suppose it has."

"And without a car, I couldn't go very far…." He continued looking out into the rain, and Arty could pretty much guess the rest. Jamie had seen his flier and jumped at it. "I need to work so I can support myself. Aunt Livvy and Uncle Max are good people, and they wouldn't leave me out in the cold or anything. But my dad wants me to come back to the farm. He doesn't get that I don't want to spend my life farming. I hated it. And it wasn't as if I could afford to go to college on my own…." As if someone turned off a spigot, the rain let up and reduced quickly to drips and drizzle.

Arty knew that same feeling. Even if he'd had the grades to go to college, he would never have been able to afford it either. Still, with his early theater work, he had gotten quite a number of lessons—not only in acting and being onstage, but also in running the business side of things. Those lessons had paid off in ways Arty never would have imagined. His experiences had helped him develop the discipline to save in good times for when it rained cats and dogs.

"I know my aunt and uncle are trying to help, but after this, I don't know what I'm going to do for money…." There was a lot left unsaid, and Jamie's voice tinged with worry.

They still had to catch plenty in order to get into profit territory for this run. Granted, Arty was prepared to walk away from what he'd put into equipping the boat just so he could help make his dad whole again. And he wanted the guys to make some money. They deserved it, with the way they were working. He sighed and closed his eyes, praying to the god of fish, and the fools who tried to catch them, that this trip actually worked out.

Arty was about to tell everyone to come topside to start getting things ready when the rain picked up again. It looked like the rest of the day was going to be a washout.

"I left for many of the same reasons as you. I wanted something different. But I guess I never imagined anyone would be running to this particular life."

He smiled, and thankfully Jamie turned, nodding himself. "You sort of stepped out of the frying pan and into the fire."

"I guess so. When Aunt Livvy said she lived near Sarasota, I thought it was closer to the city. I figured I could get around pretty easy and find a job. Instead...." He shrugged. "Well, I think that's enough. I don't like dumping my crap on other people. I'll figure something out." He scratched his head. Arty certainly hoped he'd be okay. "I'm going to check on Beck and Reginald." Jamie went down into the cabin, but came right back up.

"They're both asleep." He closed the cabin door.

Arty couldn't blame them. On trips like this, it was best to rest while you could, and there wasn't a great deal to pass the time anyway. Jamie sat down next to him under the protection of the cabin roof. "I have to ask, does your family know...?" He cleared his throat as though he wasn't sure how to ask the rest of his question.

"You mean that I'm gay? Yeah. Dad knows because I told him, but we never talk about it. Dad doesn't talk about anything really. We're a good Catholic family, and nothing unpleasant exists if you don't talk about it." Arty rolled his eyes. "At least that's how it is between the two of us. Does your family know?"

Jamie shook his head. "Dad would have two fits and a hemorrhage. He'd probably send me to one of those places that are supposed to fix me or something. Aunt Livvy knows. She and my dad never got along. Dad says that she's a bleeding-heart liberal, and Aunt Livvy calls my dad a stubborn old goat who wouldn't know his butt from a hole in the ground." He flashed a brilliant smile. "I wish I could talk to him about stuff like that, but it isn't possible. That was part of the reason I had to leave. If I wanted to ever be able to be myself, I had to get away."

"I understand." There was so much in Jamie that Arty could identify with. "I'm glad you came to live with your aunt." And he was glad Jamie had answered his ad. "I'm happy for a lot of things." He held Jamie's gaze with his own.

"Me too," Jamie whispered and drew closer as though they were attached by an invisible string. A gust of wind blew across the deck and into the pilot enclosure, but Arty barely felt it as Jamie drew nearer. Heat rose around him, and it felt almost like the sun had come out and the day was brightening. Jamie took a step nearer, closing the distance between them until he was right there, near enough to touch and for Arty to take him in his arms.

Arty hesitated for a second. He and Jamie were on a boat in the Gulf with nowhere to go and absolutely no privacy. Still, Jamie closed the distance between them, their lips meeting in a heated, if somewhat awkward kiss, sending a sizzle of excitement racing up Arty's spine. A heated, if somewhat tentative, kiss, and Jamie pulled back, blushing completely red.

"Have you kissed someone before?" Arty thought of making a snide comment about goats or something, but this wasn't the time.

"Was it that bad?" Jamie asked, the light dimming in his eyes.

"No." Arty tilted his head slightly to the side. "But I bet you're a fast learner." Jamie drew close once again, and damned if Jamie didn't prove that he was a quick study indeed. His arms slid around Arty's neck, and he pressed closer, deepening the kiss. Arty wound his arms around Jamie's waist, pulling him between his knees, drawing their chests together as he took charge of the kiss, demonstrating what he liked, and Jamie followed suit immediately.

"Arty," Beck called, and Jamie backed away, rubbing his lips guiltily, and Arty got his mind back where it should be. He had to stop himself from growling. The precious quiet moments alone with Jamie were starting to be very important to him, and he resented the interruption, even though he had no right to. "Do you think there's any chance this is going to let up?" Beck asked. He gazed at both of them, and Arty met his eyes full-on, not backing down, even when Beck's lip curled a little. He stepped slightly to the side so Jamie would be behind him and out of Beck's direct line of vision.

Arty swallowed and got his attention back on the weather rather than Jamie's sweet lips. "The marine forecast keeps calling for this to end, but it doesn't look like it." He moved off to the side. "The radar showed an end, but now it looks like more rain has built in behind, so I think we're going to be in this for a while. At least it seems to be lightening up." He turned to Beck. "What are you thinking?"

"There isn't electrical activity, just rain. We could put on our gear and give it a shot. Sitting around here isn't doing us any good." Beck climbed up on deck, joining them under cover.

"How is Reginald?" Arty asked.

"He's getting up and wanted me to come talk to you. I think he feels a little ridiculous about what happened." Beck looked out over the water. "God, this is depressing. But we aren't making any money standing here." Beck reached for his gear and pulled it on. Arty got out some extra for Jamie, and the two of them got a few lines in the water. Arty found what looked like a good spot, and after an hour, the rain finally stopped. The guys took off their wet gear and hung it up, and Arty found his attention divided between his instruments and Jamie. Though whenever he looked at Beck, it seemed the guy was looking back. Arty needed to figure out how to deal with the distraction that was his young and hot crew member before it got the better of him.

Chapter 6

"THAT BOX is full," Beck said after four more days. Once the weather finally broke, the sun came out and stayed out. Jamie's hands were sore, his back ached, and his legs were like mush when he collapsed into bed at night. They had had quite a bit of luck, and with only one more box to go, it looked like their outing was going to be a success… and come to an end toward the earlier part of the estimate. Jamie was both sad and excited. He didn't know what returning to port was going to mean for things between Arty and him.

The two of them had had no time to themselves except when they fell into bed at night, and even then, with the others only separated by a curtain, it meant there had been no privacy at all. The issue was only exacerbated by the fact that Beck seemed to watch him and Arty like a hawk. Jamie had gotten so much side-eye over the past week that he wondered if Beck was part owl. It gave him the creeps a little, but he did his best to ignore it. He and Arty hadn't done anything wrong, and if the guy had issues, then they were his and no one else's. Besides, all he and Arty had been able to do was steal a few kisses. It was supremely frustrating. But those few moments when they had been alone were magical just because everything except Arty seemed to slip away for a few seconds. Under normal circumstances Jamie would have taken things in hand, but even that was denied to him in such close quarters. So desire and heat only built and grew to the point that his imagination took off at a moment's notice.

"Find us some fish," Beck called to Arty. So far, the day had been incredibly slow, and everyone was getting antsy. Jamie was ready to set foot back on dry land, and they had already passed the farthest point in their plan and had been heading back toward port.

"I'm trying." Arty was glued to one of his instruments. "I'm not sure why Dad gave me this location. The bottom seems to be nothing but sand, and that means there aren't going to be any fish." He was growing frustrated, and Jamie wanted to go over and soothe him, but didn't dare. Instead, he busied himself cleaning up some of the work area. He'd already cut bait, and the lines were ready. It was matter of Arty finding what he was looking for.

A whistle rose from the pilothouse, and Arty continued forward. "Drop the anchor, right here," he called back. Jamie put it in the water. "Let the boat settle and then drop the lines. There's a rock ridge down there that's pretty tall. Must be some sort of old upthrust."

The lines went down and came back up almost immediately. There were fish indeed—lots of them. The first were snapper, which Jamie took off the lines, took care of, then put back in the water. And then the grouper bit. Jamie baited hooks and filled the box with ice.

"Wow," Jamie called.

"I guess Dad really knew what he was doing. Makes me understand a little more about him, because this is like fish gold," Arty said, joining them and adding a few more lines as they fished nonstop. It was like they were afraid to quit. No one ate, and Jamie passed out drinks when he got far enough ahead. After an hour, they pulled up the anchor, moving slowly, and then dropped their lines again.

"The box is almost full," Jamie said as Beck hauled in the biggest grouper of the trip. It must have weighed close to a hundred pounds. They got the beast off the hook, and Beck held it up while Arty took pictures. Then they all took turns posing together with the fish before Beck put it in the box, and they covered it with ice. To be safe, the other boxes were all topped off, and then the anchor called for. It was an amazing end to their trip.

Jamie pulled up the anchor, and Arty hit the throttle, sending them skittering over the waves in a final push for home. "Do we have enough ice made?" Arty asked.

"Yes. The boxes are full to the brim, and the earliest of the six is still super cold. But we need to get back to keep everything as fresh as possible," Reginald said as a sort of warning.

"I'm on it." Arty turned away, and Jamie went into cleanup mode while the others stowed all the gear. There was a sense of expectant jubilation as they made their trip back. The fish boxes were full, thankfully shaded, and packed with ice. Everything was looking good.

JAMIE WENT below to get out of the sun and glare for a little while now that the gear was cleaned and stowed. Their trip had been a success, and all they had to do was get back to port and unload their cargo. The hum of the engines formed a comforting backdrop until it was gone, and silence reigned as Jamie lay in his berth. Something was wrong.

He threw his legs over the side of the bed, pulled on his shoes, and climbed on deck.

"I don't know what's wrong. I heard something that didn't sound right and turned them off," he heard Beck say. Arty hurried back, pulling up the engine cover. Jamie joined them all as heat rose out of the chamber in a wave.

"We need to let it cool before we touch anything," Reginald offered. "Do you think it was overheating?"

Jamie took a look, but didn't see anything obvious. Arty pulled out a tool kit and set it on the deck while the boat bobbed in the waves. He leaned over, looking down into the massive black engine, trying to see what was amiss. "Did the power fall off? What sort of sound did you hear?" he asked Beck.

"I'm not sure. It just didn't sound right, and the boat was dropping speed. I...," Beck said, and Arty sat back out of his way. "Dad and I have worked on engines together sometimes, but mechanics aren't my strong suit."

"I've spent—" Jamie was about to volunteer, but Beck grabbed the tool kit, sitting down on the deck so he could get closer.

"It's probably the turbo charger. Maybe it's gotten clogged or come loose." He leaned closer, but Jamie was already shaking his head. He doubted that was the issue.

"It could be the—"

"Let me check it," Beck plowed on after shooting Jamie a dirty look. Clearly he thought he was the guy in charge, at least for now.

"I don't think so," Jamie said, this time a little more loudly, and Beck looked ready for a fight. Jamie ignored him. "The connection is there, and it looks secure." He pointed, and Arty and Reginald both nodded. "We should look for the most obvious causes and work back from there."

"Jamie, you take charge of trying to fix it."

"Him!" Beck howled. "What does he know about marine engines?" Beck slammed the tool kit on the deck.

"There's no need to fight." Arty's voice was strained, and Jamie figured it might be best if he backed off. "We're almost a day from port. If we don't get this running, then the Coast Guard is going to take that long to get here and even longer to pull us back. There won't be any fresh ice in that entire period because we have only battery power, and that isn't going to last that fucking long. We'll have a hold full of spoiled catch, a fine from the state, and nothing to show for all our work. So back off, work together, and get the engine running."

Jamie had never heard Arty speak that way. He was usually so easygoing. But flames nearly shot from his eyes, and he and Beck held this staring contest that Beck was certain to lose. Arty approached, and finally Beck lowered his gaze.

Jamie wasn't sure he wanted to say anything at all, but then Arty turned his gaze to him. "Let's check that the engine is getting enough fuel to rule that out, and then we can go from there."

"You do whatever you want," Beck growled and stalked away. Jamie sighed and lay on his belly on the deck to get a closer look. He checked the fuel lines, but they didn't seem to be the source of the trouble. Then he pulled off the air filter housing and opened the top.

The smell that came out was enough to knock him over. The inside was encased in salt and dirt. What a mess. "Is there an extra filter?" Jamie asked.

Arty went below and shook his head when he returned.

"Okay." Jamie pulled the filter out of the housing, got a plastic bag, and knocked off the debris that he could onto the plastic. "The engine was probably starved for air and reached a critical point." There was canned air in the toolbox, and he sprayed it over the filter, sending a cloud of dirt and dust into the air. Reginald took the housing and worked to clean it while Jamie did what he could for the filter.

"That can't be it," Beck groused.

"Most of the time it's the simplest cause." Jamie finished with the filter and put the cleaned housing back on the engine. He made sure everything was right and then stepped back. "Try starting it." He hoped to hell that was the only issue and that the thing actually started. It had been giving Arty troubles, but a clogged filter and restricted airflow would do that.

Arty went to the pilot area. Seconds later the engine turned over and roared to life. "That sounds a lot better. I'm going to increase speed slowly and see what happens." They began moving closer to home and to the end of the journey.

Jamie put the toolbox away and glanced at Arty, hoping for some sort of indication as to what was going to happen next. Beck seemed to watch both of them intently, so Jamie simply went about his tasks and continued to wonder.

JAMIE LAY in bed, staring at the roof of the cabin just above him, wondering if Arty intended to stop, but the engines continued their drone, and he figured he should try to get some sleep. Once they arrived, there was going to be plenty of work. He closed his eyes, but couldn't sleep.

Beck and Reginald were in their bunks, snoring in stereo. Jamie slipped out of his bunk and wandered through the cabin, opening the door and climbing on deck, where Arty sat at the controls. He closed the door and joined him, feeling bold, like this was his last chance to make his wishes truly known.

He stood behind Arty, winding his arms around his waist, making the most of the time they had alone. "How much longer do we have?" That question had so much meaning for him. "This was a good trip… with a few exceptions."

"Yeah, and it's too bad that one of those exceptions had eagle eyes and can't mind his own damned business." Arty sighed. "But beggars can't be choosers, and we got through this trip in pretty good stead."

"Will you be going back to New York?" Jamie asked.

"Eventually, yes. I don't plan to stay here, but I can't let my dad flounder. Why?" Arty turned with a half smile in the single light from overhead.

"I don't know. I was wondering if I could go to New York with you. I don't want to stay here, and maybe I could get some work there. I'd like the city, I think, but it would be easier if I knew people there." Jamie also liked the idea of being around Arty and getting to know him better. They had just met, and he didn't want them to go their separate ways when Arty returned. The fishing trip had been hard work. On a boat in the middle of the Gulf of Mexico was the last place he'd expected to find someone who made his heart beat faster with just a look or a furtive touch.

Arty chuckled. "Of course you can come. I'd be happy to introduce you to some people there. I have friends, and you said you wanted to try your hand at acting." Arty's smile brightened. "You have a great look, and I think there would be a number of people who might be interested." Arty placed a hand on top of Jamie's. "Not that there are any guarantees. But you aren't afraid of hard work, and my friend Ryan has connections. He's in fashion, but I bet you'll really like him. He's great fun. So, give it some thought. You don't have to make any decisions right now." Arty pointed ahead, and sure enough there were lights on the horizon. "That's our destination."

Jamie was glad Arty didn't call it home. It hadn't felt that way for Jamie, and he doubted it did for Arty either… not anymore. Arty leaned back against him, and Jamie stayed close. It was nice being here, just the two of them, alone together. Jamie kissed the base of Arty's neck and closed his eyes, wondering about, and hoping for, what would come next. At least for a few more hours, he could pretend that Arty might be his.

EVERYONE WAS awake and on guard as they passed under the bridge and into the bay, the lights of the dock and fish plant just ahead in the early morning. It was exciting, and the prospect of being back on land made Jamie impatient. They approached the dock and tied up the boat. It seemed they had someone waiting for them. "Morning, Gerald," Reginald called as they slipped into their berth and pulled up alongside the dock.

"Welcome back," Gerald called as Arty killed the engines. "We got word you were coming and have the plant ready to take your catch."

Reginald and Beck both turned to Arty, who had been on the phone constantly as soon as they had come in range of the shore. "That's good of you, Gerald. Come on board and we'll talk rates. We are fully loaded with amazing grouper." Arty seemed happy, but judging by the calls he'd been making, he had something up his sleeve.

"We'll pay the usual rates," Gerald answered, the smile and the welcome in his voice slipping away.

"That's the thing, Gerald. We didn't borrow any money from you for this run, and as such, no agreements were signed. I've been on the phone with Sampson and Trident, and they're willing to pay more… considerably more." Arty turned to the others who were sitting at the restaurant and some who had come to check on their harvest. A boat coming in was always welcomed home. It was tradition. "Twenty percent more."

Jamie wasn't privy to exactly what was going on, but they had all agreed that Arty was going to be responsible for selling the catch and getting the best price.

"Everyone here sells to us. We're part of the community."

"Yes. And you're such a good corporate citizen." Disdain dripped from Arty's voice. "I've been calling around, and the other plants regularly pay quite a bit more." A crowd was gathering, and Arty spoke more loudly. "It comes down to this. Since you've been loaning all the fishermen here money, you've controlled their catches and they have to sell to you. We don't. So I did my homework and learned you've been underpaying." Now everyone on the dock was interested.

Gerald stepped right to the edge of the dock, eye to eye with Arty. "So help me, I'll…." Jamie moved through the crowd and into position right behind Arty, gently touching his shoulder just to let him know that he was there and had his support. He just felt that Arty might need it, and he didn't want him standing alone.

"What? Threaten never to buy my catch again? You need us, Gerald. Trident and Sampson are willing to deal with us fairly, all the time. They want our business, and they don't see us as their captive audience." The tension between the two spilled over across the dock and onto the boat. Jamie wasn't sure who would back down, but Gerald flinched and stepped back.

"All right. Let's go to the office and strike a deal," Gerald said.

"You know I'm going to share the deal I get with everyone else. So you may as well say what you're offering so they all know." Arty stepped into the gunwale. "We deserve a fair price for our catch—all of us do.

You all know me, and I'm doing this for you as well as for the four of us."

"But who will finance our trips?" one man asked.

"Sampson and Trident have similar arrangements, and their contracts don't discount what we bring in as additional interest." Arty turned back to Gerald, who was grinding his teeth. "I want to be fair to everyone, Gerald. You get good, fresh fish, and we get a fair amount for our work. That way, we all win." The aggression had already slipped away as he handed Gerald the details of the other offers.

Gerald's lips pursed, and then his face relaxed a little as he looked over the offer. "Fair enough. If our pay scales are out of date, we will make them current. And we'll meet this price and do right by our fishermen," Gerald vowed.

Damned if Arty hadn't done it. He was quite the dealmaker. Granted, a lot of this was Gerald trying to save face, and Arty let him have that. Arty had what he really wanted, a good price for the catch. He extended his hand, and Gerald shook it. The other men looked at each other, smiling, and Arty patted Gerald's back as he strode back down the dock.

"Take the boat to the loading chute and we'll get to work." Gerald continued on his way, and they cast off the lines while Arty backed the boat out of the slip.

"That took brass balls," Reginald said.

"Yeah, but we made a lot of friends, and Gerald needed to come down a peg or two. He's been using his position to push people around here for long enough. He needs to be fair, and now that folks know he hasn't been, they'll keep an eye on him or do business with someone else."

Jamie thought it was damned heroic what Arty had done. Yes, he'd gotten a better deal for them and their shares would be more, but he'd also helped everyone else in the process. Pride…. He was proud of Arty for standing up to Gerald. Anyone who would take care of others that way might have his back too. "Would he really take you on in front of everyone else?"

"That was part of the plan. I had to have witnesses and support. Gerald thought he was the king of the hill, but he needs the fishermen or he doesn't have a business." Arty maneuvered the boat up alongside the plant to the chutes, which were extended on board. Then he killed the engine.

"Bart," Arty said as a huge man came on board. They shook hands. "Are you ready for a great catch?"

"You bet." They started unloading the boxes, sliding the fish and ice down the chute and right into the plant, where it would be weighed and processed immediately. There was no waiting or their catch would lose its freshness. Unloading took a surprisingly short amount of time.

"Those are some beautiful fish. Let me get you a receipt for the weight and type, and we'll get to work." Bart hurried inside. In the meantime, they cleaned out the boxes. Bart returned with a detailed sheet of every fish, its weight and type, and a net amount that Arty shared with all of them. "One of the best runs of the year. You staying with your dad?"

Arty nodded.

"Then go ahead and get some rest, all of you. I'll call over when the check is ready, and you can come pick it up." Bart smiled and left the boat. Once the chutes were returned to the plant, they pulled away and returned to their berth.

"Go on, guys, head on home. We can clean up the rest of this tomorrow morning." Arty yawned and shook his head, silencing the engines. He shook hands with Reginald and Beck, then watched as they left the boat, heading out down the dock and across the parking lot.

"You going to your aunt's?" Arty asked, and Jamie shrugged. "Then come on. You can shower and rest at the house."

Jamie followed Arty down the road to the small white house. "Dad, I'm back," Arty called once they were inside. Arty set down his bag and peered around the corner into the living room. "Did you sleep in the chair?"

"How did it go?" He seemed to ignore Arty's question.

Arty handed his father the sheet he'd been given, and while Jamie had never seen Arty's dad before, he knew surprise when he saw it. "What do you think?"

"You did well, boy." He turned and must have caught sight of him. Jamie stepped forward.

"This is Jamie. He went out with us. Jamie, my father, Byron." Jamie extended his hand, and the older man shook it. "He's going to stay a little to rest up." Arty didn't waste time. "The bath is down the hall on the left, and you can take my bed. It's just across the hall. Go get cleaned up and get some rest."

Jamie wasn't going to argue. He was too tired to put up a fight, so he retrieved his bag and trudged down the hall.

The shower was hot, and it felt darned good to get the dirt and stink off him. He smelled like fish and sweat, and God knew what else. But all that went down the drain. And once he was done, he put on comfortable clothes, hung up the towels, and padded across the hall, doing his best not to listen to Arty and his dad. Though there wasn't all that much to hear—just Arty talking and his dad grunting. He closed the door and sat on the edge of the bed, wondering if what Arty offered was a real chance at something, or just another disappointment.

The pillow and blanket called to him, as did the fact that the world wasn't rocking and swaying. He lay down with a sigh, pulled up the blanket, and was asleep in seconds. His hopes would wait. They had long enough already.

Chapter 7

ARTY QUIETLY went into the bedroom and closed the door. He was clean and felt human again after his shower. The amount of dirt that went down the drain must have been enough to make one hell of a mud puddle.

Arty wished he understood his father. They had done well, very well. The catch had been excellent; the result of the trip was more money than they'd made in a long time. Arty got a better price for his fish, but all his father did was humph and sulk. Maybe his father was jealous of the fact that Arty had had some success. Though he doubted that. His dad wasn't the jealous type. Still, he would like to have heard something positive about the fact that Arty had earned enough money to get his dad's bills current, and pay off some of the past debt. Yeah, it was a single run, and in the end, their luck had been good, but it was a big start to digging them out of the hole they were in.

Taking a few minutes to think, Arty realized he had been here about three weeks, which meant he had another three weeks to go. And if the fishing remained good, he could return to his own life again and leave his dad on a sound financial footing.

He stifled a sigh and turned to Jamie, who was curled under the blanket on the far side of the bed. Now *that* was a gorgeous sight. Arty sat on the edge of the bed as gently as he could, the lure of sleep calling to him like a siren song. He pulled up the spread and climbed under it, separating him from Jamie. That was the safest course of action. Sure, the two of them had kissed and danced their way around each other while at sea, but they were back now, and things were different on land. Jamie had options, and Arty wasn't going to force himself on him like some letch. He lay on his back, his eyes heavy, breathing deeply. There were plenty of things he needed to do, but right now, none of them mattered. Rest, he needed rest.

Arty woke some time later to light peering in from behind the curtains. He wondered what time it was. Jamie had shifted and pressed right behind him, an arm over Arty's shoulder. It seemed as though he was still asleep from his breathing. Arty didn't want to disturb him, but he desperately needed to get up. He carefully unwound himself from the blankets and Jamie.

"Where are you going?" Jamie asked groggily.

"I'll be back. There's no need to get up." Arty's legs were unsteady, but that was just from being on the boat for so long, and the fact that he was still half asleep. He went across the hall to the bathroom, peed, and got a drink of water before returning to the room. Jamie stood next to the bed and shuffled past him and out of the room to the bathroom. Arty got back into bed, closing his eyes, listening for Jamie.

Arty wasn't a smooth operator when it came to other guys. He didn't have a way of asking a guy back to his place without actually saying what he wanted. Arty had never understood that subtle language. He was just a kid from the coast of Florida who lived and worked on the water. But he was keenly aware of Jamie and listened for his return, wondering what he should do when the bedroom door opened. He thought of pretending to be asleep, but that was childish. Instead, he lay still, awake, and when the door opened, the covers he'd been using suddenly seemed too warm.

The shorts Jamie wore hung low on his hips, and his T-shirt clung to his chest just enough to entice. Arty watched as Jamie walked around to the other side of the bed. The mattress shook as Jamie got back on, and then Jamie pressed right to him, with warmth and a sizzle of energy when his hand slid around Arty's waist. "That boat was way too small," Jamie whispered, holding Arty a little tighter.

He slowly rolled over, and Jamie closed the gap between them with a kiss that rocked Arty's world. Arty hugged Jamie tightly, his hands roaming as his willpower crumbled to a pile of dust. He had wanted this since first seeing Jamie on the dock, crushing his hat in his hands. Now he got to know what those lips really tasted like and what Jamie's skin, smooth and warm, felt like under his hands.

For a second Arty wondered where his father was, but after two seconds, he no longer cared. All that mattered was Jamie, right here and now. Arty tugged at the bottom of Jamie's shirt, getting it over his head, followed by his own. Chest to chest, heat to heat, he sighed as they pressed together. This was what he needed, what his spirit wanted, and he wasn't going to be denied any longer.

He became a little frantic, desperate to get all of Jamie. He needed to feel him, know what he was like, put a road map of Jamie in his mind so he could carry it with him forever. They fumbled a little, Arty's hands shaking, but soon their shorts joined the shirts on the floor on the far side of the bed. Arty sighed as Jamie came to him, nothing but thin cotton between them, with no one else sleeping a few feet away, a closed door between them and the rest of the world.

"God," Jamie whispered, his hands sliding around Arty's neck, his eyes shining in the dim light. "You really are beautiful."

Arty snickered softly. "I wouldn't say that. You're the one who will turn heads. You certainly did mine." He tugged Jamie lower, covering his mouth, his tongue sliding forward to taste him better, to get more. He wanted more… hell, he wanted it all. Arty rolled them on the bed, holding Jamie. The thing was, he didn't want to let him go, not now, not ever. Jamie was special, he knew that, and being with him seemed magical. Maybe it was the weeks of anticipation and buildup. But in his life, things that were built up to such heights usually turned out a disappointment. Jamie delivered, and so much more.

He kissed down his neck, Jamie shivering when Arty found a spot right at the base, teasing and worrying it until Jamie gasped and clutched at him. Arty wanted to drive him wild, and judging by the gasps, he was succeeding. "We have to be quiet," Arty whispered and then smiled. "So I'll make a deal with you. If you don't make a sound—" He ran his hands down Jamie's ripped chest and over his fluttering belly, teasing the waistband of his stretched boxers. "—I'll more than make it worth your while."

"How?" Jamie asked, eyes wide and mouth parted in anticipation.

"Have you ever been with anyone before?" Arty asked, and Jamie colored deeply. "I see."

"I know what's involved in things like this." Jamie sat up and slid up to the head of the bed, gathering the covers around his waist. "I'm not a virgin or anything, but I spent more time on the farm watching the animals do... what animals do... than I got to spend time with someone like me." He pulled up the covers.

"I take it things didn't go well," Arty supplied and wished he'd never asked the question in the first place. He had only wanted to make sure that his impression was correct so he could take his time with Jamie. Arty's intention wasn't to kill the mood. But then, if there was this kind of hurt and doubt lingering in Jamie's mind, it was something they needed to work on together. Arty knew how it felt to carry secrets and to have them come back to hurt you.

"No. I suppose this story has been told a lot. I liked him, I thought he liked me... and he did. But when it came down to it, he was too scared to do anything." Jamie sighed. "At least he didn't go around telling everyone else, probably because he was afraid I'd tell on him."

"You know that's okay." Arty leaned forward. "You are who you are, and that's more than good with me." He gently kissed him, and Jamie wound his arms around Arty's neck, spreading heat throughout his entire body. "You know, you're really sexy."

Jamie colored again.

"You are." He skipped his fingers over Jamie's chest, swirling them around a nipple, loving the hitch in Jamie's breath. You could tell so much about someone by how they were breathing. He smiled as he trailed his fingers lower, and Jamie's breathing became more shallow, his body reacting, anticipation building. It was beautiful to behold. Arty knew that burst of wanting; he felt it himself. Jamie was magnificent, and he wanted to know all of him, from the way his hips narrowed just above his boxers, now tented with desire... to the power and strength coiled in his shoulders and arms. "Lie down," he mouthed, and Jamie slid down the bed. Arty tugged down his boxers, freeing Jamie's straining cock, which bounced on his belly, reaching his navel.

The man was gorgeous and strong, and Arty stroked down his smooth glistening chest, over his hard, ripped belly to his cock, stroking him slowly, as Jamie gasped. "This is how it should feel when you're with someone you care about." He leaned over him, not letting Jamie go. "That rush of pleasure, the loss of words... the heat, even the sweating. It's all your body reacting to me, and I feel the same. I can't think about anything but you." He kissed him, tasting those sweet lips.

"You talk a lot," Jamie said, and Arty nodded.

"I love to talk during sex. It's how we get to know one another." Arty brought his lips to Jamie's ear. "And I want to know you... all of you." He sucked on his ear, still stroking Jamie, feeling the quivers that ran through him. "Now, what do you like?"

"I don't know. Normal stuff," Jamie answered with a half smile, clearly a little nervous. Arty hadn't meant to make him that way and backed off, smiling.

"I see." Arty drew closer, inhaling the increasingly musky scent that built by the second. Then he parted his lips and drew nearer, sliding them around Jamie's cock. Jamie gasped, and Arty sank deeper, taking more of him as Jamie quivered. He raised his gaze and saw Jamie's eyes glazed over, his hips rocking slightly. Thankfully Arty was very good at this, and he took more of Jamie, earning yet another growl of happiness.

Arty tapped Jamie's hip to remind him to be as quiet as possible while doing his best to drive him wild. Jamie wound his fingers in Arty's hair, and Arty worked Jamie's glorious cock, sucking for everything he was worth. "I'm gonna...."

Arty backed away, leaving Jamie breathing heavily. He kissed him hard. "I don't want things to be over before they really get started." A squeak from outside the door reminded him that his dad was out in the living room and that they didn't have all the time in the world. It wasn't likely his father was going to come in here, but still....

Arty pressed Jamie down onto the mattress. Jamie wound his arms around him, hands sliding downward until Jamie grabbed his butt, holding him closer. They moved together, bodies sliding against each other. Jamie buried his face in Arty's shoulder for a few seconds, and then they kissed hard. Arty let himself be transported, and the worries of the world passed away. Seconds seemed to last an eternity, and Arty made the most of each moment of happiness, committing them to memory because he knew they didn't come around all that often.

"God, Arty…," Jamie groaned into his ear.

"Yes. You're amazing," Arty whispered, and Jamie shivered under him, their intensity building. They had spent days so close to one another that Arty thought he'd burst. And now, he just wanted as much as he could get.

The sound of a crutch hitting the floor muffled into the room, but Arty was too far gone to stop. He held Jamie closer and Jamie did the same, the two of them driving each other to mind-blowing completion.

Neither of them moved for a long while. Arty stroked Jamie's forehead, and then he slipped off the bed and grabbed a towel from underneath it. He wiped them both up, folded the towel, and tossed it into the dirty laundry before joining Jamie under the covers.

"Do we need to get up? Won't your dad wonder?"

Arty shook his head. "Nope. Dad always sleeps for hours when he gets back from fishing. He'll expect the same from me." Arty tugged Jamie closer, loving his heat and the fact that he was here with him. Sometimes the greatest joy came from the simplest things. Arty closed his eyes, and sleep overcame him once again. Jamie was right, and they were going to need to get up pretty soon, but for now, it could be just the two of them.

ARTY DOZED and, after a little while, woke again and slipped out of bed. Jamie was sound asleep. Arty didn't want to wake him, but he was also reluctant to leave him after their first night together. Too bad those times wouldn't last forever.

They had both had a hard week and a half, and he had some things to do. Arty grabbed some clothes and dressed in the bathroom across the hall and then went out in search of food.

"Hey, Dad," Arty said when he entered the kitchen. His dad nodded and continued watching television. "You know that stuff is going to rot your mind."

"Smartass!" his dad retorted with no heat. Arty poured a cup of coffee and sat at the table.

"Don't you have a doctor's appointment?" Arty seemed to remember that there was one coming up.

"Tomorrow." His dad emptied his mug and took it to the sink. Arty watched him move, noticing the pain, even if his dad tried to cover it. "Where's your friend?" His dad set the mug in the sink and maneuvered his way back to the living room on his crutches.

"Still asleep. He worked really hard the entire trip." Arty picked up his mug and followed his dad into the living room, determined to do more than grunt or just sit in the same room and say nothing. There had been hours of that growing up, and Arty wanted something different now. "He baited hooks, cut bait, and worked as hard as any of us."

His dad nodded. "You were eager the first time you went out too. Remember?"

"Yeah. Then it became something different." Arty sat on the sofa as his dad lowered himself into his chair with a sigh.

"Work always does." His dad pulled the recliner's footrest.

"It wasn't the work, Dad," Arty clarified, but his dad had already turned on the television and was zoning out, not interested in whatever Arty had to say. "Dad...," Arty pressed and stood, picking up the remote off the side table and hitting the power button. "We need to talk."

His dad turned to look at him. "Then talk, Robert," he demanded, looking at Arty as though he'd gone crazy.

"Arty?" Jamie said, coming down the hall.

"Is he your *friend*?" His dad's inflection was hard to read, and Arty chose to ignore it. Sometimes it was best to beat his father at his own game. If his dad didn't want to talk about what was going on, then why should Arty volunteer any information about his own life?

"Are you hungry?" Arty asked Jamie and got up, heading to the kitchen. He found some eggs and ham in the refrigerator and made a scramble with some onions. It was basic, but they needed food and it was easy to make. Arty pulled some orange juice out of the fridge and poured two glasses.

"Can I ask why they call you Arty? I heard your dad call you Robert. But with a nickname like Arty, I thought your name was Arthur."

"Nope. Robert Todd—R.T. or Arty. It was a nickname I got as a kid in school and it stuck." He shrugged and set their plates on the table. "Dad, do you want some? I made enough." His dad came in, and Arty made a plate for him before sitting down.

"Arty says you did good," his dad said to Jamie. "He said you worked hard."

"I did. The entire process went pretty well. One day was a complete washout, though. It rained nonstop."

Arty nodded. "The deck got slick, and Reginald went overboard in all his clothes and rain gear. Jamie helped get him out. He thought quickly and averted a difficult... well, more difficult situation."

His dad patted Jamie on the shoulder, which was more than Arty had ever gotten from him. Then he turned to Arty. "You should be more careful. You were the captain. It was your responsibility to make sure everyone was safe." The admonition had Arty grinding his teeth together, but he said nothing. His dad was right in a way, but no captain could foresee everything. Sometimes it was how the situation was handled that counted. Still, it grated that his dad just assumed that he'd messed up. Arty lowered his gaze and ate his food. The sooner he got back to New York, the better.

Jamie didn't seem to notice. "You should have seen him on the dock with that guy from the fish plant. He was brilliant." Jamie took a bite, grinning, and Arty's heart leaped that Jamie was standing up for him. Jamie was pretty amazing, and the thought of just letting him go sent a cold shudder running through him. "He got a better price for our catch and for the rest of the fishermen as well. That guy was being cheap, but Arty did the research."

"Yeah." Once again that gaze came his way. "And you'll make it more difficult for us in the future. He won't want to deal with me."

Arty shook his head. "I already opened negotiations with Triton and Sampson. They will be glad to work with us in the future. We—you—were being cheated." Arty's indignation hit the boiling point, but his dad just dropped his fork and pushed away his plate. They stared at each other, and Arty thought he might, for a second, have seen pride flash in his dad's eyes. But if it had been there, it was gone in a few seconds, replaced with his father's usual stoniness. Then his dad got up from the table and left the room.

Arty really didn't understand his father. Then again, his dad didn't understand him either and didn't even seem to want to try. Arty had done his best to help his dad, and his efforts had met with success. The boat had been full, the fish sold at top price, and a large portion of his dad's debt could be wiped clean. Arty didn't need to be hailed as a hero, but a thank-you would have been nice.

"I didn't mean to make him mad," Jamie said. "But you needed someone to stand up for you and—"

"I know. It wasn't your fault." Arty patted Jamie's hand and shook his head, watching where his dad had gone even as he basked in knowing that Jamie had understood what he needed and stood by him. He shrugged and did his best to let go of the disappointment. "I always seem to be aggravating him somehow." Arty finished eating and then took care of the dishes.

"What's next?" Jamie asked.

Arty peered out the windows. "I was thinking we could wander down to the docks and maybe start some of the cleanup. I have to arrange to have the tanks pumped and the boxes cleaned. There's always a lot of work once a trip is over."

Jamie got to his feet. "Then come on. The work isn't going to do itself." He was already heading for the door.

"Do you ever do anything halfway?" Arty grinned. Jamie had this energy that was contagious. "Let's go; we may as well get done what we can before the fatigue catches up with us. And it will. We were all running on adrenaline and drive for a long time." He pulled open the back door. "Afterwards, we can stop at the Pelican for a beer." They would deserve it.

HOURS LATER, they had made good progress. The trash had been bagged and arrangements made for the tanks to be emptied. Much of the cabin had been cleaned and the gear stowed. Things to be washed were bagged and sitting on the dock.

"I have the boxes washed out, and I added a little bleach to the water to help sanitize them. The lids are open and they are nearly dry." Jamie looked up from his work. "The decks have been hosed down, but I wasn't sure what to do with all the gear. I didn't know where it went."

"We can leave that until tomorrow," Arty said. "We've made a good start, and I think that's enough for today. Why don't we haul the trash to the dumpster, and we can take the laundry to the house before stopping for a beer." He needed to get the wash done so the gear could be returned.

"When are you going out again?"

Arty shrugged. "I'm not sure. A lot will be determined by what they say at Dad's doctor's appointment tomorrow." He needed to find out where his dad was with his recovery before he made any definite plans. "If I have to go back out, I'll probably go Monday." And hope for a good yield this time as well.

"Then let me know and I'll go out with you again." Jamie smiled, and Arty nodded. Now that was the best news he'd had all day.

"Wonderful. Though I doubt Beck will go, and I'm not sure about Reginald either." He was going to have to put together the rest of the crew. "Let's get this taken care of." Arty hefted the trash, and Jamie grabbed the laundry. They hurried down the dock and across the lot, where he dumped the trash in a dumpster, and they headed to the house. Arty found his father asleep in his chair, which worried him. His dad never just sat around, and he didn't nap all the time.

Arty started a load of laundry, and then he and Jamie headed down to the Pelican, where he was welcomed like some conquering hero. "You saved all of us," Clive, one of the longtime fishermen and one of his dad's cronies, said almost as soon as he sat down.

"I just did my homework."

Clive shook his head. "No. You upended the game. None of us has the wherewithal to go anywhere else. Gerald holds paper on all of us, and we're beholden to him for money whenever we need to outfit our boats." He slapped Arty on the back, guided him to a table, and motioned for a server. "You could have taken your bounty and gone on your way, but you shared it with us all." He ordered a beer for him and for Jamie.

"Gerald isn't going to see it that way," Arty said cautiously. "I think I may have stirred up a hornet's nest."

"Yeah, you probably did. But you'll go back to New York. Gerald can hate you if he wants, but you'll be gone, and the rest of us can hope to make a better living." Clive leaned closer. "And we all know to keep an eye on the little weasel now." He smiled his gap-toothed grin and chugged his beer.

His father's comment had raised his wariness, so when Gerald came into the restaurant, Arty waved him over and offered to buy him a drink. He didn't bring up anything that was said earlier in the day, and he hoped Gerald would see it as a peace offering of some sort. Everyone here was just trying to make ends meet, and they needed each other. Gerald accepted the beer and then moved away to join another party.

Clive said nothing, and Arty was relieved about that. Everyone was interdependent, and rocking the boat too much only capsized them all. "So when are you going again?"

"Possibly Monday. I'm hoping that will be my last run and Dad will be well enough to take over again soon." Arty finished his beer and thanked Clive, who caught the eye of one of the other fishermen and excused himself.

"Well, that was unexpected," Arty said.

Jamie drank his beer and glanced around. "Why is everyone staring at us? I mean, I can understand them looking at you because of what you did, but…."

Arty had noticed it too and he'd tried to ignore it, but they seemed to be the object of fascination. Just then a waitress came over and asked, "Can I get you something else?"

"Maybe a snack. What's good today?" Arty asked.

Susie, their server, came closer, as though taking their order. "I'd say the two of you." She winked.

"Excuse me?" Arty asked. "I don't get it."

"Well, everyone is talking about what you did for all the fishermen. They think you're a kind of hero. Then Beck, the bigmouth ass, started in about how he was trapped on the boat with the two of you and he would never have gone out if he'd have known that you had the hots for each other. He was talking real loud and drinking too much for that time of the day. Reginald told him to shut his mouth and mind his own business before he dragged him away." She smiled and turned to Jamie. "So is it true—are you a couple?"

"Susie," Arty said, and then figured, what the hell. If he acted like they had something to be ashamed of, then that would be picked up.

"Jamie and I like each other. But nothing happened while we were out on the Gulf." He rolled his eyes. "You know how big those boats are. Like anything can go on and not have the entire crew looking in." It was ridiculous. "And Beck had better learn to watch his mouth," Arty said more loudly. "If he'll gossip about me, then he'll tell stories about anyone."

Susie seemed satisfied. "The grouper bites are pretty awesome today. I suspect it's some of what you brought back."

"Then we'll have those, some of the fries, and an extra plate." He figured they could share.

"No problem. I'll also bring you both another beer. I got plenty of people who want to buy you one." She tapped the table and then hurried away. It shouldn't surprise Arty how much people talked, but it still did, sometimes.

"Is there going to be trouble?" Jamie asked. "Back home there would be." He seemed a little nervous.

"I doubt it. You and I are going to have a bite to eat, another beer, and then go back to the house. Once our bellies are full again, I suspect we'll be tired. And as for whatever rumors are going around, they'll die out when something else happens." Arty accepted the beers from Susie, and a couple more of the old-timers stopped by to ask about his dad and tell stories about the one that got away. It was a cliché, but truer words were never said than fishermen telling whoppers about the time they caught a great white that turned out to be a minnow with some fight.

Once they had finished eating, Arty paid the bill, and they left to walk back to the house. "You really seem to belong here," Jamie observed.

"I don't know about that," Arty said. "They'll overlook certain things right now and will probably give me the benefit of the doubt because I helped them and because of my dad. But I never really belonged here." The night air held a slight chill. His dad had never been someone who listened to rumors, and this one should die away soon enough; at least he hoped so. Though his dad had already been told he was gay, so it wasn't the worst thing in the world.

"So you'll definitely go back to New York?" Jamie paused. "Can I go with you? I don't fit in here, any more than I did back in Iowa. My aunt doesn't understand, and she's got enough on her plate. I thought I would like it here, that I could start again, but…."

Arty understood. "This is the same as home, beneath the surface. You can work yourself to death and get nowhere. It's just like the farm, except with water."

"Exactly."

Arty smiled. "I was serious if you wanted to come to New York. My friend and I will help." He liked the fact that he and Jamie might have a chance to see where this attraction led them.

"That's awesome. I've waited tables before, and I've worked with all kinds of animals. Of course, that probably isn't going to be of much help in New York. Maybe I could walk dogs and things. I see people doing that on TV."

"What is it you really want to do?" Arty had a pretty good idea. But he had to ask.

"I want to get into theater or TV. I loved that in school." Jamie turned away. "I know it's hard and every other person in the city wants the same thing. Mostly I guess I want a different life and a chance at something better." He wiped his nose and sniffed a little. "Maybe if I could make something of myself, then my dad would see it and realize I'm more than just some huge disappointment."

Arty shook his head slightly. "Why is it that we're all trying to get either our father's attention or his approval?" He'd been trying to do that…. Hell, he still was. Not that it did a damn bit of good. "I can't guarantee anything, but I'll introduce you to my agent. I don't know if she'll be willing to take you on, but it isn't going to hurt to meet." Hell, his own dreams had taken their ups and downs, and he'd been working at them for years now.

"Then we'd better hope that the next run is as good as this one. That way, I'll have made enough money to get to New York and maybe have a little to get me by until I can get a job and earn my own way." Jamie smiled, full of excitement and wonder. Arty remembered that same feeling when he'd first arrived in New York. Everything was new, and the world was open to so many possibilities. Then the world came crashing in, and reality reared its sobering head. Still, he wasn't going to dash Jamie's hopes. He deserved to delight in them for as long as they lasted.

"I'll call Ryan tonight and make sure it's okay with him. You should phone your aunt and let her know where you are and that you're okay." Arty started walking back toward the house. The streetlights cast a meager glow, but he knew the way by heart. Jamie wound his arm through his, letting the shadows conceal what didn't need to be on grand display.

They approached the house, but Jamie didn't slow down, so Arty just continued past it, wandering farther from the Gulf down streets he'd known as a kid, but which now seemed so different because he had someone to share them with. "Is this where all the fishermen live?" Jamie asked.

"It used to be. Now half the homes have been bought up by people from up north because they're affordable." Arty paused. "I used to know everyone in each of these homes. I played with their kids and we all grew up together. Some of them are still here, but a lot of them are gone… just like me."

"Are you glad you came back?" Jamie asked, a little tentatively.

"Not for the reason I had to, but yeah…." Arty paused because he wanted to get this right. "In some ways, I wish I hadn't come. This trip brings back a lot of things that I thought I'd left behind." But then, nobody ever truly leaves behind their childhood. A person could go to New York or Manitoba—it didn't matter—but their past would follow them. And maybe it should. "But then I met you…." He let that hang in the air. There were so many things he wasn't quite sure how to put into words, and part of him was as suspicious as anyone who grew up on the water. If he talked about it too much, then he might jinx it. So instead, on the quiet street, with no one around, in front of a dark house, being serenaded with cicadas and the night insects, he leaned closer, sharing a kiss with Jamie that made him want to hurry back to the house.

"I think I understand."

Arty sure as heck didn't. "I wish you'd explain it to me. Because most of the time, I have no clue." He really didn't. His own father was a mystery to him, and maybe he'd always be that. Nothing was ever said that he deserved whatever attention he thought he wanted from his dad. No one ever got everything they wanted in life.

"This is a place of good and bad for you. It's where you grew up, and it's all of this—" Jamie motioned around him. "There's the Gulf, and friends, and lots of memories. But there's also stuff you don't understand, and here, you feel more like a kid than a grown-up. It's the same for me on the farm. My dad gave me as much work as I could handle, but he never let me make decisions. I was always a kid to him." Jamie turned to him. "And it seems both our fathers keep a lot of things to themselves. Whatever they're feeling is locked away, because if they talked about it, then they'd come across as weak or something." He tensed and his voice grew stronger, darker.

"Yeah." There was nothing Arty could do but agree. "If they'd just open up to us, then maybe we could understand." There was so much he wanted to know, but his father was like a closed safe, full of information that was locked away from him. "But they won't change. Not for either of us." He slowly started moving again, turning the corner. A breeze came up off the water, chilling them both, and Arty guided them back to the house. It was time to go in before the cold settled too deeply. Not that it would last against the morning sun, but that was a long way off.

It only took a few minutes to get back to the house, something Arty wished he could delay. It was nice being alone with Jamie, having him to himself for a while. They separated before going inside. Jamie went to Arty's room to call his aunt, and Arty sat at the kitchen table to call Ryan as his dad slept in front of the television.

"How is it going?" Ryan asked right away when he answered. "Did the trip go well?"

Arty smiled to himself. "It was good. Dad goes to the doctor tomorrow, so we'll find out more then." He cleared his throat and peered into the living room. "I met someone."

"The guy you told me about from the boat?" Ryan asked.

"Yeah. Jamie's from Iowa, and he's going to go out on the next run with me. He's sort of staying here for a little while." Just the thought made Arty's heart beat a little faster. "And he wants to come back to New York with me."

Ryan groaned. "Another of your provincials," he said haughtily and then laughed. "Let me guess: you want him to stay with you." There was something jovial about the way Ryan said it, as though he'd expected nothing else.

"It won't be forever...," Arty argued.

"It's okay. But I have to ask how well you know him." Ryan grew serious.

"We spent eight days on a small boat in the middle of the Gulf of Mexico. There aren't many secrets after something like that. I'm hoping to go out once more, and then things with Dad will hopefully be settled and I can come home."

"And bring a boyfriend with you." Ryan's voice grew deeper. "Are you sure about this? You left New York a few weeks ago, down in the mouth, and now you're like the Energizer Bunny. I'm wondering if Florida might be good for you."

Arty paused. "Are you kidding?" he asked more loudly than he intended, then stood, went outside, and pulled the door closed after him. "My dad sits and watches television all day. I have no idea how he feels about what's going on or if he's even happy that I'm here. He growls and tells me nothing. No, I don't belong here any longer. The people have been nice, but my life is in New York. This will never be home for me."

"Okay. I just wanted you to be sure." That was Ryan, always playing devil's advocate. "When are you coming back?"

"In a couple of weeks, I hope. After I go out one more time, I'm hoping Dad will be able to take over again." God, just two more weeks and Arty could go back to New York. He was so ready.

"And Jamie is going to come with you?" Ryan asked. "I know you like the guy, and if you want him to come, then I will be happy to have him stay, you know that. But you just met him. Are you sure you want him to stay with us? Don't you think that's moving a little fast?"

Arty wanted to get angry, but that was the same question he'd been asking himself. "He wants to come, and things are good between us. So, I figure he should come. If it doesn't work out, he can find a place of his own. But, Ryan… I really want to find out if things can work between us. He's a good guy and he's down to earth. Jamie works hard, and he doesn't expect things to just drop in his lap. How many people are like that? Everyone seems to expect that good things will happen for them just because it's their due… or if they work hard, it will come to them. That doesn't always happen." He spoke quickly, as if he had to get the words out. "I have shit luck with guys, you know that."

Ryan chuckled. "Yes, you do, my little loser magnet. That's why I have to ask if you know what you're doing. The last thing we want is to have another Jerry Jerkoff staying with us. Remember him?"

Arty practically choked. "I dated him exactly twice, and then I dumped him when I found out what kind of pig he was." When he met him for their second date, Jerry had told him to come in, and Arty had found him on the sofa with the goods hard and porn on the TV. Apparently, he was really into himself. "Give me a little credit."

"I'll do my best. But your love life has been so entertaining." Ryan was such a shit sometimes.

"What love life?" Arty countered.

"That's what makes it entertaining," Ryan retorted, and Arty growled under his breath. "Come on. You have the worst luck, and it isn't like mine is much better. Remember Claude?" He started giggling and then outright laughing. "He was one sick puppy."

"Yeah, and you dated him for three months," Arty added.

"I can be as freaky as the next guy. Sometimes it's nice to nibble at the freak buffet, but I didn't want to make a steady diet of it." At least Ryan could make fun of himself. That was part of why Arty loved him. "Anyway, you really like this guy?"

"He's...." It was hard to put into words. "I don't know. That's the thing. I've been sure before, and the guys always turned out to be losers. So, with Jamie, I don't know." He hated this doubt. "But I need to try to find out."

"Okay. Then bring him, and I'll be here to help you." That was Ryan. "Now, I have to go because I have a date tonight and I need to get ready. He invited me to this club downtown. It's supposed to be really fun, and apparently clothes are optional." He remained quiet for a second, just long enough for Arty to inhale sharply, and then he burst into laughter. "I got you. Go and see how things work out with Jamie. I'll talk to you soon. Be sure to call me before you go out to sea so I won't worry when you don't answer my texts." Arty hung up, half smiling. Sometimes he thought it was too bad he hadn't just fallen in love with Ryan. They had both talked about it, but it would never have worked.

Ryan was too good a friend, and there was no mystery between them.

"Is everything okay?" Jamie asked. "You were on the phone for a long time. I put the wash in the dryer and started the next load." He stepped outside and closed the door.

"You do laundry?" Arty asked, tugging Jamie closer.

"Of course. Do you find that sexy?" Jamie asked in a mock husky voice that made Arty smile.

"Yes, I do." He tugged Jamie nearer, their heat mixing against the chilly evening air. Their lips met and Arty closed his eyes. There was no way he was going to get enough of that taste or the way Jamie made him feel. How could he have known that when he'd come back to Florida to help his dad, he'd find someone like Jamie? Arty pressed him into the darkness and then against the house, his hand sliding under Jamie's shirt and up to pluck one of his perky nipples. Jamie moaned softly, just loudly enough for Arty to hear and to stoke his growing desire.

Jamie shivered, and Arty gentled the kiss and slowly moved back, his hands slipping away from Jamie's heated skin. Jamie breathed hard and stayed where he was, the darkness covering what Arty hoped were thoroughly kissed lips.

"I should go inside." Jamie's voice broke a little, and then he slipped away and walked toward the door.

"Jamie, I don't mean to overstep," Arty said in a whisper.

Jamie stopped. "You didn't. I'm only going inside because I don't want to beg you to strip me naked right here and now and then take me on the ground." He came closer. "I want you as badly as you seem to want me. I don't fully understand what I can offer you, but I want you. Just not out here." He turned and went inside the house, closing the door.

Arty took a deep breath and followed him inside the house. He found Jamie and his dad sitting in the living room, neither of them saying a word. Arty sighed and joined them, sitting next to Jamie on the sofa. They watched a basketball game, which interested Arty about as much as watching dental work, but his dad seemed interested, and Jamie shifted to the edge of his seat as the game progressed.

Jamie whooped at what was an important point, and Arty's dad turned and smiled. "You follow the Heat?"

"Yes. Even when I lived in Iowa, they were my team. My dad preferred the Chicago Bulls." Jamie turned to him. "Part of me chose to watch the team because my dad hated them so much," he added in a whisper and then came out of his seat as the Heat scored a three-pointer.

"I'm going to go into the room to read. You two enjoy yourselves." Arty stood, walked down to the bedroom, and closed the door. He found a book he'd wanted to read and lay on the bed. After a few minutes, the bedroom door opened, and Arty set his book aside when he saw Jamie.

"Are you angry?" He came in and sat on the edge of the bed.

"No. Of course not. You go watch basketball and have a good time." Arty patted Jamie's hand. "Enjoy yourself. There's no need for you to be anything but happy. Please." He smiled and nodded. Jamie leaned over the bed, kissing him gently.

"I better get back before the break is over." He got up and half floated out of the room, closing the door.

Arty picked up his book and tried to read, but too many other things kept running through his head.

A cry drifted in from the living room. They were happy, and when Arty cracked the bedroom door, Jamie and his father were discussing basketball. He closed it again and plopped on the side of the bed. His dad had said more to Jamie in the last hour than he had said to Arty since he arrived. Part of him was jealous, and he hated feeling that way. He and his father just didn't have anything in common.

Another cry wafted into the room, and Arty gave up, figuring he could either sit here alone, or join them and be part of the action. Arty was tired of being on the outside looking in.

Chapter 8

JAMIE LOVED basketball, and football as well, and he was pleased when Arty joined them in the living room. He didn't seem to understand the finer points of the game, and Jamie did his best to explain some of the strategy.

"Arty never liked sports," his dad said, his attention still glued to the television. Jamie wanted to argue with him, but Arty shook his head and sat back. These two men who sat in the same room were as far apart as Jamie had ever seen two people. Even he and his dad spoke to each other. They might have argued most of the time, but at least it was communication. This quietness was disconcerting. Still, it was none of his business.

"It's okay. Basketball isn't as interesting for me as it is for you and Dad. I just came out to be with both of you." Arty got up and went into the kitchen, then returned with a tray of chips and three bottles of beer. He handed one to his dad, and then one to Jamie.

"Thank you," Jamie said as his phone vibrated in his pocket. He pulled it out and groaned when he saw the number—it was his dad in Iowa. The game went to commercial, so he got up and left the room. He didn't want to disturb the others.

"Hi, Dad," he said from the kitchen.

"Where the blazes are you? Your aunt called and said that you had been gone for over a week and then called to say you were staying with a friend. What do you think you're doing?" His angry voice on the other end of the line was loud enough that the others could probably hear.

"I was working. I'm staying with the captain of the boat I was on because we're going out again next week and there's a lot to do." He stood taller, even though his father wasn't there to see him. It was like he had to steel himself against the older man.

"When are you coming home? I need you here. There's work to be done, and this is where you belong."

Jamie shook his head. Arty's hand slid over his shoulder, and Jamie stiffened at the surprise and then relaxed and leaned back into the touch, taking strength from it.

"The farm is where *you* belong, Dad. Not me. I'm working here, and then once I have enough money, I'm going to New York. I have things I want to do." He held still, waiting for the explosion that was sure to come. If he listened, he could probably hear it without the aid of the telephone.

"You are not! You'll come back here in two weeks and that's final." The snap in his voice was the same one that he'd used with Jamie his whole life. In the past, Jamie had always given in, but it wasn't going to work now. "I need you here. I can't do this all by myself," his father added, throwing in a little guilt for good measure.

"You've never done it. You always had me to do all your damned work, and now you can't figure it out. Well, I'm an adult now, and I get to make some of my own choices. I don't want to clean up cow shit and spend hours on a tractor going back and forth planting corn and cutting hay. That isn't how I want to spend my life." Jamie turned to Arty, who glanced toward the other room and then moved a little closer. He could feel Arty's heat through his shirt. "I want more."

"Kids always want more. But you have a life here."

"I'm not a kid, Dad, and I don't want what you want. That's not my life. I'm going to New York, and I won't be back except to visit on holidays." He sighed. "I just want my own life, Dad."

His dad sputtered, something Jamie had never heard before. "You aren't going to get a cent from me."

"I already have access to my accounts."

His dad groaned. "My name is on all those accounts, and I'll close them out tomorrow…. You won't have anything."

Jamie took a deep breath. "Don't worry about doing that. I already closed them and opened new ones that you don't have access to." He turned to Arty and shook his head. "You need to accept that I'm going to go my own way. I only answered your call to let you know I'm fine, I found work, and that I'm not coming home for a while. So you will need to find someone to help you work the farm. I'll send you an email of all the things I did there, and maybe now you'll get off your butt and work." Jamie was so angry. He pulled the phone away from his ear as his father started yelling. He pressed the End button and put the phone back in his pocket. It rang again, and he declined the call, as well as the one after that.

It kept ringing, so he turned it off. "Are you okay?" Arty asked. Jamie felt like a caged lion and began stomping through the small yard.

"He…." Jamie threw his hands in the air, sputtering. "He thinks…." Jamie continued pacing in the yard, needing to work off his anger. "Damn him. He only thinks of what he wants, and nothing else matters."

"At least he cares enough to be angry," Arty said softly, and Jamie whirled on him, ready to snap. "My dad doesn't argue with anything. He barely talks to me at all."

"He didn't say anything when you left?" Jamie asked, and Arty shook his head. "Nothing?"

"Not even goodbye," Arty said with a shrug.

"All my dad cares about is his farm and how much he can make from it. And to save money, he got as much labor out of me as possible. I tended the gardens. I spent so many hours on that tractor my butt took on the shape of the seat. What was my dad doing?" Jamie shook his head. "I have no idea, but he was always sitting at the table when I came in, and then he'd have something else for me to do. I felt… feel that I'm nothing more than a workhorse for him." He stopped moving, the energy gone, his anger draining away, at least for now. Yes, he'd told his father he was going to New York. Now he needed to make it happen and somehow build a whole new life. It was almost enough to scare him into going home… almost.

"I'm sure there's more to it than that," Arty said.

"Just like there's more to your father," Jamie argued, and hoped he hadn't made Arty angry. Arty laughed and threw an arm over Jamie's shoulder.

"Come on. Let's watch the rest of this basketball game and then go to bed."

Jamie was really starting to like the idea of going to bed. Maybe he should figure out how to spend more time there. Especially with Arty.

JAMIE YAWNED as the game ended and the analysis began. Arty had already gone in, and Mr. Reynolds flipped through the stations to try to find something to watch. Jamie said good night and padded down the hall to the bedroom. The lights were off, and in the dimness, he saw the curve that was Arty under the covers. Jamie went into the bathroom, got cleaned up, returned, and climbed under the covers, wearing only his underwear. He wasn't sure how Arty normally slept, and he didn't want to presume.

He needn't have worried. Arty was dressed the same way he was, and mumbled something before moving closer, drawing Jamie into his embrace, and then settling once more.

"I don't know if I can sleep when the bed isn't rocking," Jamie whispered.

"Hmmmm," Arty responded. "Don't worry. It will rock again soon enough." Arty snickered, and Jamie groaned softly. The will was there, and judging by the stiffness that pressed to his butt, some part of Arty was awake, but he was already half asleep. Fatigue had caught up with Jamie, and he closed his eyes. When he opened them again, it was several hours later. The house was quiet, there was no television in the background, and Arty was breathing softly in his ear.

"Are you awake?" Jamie asked, and Arty hummed faintly, his weight shifting until Jamie lay on his back with Arty on top of him. He didn't have much time to think about it before Arty kissed him. Jamie wrapped his arms around Arty's back, smooth skin passing under his hands until they found the curves of Arty's ass. Then he pushed his boxers down over them and past his hips, holding tight as his own boxers slid lower. "You most definitely are."

Arty humphed, and Jamie cut him off by capturing his lips once again.

"We need to be quiet," Arty whispered. "But maybe tomorrow, if I can arrange it, you and I can take a day trip out on a boat into the Gulf, and then you can talk and yell all you want."

Jamie shivered as Arty kissed away his moan and slid down his body. Jamie closed his eyes, taking in every sensation. He clamped his lips shut and swallowed hard as Arty swirled his tongue around his nipples, then down his belly, dipping into his navel before his hot breath ghosted over Jamie's throbbing cock. He gripped the bedding when Arty encircled his cock with his lips and then went deeper, encasing him in wet heat that threatened to blow his mind to bits. He kept his mouth closed even though the need to groan and cry out was almost overwhelming.

"Arty," Jamie whispered urgently, and Arty stopped, taking his lips once again.

"I want you, Jamie," Arty said, and Jamie wasn't sure what that meant. His inexperience left him wondering as Arty reached for the nightstand, his weight shifting and then returning. He had a small square in his hand, and Jamie recognized the condom. He nodded, and Arty tore it open and then stroked him hard before rolling the condom over Jamie's aching cock.

Instantly he got the message, and he gasped before he could stop it. *Arty wants me inside.* That blew his mind. "Have you done this before?" Arty whispered in his ear, and Jamie rolled his head back and forth on the pillow. "Baby, you are going to love it." Arty grabbed a bottle off the nightstand and straddled Jamie's hips. Jamie saw his movement and felt the coolness through the latex before Arty sat back, and Jamie was surrounded by the tightest heat and pressure he could possibly imagine.

Up until now, Jamie's encounters had been a few fumbling attempts that came to an abrupt end before they got to this sort of experience. And, man oh man, what he had been missing! Jamie swore he could feel Arty's heartbeat, and damn, to be connected to someone else this way was mind-blowing. Arty sank deeper, and Jamie whimpered as the intensity grew. He was afraid to move, and yet instinct compelled him forward.

Arty held Jamie's leg, and he kept as still as he could before slowly beginning to move. God, this was incredible, and he wished he could talk and tell Arty all about how he made him feel. His entire body was on fire, and his heart felt as though it were going to burst. The connection, the closeness to Arty, was nearly overwhelming, and the way Arty gave himself to Jamie only made Jamie want to give of himself in return. A union, a coupling that he wished would last forever.

Jamie held Arty's hips as they moved. He needed to steady himself as Arty undulated above him. God, the sight, even in the dim light, of Arty's pelvis rolling, his chest glistening and stretched as he arched back. There wasn't enough light to see a great deal of detail, but what he could see only added to the thrill of the moment.

"Arty... I...," Jamie whispered as Arty's body clenched and tugged at him. It was overwhelming, and he inhaled deeply, surprised by the way Arty seemed to read him, then change things up, keeping Jamie on edge. Again and again, he thought he was getting close, and Arty would back off, only to drive him upward once more. Jamie held on to Arty for dear life and let him have control. Hell, Arty must have had legs of steel with the way he controlled their lovemaking. Jamie was seconds from begging when Arty held him tighter, pulling and tugging him toward the edge... but this time, letting him go over.

Jamie floated and let out a monster breath as calm serenity settled over him. He didn't move, but kept his eyes closed, and just stayed in the moment for as long as it lasted. Then, and only then, did he open his eyes and tug Arty down into a kiss.

Slowly Arty lifted himself upward, and Jamie came free. He stifled an overstimulated yelp and then settled once again. Arty grabbed some tissues for cleanup while Jamie got the condom off and tied up. Arty took care of the debris and, once they were less sticky, joined him back in bed.

"Is that what you call being a power bottom?" Jamie asked, and Arty chuckled.

"I guess so." He held him closer. Jamie didn't move, and his eyes grew heavy once again. He now understood guys falling asleep after sex. He'd always thought the movies were kind of dumb on that part, but then he'd never met Arty and his own particular brand of athleticism. "Go to sleep. We have work to do in the morning, and we need to get ourselves back on a normal schedule."

"Okay." Jamie tried not to think too much about what was going on right now and where all this was going. Oh, he wondered, but he was too content and happy to examine it too closely. He knew things couldn't be as perfect as he thought they were right at that moment. But he'd enjoy it while it lasted.

"REGINALD, HAVE you got all your gear, and Beck's, off the boat?" Arty asked the following afternoon when he and Jamie met the older man at the White Pelican. Arty had cut checks for each of them, with their share of the profit from the trip. Jamie had no idea if what he received was good, but Reginald seemed impressed, and even Beck didn't make any snide remarks.

"Yes. It's all off and we cleaned up as well. You should be good to go out again whenever you're ready. Do you have a crew?" Reginald asked. "Beck is returning home to Tampa, and I'd go out again, but that last trip was more than this old body can do anymore."

Arty extended his hand, and Reginald shook it. "You did a great job, and we all made it work. I fully understand. I'll post that I'm looking for two people, and I suspect I won't have much trouble this time around."

"I'll go out with you," a voice said from one of the other tables.

"I'd be glad to have you, Katherine," Arty said with a smile. "Now, I just need one more."

"I'll go," a man said, and Arty nodded. He seemed to know both of them and turned back to the table, clearly pleased.

"I'm planning on Monday. I'm sure both of you know the drill, but we'll meet here on Friday to finalize details." Both of them nodded, and Arty's face practically split into a grin as he turned back to Beck and Reginald. "Thank you again for all your help. Have a safe trip back home."

Beck shrugged and was already standing. "My vacation time is up this week, and my wife wants to have some time together before I go back to work." Arty shook his hand as well as Reginald's, and then the two of them left. Arty seemed relieved.

"I was hoping that would happen," Arty said softly. "Beck is a good enough guy, but I don't want to go out with him again. It's one thing to be straight, but another to be closed-minded and adversarial. He got the job done, I'll say that for him, but...."

Jamie nodded. "I wasn't very comfortable around him either." Jamie glanced at Katherine and the other man. "What about them?"

"Katherine is cool. We went to school together, just like everyone else around here. We were good friends. She and her wife live a few miles away. And Lyle is a great all-around hand, and let's just say that he bats for the same team. But he doesn't think anyone knows, so we don't mention it." Arty smiled.

"I see. So...."

Arty leaned over the table. "It will be like last time. We're working, so no fooling around. We'll just have to get it out of our systems before we leave." Arty winked, and Jamie felt his temperature rise within seconds.

"Is it okay if I join you?" Katherine asked and moved over from where she was seated alone. "I was serious."

"So am I. I'll be glad to have you. I know you can do the work. Jamie here cuts good bait and has learned some of the basics. While he provides excellent support, someone with your experience is going to be very welcome. I have the exact locations of the places where we had good luck, and the fish will have had a chance to migrate in again, so we can check those areas and a few others that might look good."

"Hopefully, your luck will hold," Katherine said, and Arty nodded. "People who fish for a living are very superstitious," she said to Jamie.

"Yes, I understand. Arty has already informed me that there are no bananas on board the boat. Though why, I don't understand." Jamie snickered.

Katherine got this mischievous look on her face. "I think it was because of sailors and their reputations on long ocean voyages. You know, no phallic fruit to make people think of the buggery going on belowdecks and all that."

Jamie tried to keep from guffawing and nearly failed. He figured he was going to like her a lot. "Is there anything we need to do to prepare for this next trip?" he asked Arty.

"No. Just outfit the boat. Katherine, let me know if there are any special foods you might want, and coordinate it with Lyle here. We eat a lot, but it's pretty basic. I'm sure you know that. I'm really hoping this can be a quick trip, but of course, that's up to the fish and the weather more than anything else." Arty ordered some of the wonderful grouper bites and a round of drinks.

Lyle joined them after a while, and the four of them got acquainted and talked over the run.

"Say, Katherine. Do you still have your father's old cabin cruiser?" Arty asked.

"Sure. I've been working to restore the old girl. She's looking pretty wonderful now. Why?"

Arty glanced at Jamie. "I was wondering if I could borrow it for a day. I'd like to take Jamie out for a little fun. Fishing is a completely different experience from just enjoying being out on the water. I was thinking I could take it up Longboat Key, maybe stop and have lunch somewhere, and come back. The weather forecast is sunny and calm."

She nodded, reached into her pocket, pulled a key off her ring, and handed it to Arty. "Go ahead. I know you'll take good care of her. I don't get to take her out as much as I'd like, and it would be good for her to get used." She winked, and Jamie wondered what that was for. "You two have a good time."

Jamie tried not to blush and failed. But Arty didn't pause too much, and he went into his plans for the run and all the things that had to be done. He had arranged for a lot of it already, but there were still a few things left that he assigned to Lyle and Katherine to take care of. By the time the food had arrived, they had things worked out, with a plan to finalize everything on Friday. Another run, another chance to make some money, and Jamie was one step closer to going to New York with Arty. That was the prize he kept his eye on. A new life and maybe, if he was lucky, a new love to go along with it.

His phone vibrated, and Jamie pulled it out of his pocket. He groaned and answered the message quickly. "What is it?" Arty asked.

"I'll tell you later," Jamie said as calmly as he could, putting his phone back in his pocket. Lyle excused himself, and Katherine watched him go before turning back to the others.

Lowering her voice, she said, "Gerald has a bee in his bonnet for you. He put the word out that no one was to go out with you if they wanted him to loan them any up-front money for future fishing runs. The little shit." She smirked.

"And yet you came with us," Jamie said, glancing at Arty with concern. His mind went to how Gerald could make trouble for them. Jamie didn't know Gerald very well, but he'd had experience with plenty of guys being assholes over the years.

"I'm not going to let that little man tell me what I can and can't do," she said. Jamie liked her even more. "Lyle is the same way. But Gerald said he's going to block you from docking here... or others who work with you."

"He can't. Dad owns the dock and the small piece of land it attaches to," Arty said. "And as much as Gerald might sputter, he can't block access to it either. That would be illegal and make him look like a real dick." Arty sighed. "Though I wondered how he was going to try to get back at me. He always had an inflated ego. And as we know, has no compunction about cheating people." Fire burned in Arty's eyes as he spoke more normally. "What I really want to know is, how much money has he stolen from the families here? How many kids have had to go without, because he wasn't paying the market price? I'm sure there are other fishermen who are in the same position as my dad because he was swindling them." Arty looked around, but Jamie didn't dare. He kept his gaze at the table, but heard some rumblings from other tables.

"Damn, Arty, you missed your calling. You should be in politics," Katherine commented, but Arty shook his head.

"Theater," he added. "Life is theater, and sometimes all you need to do is put on a good show. Gerald is only looking petty, and he'd be better off to keep quiet and go about his business. Dad was worried about what Gerald would do as well." Arty seemed more tense than Jamie had ever seen him. But that's because he knew Arty now. To the world, Arty seemed calm, but under the table, Jamie saw his foot bouncing on the floor. "I probably should have been more careful, but I was so angry over what he was doing. Nobody deserves to be taken advantage of." Arty still seemed to be playing to the gathered group.

"I know that, and so does everyone else. He's in a pretty tight box right now, but who knows how long he'll stay that way? People will go on, memories fade, and Gerald is a shit who can hold a long grudge." Katherine made a good point. "I need to get back to my partner, Susan. But you two have fun tomorrow and don't let this business with Gerald get to you. There are plenty of people who are grateful for what you did, and so are their families." She tapped the table a few times. "I'll see you both on Friday." She stood and stopped at the bar area to pay her bill before leaving.

"What are we going to do about Gerald?" Jamie asked. He was concerned that the asshole was going to make real trouble for Arty and his dad.

"Nothing right now. Let him sputter a little. It makes him feel better and soothes his ego. But he was caught cheating people, and no one here is going to forget that, no matter what Gerald tries to do. They have options now, and if everyone got together, they could put him out of business. Not that anyone wants that, including me, but it could happen." Arty paid their bill and then they left the restaurant, giving up their table for someone else.

Jamie was still concerned, but there was nothing he could do about it and it really wasn't any of his business. Still, it worried him as they walked back toward the house. "What was the message you didn't want to worry me about?" Arty asked.

"My dad is freaking out and threatening to come out here to find me and bring me home." Jamie and Arty stopped walking. "I know he cares for me in his own way, but this behavior is getting just a little obsessive."

"Do you think he'd hurt you?" Arty asked.

"Not physically. But God knows how he thinks coming out here is going to change anything. He can't tie me up and force me to leave. He doesn't even know where I am, exactly."

Arty paused. "Are you sure? Is your phone on his account? He might be able to track it because, in effect, he owns it."

Jamie scoffed. "Are you kidding? My dad would never pay for anything like my cell phone. I've always taken care of my own bills. I don't have the greatest service, but at least the phone is mine." That was one thing he didn't need to worry about. "But Dad probably has a pretty good idea of where I'm at."

Arty shrugged. "At least you're not at your aunt's place. Then he'd know exactly where you are. Maybe he'll calm down after a day or two. Then you can call him and make him see reason." The idea made sense, but Jamie knew that sometimes sense was something his father didn't have a lot of.

"Who knows what he'll do?" Jamie was starting to get a little nervous about how far he was pushing his father. He and his dad fought sometimes—when Jamie had defied him or had complained about how hard his father was working him—but he had never turned his back on his dad this way before. It was hard. His dad was the only really close family he had. Jamie was well aware that his aunt, his dad's sister, had divided loyalties. She did care about Jamie and had tried to help him, but she was first and foremost his dad's sister.

"What do you want him to do?" Arty asked, which seemed like a strange question.

"I want him to stay home and take care of his own business, and let me have a life of my own." They moved closer to the side of the road as a car slowly came toward them and passed. "I want a little freedom. What do you want from your dad?" He wasn't sure he wanted all this examined too closely, so he turned the tables.

"I want him to talk to me, to be proud and to be my dad. To act like a dad. I barely know him at all." Arty continued down the road and Jamie followed.

"But what is a dad to you?" Jamie asked. "Does he yell and try to force you to do what he wants? When you left for New York, did he try to stop you?"

Arty shook his head. "No."

"When you were a kid, did he force you to work on the boat because you were free labor? Did he watch what time you came home from school and scold if you were late because there were chores to do?" Jamie put his hands on his hips.

"No. I went out with him when I was off school, sometimes. But he never forced me. After Mom died, and it was just the two of us, the house was pretty lonely and really quiet." Arty sighed. "I miss my mom. She was full of life. She worked hard, but she was fun. She used to take me out to watch the dolphins. Believe it or not, it was my mom who taught me boating and boat safety. She loved the water and she was patient with me. Even when I was a teenager. I lost her to cancer when I was thirteen, and after that, it was just Dad and me." Arty leaned on a fence post in front of the house. "What was your mom like?"

"I remember her taking me out when I was maybe eleven or so to watch a cow being born. I asked if I could have him and she said I could. So Bubba became my cow. I fed him and watered him. Dad said he was a steer, not a cow, but I just thought of him as my boy cow. I didn't know then what it meant." Jamie came closer. "I was eleven when I got him, and then a year later, Mom died in an accident. She fell out of the hayloft and broke her neck." Jamie wiped his eyes. "I would go up there all the time to talk to her when I couldn't talk to Dad." He wiped his eyes again and blinked. He was not going to cry over this. Not now.

Arty stayed still, but Jamie felt his gaze on him. "I know there's more."

"Yeah. I came home from school to feed Bubba, but he was gone. Dad said that he was big enough and that it was time."

"Oh God, no."

"Yeah. I didn't eat beef of any kind at home for a year because I was afraid some of it might have been Bubba. If Dad pulled it out of the freezer, I'd become sick and that was it. I know what farming is and that livestock is raised for food or to be sold. I never named another animal in my life after that. Not even a dog or any of the barn cats. I learned my lesson."

"But your mom gave you Bubba," Arty said. "He didn't talk to you or anything?"

"Nope. He made his decision, and that was that. Dad said he was trying to teach me a lesson, and maybe he did. But the lesson I learned was that my dad was one cold son of a bitch." Jamie took a deep breath and released it. "I think that's enough for one day." Lord, they had taken a long walk down Maudlin Road.

"Yeah," Arty agreed.

"What are you going to do for the rest of the day?" Jamie asked.

"I have a number of arrangements to make, and I have to take Dad to the doctor in half an hour. You can ride along into town with us if you'd like, or you can stay here. It's up to you."

"I'll take a walk around here, if that's okay."

Arty led the way inside, and Jamie turned on the television while Arty and his dad got ready to go. Mr. Reynolds shuffled out to the truck, and Arty drove off. Jamie turned everything off, then went outside, locked the house, and set off for a little exploring.

"DAD, YOU have to do what the doctor says and take the pills," Arty was saying as Jamie came in through the back door. "The infection isn't clearing up the way it should, and if there's no improvement soon, the next step is an IV at the hospital. Is that what you want?"

"I want to be left alone," he growled. Arty stormed into the kitchen and stopped when he saw Jamie. "I don't know what to do. The wound on his leg isn't healing, at least not as quickly as it should be. His other leg is mending, but again, slowly. He has to stay off it more. But the stubborn jackass won't do a damn thing the doctor says." Arty slumped into one of the chairs. "I have to take him back in two weeks. If there's no improvement, they're going to put him in the hospital and start IV antibiotics."

"I'll be fine," Arty's dad called out.

Arty got back up, stomping into the other room. "Dad, the infection was so bad that the doctor thought you might lose your leg. You never told me that. Because of the ongoing infection, your system is stressed, and the bones aren't knitting like they should. Just take the pills and do what he says, okay? I want you well so you can go back to your life and your friends." Some of Arty's snappishness slipped away. "Everyone misses you. People ask about you all the time."

"No one comes here," he grumbled.

"Maybe if you didn't act like a bear with a sliver in its paw, they might actually stop by to see you." A knock on the door caught his attention, and Jamie went to answer it. A woman with a casserole dish stood on the doorstep.

"Mrs. Marshall." Arty seemed happy to see her. "Thank you for stopping by. This is Jamie. He went out with me on my last trip, and we're leaving on another on Monday."

"I brought a pasta casserole for you." She stepped inside and put it in the refrigerator. "Just heat it through for your dinner." She turned and smiled at Jamie. "It's nice to meet you." Jamie shook her hand.

"How is your dad?"

"Go on in and talk to him. Maybe you can get him to do what the doctor says. He doesn't want to take his pills," Arty said loudly.

"They make me tired!"

"Then sleep, but take the pills—they'll help you." Arty turned to Mrs. Marshall, who was on her way to the other room. "I hope she can get through to him." He sat back down and held his head in his hands.

"You're really worried," Jamie commented.

"He's my dad," Arty said with more feeling than Jamie could remember having for the man who raised him. "I have to make some calls and get things arranged or we aren't going anywhere." Arty pulled out his phone.

"What can I do to help?" Jamie asked, and Arty pulled out the chair next to him.

Arty grabbed a tablet and set it in front of him. Jamie took notes and wrote down details that Arty told him as he made call after call. Arty put the casserole in the oven a few hours later and asked Mrs. Marshall if she wanted to stay for dinner.

"I have to get home, but thank you." Arty hugged her, and Jamie wished her a good night. Then they got back to arranging for fuel and getting the other supplies together. By the time dinner was ready, Jamie had created a calendar of sorts, outlining when everything needed to happen. Arty put it aside, and pulled the casserole out of the oven while Jamie set the table.

Arty made a plate and took it in to his dad, along with a glass of ice water.

"I want a beer."

"Sorry, Dad, the doctor said no alcohol. Here, water tonight, and take a pill before you go to bed." Jamie waited for the grumble, but instead, he heard soft muttering. Maybe the two of them were talking, because Arty stayed in the living room for quite a while.

THE ROOM was still dark when Jamie woke sometime in the early morning. He and Arty had spent a quiet evening, after Arty's dad went to bed, watching old movies until neither of them could keep their eyes open. "Do we need to get used to fishing hours again?" Jamie asked, and Arty answered by throwing his arm over his chest, snoring a little louder. Jamie was grateful and closed his eyes, going back to sleep.

"We need to get up," Arty said, pulling Jamie out of a sound sleep sometime later. "It's after ten, and if we want to take a real ride, we should get moving." Arty was out of the bed and on his way to the bathroom before Jamie could say anything, so he rolled over and went back to sleep, only to be woken by Arty lightly slapping his bare butt.

"Okay. I'm getting up." Jamie got out of bed, dressed, and took his turn in the bathroom. By the time he was done, Arty was arguing with his father about his meds.

"There's food in the refrigerator, and Mrs. Marshall will be over later. So be nice."

"I'm always nice," Mr. Reynolds barked.

"You are not," Arty countered almost jovially as he headed for the door. "Maybe you could work on that." Arty was still smiling as he led Jamie down the street toward the wharf where a beautiful Chris-Craft wooden boat was moored. "This is a classic and one of the best boats ever made." Arty helped Jamie board, then started the engine and cast off the line.

"I feel almost regal."

"This boat is from another time, when boating was for the wealthy. Katherine's father bought it and worked to bring it back to life, and Katherine has continued the work." He ran his hand reverently over the woodwork.

"We should be careful, then," Jamie said, sitting down near Arty.

"I love how this boat rides. It reminds me of one of those water babies movies from the fifties and sixties, with all those women in lovely suits, smiling under water, or water-skiing in pyramids." He motored them deeper into the bay and around the point until the fishery disappeared from view. "See, boating is completely different like this."

Jamie chuckled. "For one thing, it isn't four o'clock in the morning."

"No, it isn't." Arty tugged him up, and Jamie stood next to him. Arty wound an arm around his waist as they stood together, gazing out at the horizon, the entire Gulf of Mexico in front of them. "I swear you could blindfold me, put me anywhere near here, and I would know where I was by the scent and the sound." He sighed, and Jamie leaned over to kiss him.

The water slapped the wooden sides of the boat as they motored slowly. "It's so different like this, without having to look at the water and everything like it's work."

"Exactly. I wanted to take you to have some fun." Arty smiled and pointed. "Look, a pod of dolphins."

Jamie stood next to him, watching and almost shaking with excitement. "There are so many of them."

Arty slowed as another pod drew closer and passed within a few feet of the boat, their slick bodies visible under the water. "Wow," Arty breathed and slipped an arm around Jamie's waist. "You don't see that often."

Jamie turned to him, grinning and pressing closer to him as the sun warmed the air around them. He wished this could never end. "What are those?" Jamie asked.

"Osprey nests," Arty explained.

"They're stunning," Jamie whispered, continually looking all around as more dolphins passed. He turned to him, and Arty caught Jamie's gaze. "I'll remember this forever." Jamie leaned closer, kissing him, drawing Arty nearer to him. A pelican sailed right in front of the bow of the boat, gliding away in its search for food, but treating them to yet another spectacular sight.

Arty knew he'd remember this too and continued onward, slowly turning out toward the center of the bay. "I used to love to come out here, drop the anchor, and just lie in the boat and watch the sky. It gave me a chance to think and get away from Dad and everyone else."

"Where did you do that?" Jamie asked, and Arty pointed, taking them in that direction. Jamie got the anchor, and when Arty cut the engine, he dropped it into the water. The boat rocked on the small waves and in the wake of passing craft, but Arty barely noticed as Jamie drew him into a kiss and then down onto the stern cushions. "I bet you never did anything like this." Jamie smirked and slipped his hands beneath Arty's T-shirt, kissing him hard.

They shimmied and groaned as their clothes slipped off. Thank God what they were wearing was loose and easy to get out of. "Out here you can make as much noise as you want. The wind will simply carry it away."

"Oh, thank God," Jamie said, and they proceeded to frighten away every bird or fish within a hundred yards. The future and the rest of the world be damned—at least for a few hours, passion and pleasure could rule their hearts.

Chapter 9

THIS FISHING trip went more smoothly, and the weather was perfect almost the entire time. "How long before we get back?" Katherine asked as she finished packing up the gear and helped Jamie clean up the deck.

"A few hours. We should come into cell phone range soon." Arty guided the very full boat back toward port. The coolers they usually used for drinks and extra food had been emptied and cleaned, then filled with fish, as well as all of the regular iceboxes on board. It had been a wondrous trip.

"We're almost done here," Lyle said. "I thought we'd clean up the cabin next so that would be done as well." During the entire trip, none of them ever stopped, and they were back in record time, loaded to the gills—literally. Once they were in range, everyone checked their phones, and Arty called to make arrangements for the sale of the catch.

"Do you want the catch or not, Gerald?" Arty asked when they were a mile out. "I'm getting tired of this. All you have to do is be fair with me and the rest of the fishermen, and we won't have any more issues. We can let the past rest. But it's up to you."

"You made me look—" Gerald paused.

Arty sighed. "Then I'll call Sampson." He ended the call and went to make another. His phone rang before he could redial, and Arty settled things and headed in. He knew Gerald needed the catch just as much as Arty needed to sell it.

"Is everything okay?" Jamie asked.

"Yes. We're on our way in. Are there any messages from your dad?" Arty asked. Jamie had been worried for much of the trip. He had called his dad to tell him he was going to be out of touch, and apparently the man had reiterated his threat to come get Jamie, forcibly if he had to.

"Yeah. There are about eight. He must have called every day. Dad is nothing if not persistent. Judging by the messages, I don't think he's done more than talk up to now." Still, it was enough to add to Jamie's worries, and Arty put an arm around his waist to comfort him as they passed under the bridge into the bay.

They approached the dock ten minutes later, and Gerald was there to meet them. Arty thought it strange, but once they moored the boat, he cut the engines, got off to greet him, and shook his hand. "I've been giving things a lot of thought," Arty said.

"Yeah." Gerald met Arty's gaze.

"It's time we buried the hatchet. You treat the fishermen well from now on, and you'll have no more trouble from me." He didn't need to tell him that Arty was planning to return to New York just as soon as he could. Two runs and coming back dog-tired for the second time was enough. Gerald shrugged. He seemed wary, and Arty didn't blame him. "We all need each other here."

Gerald nodded. "That's very true." He didn't say anything more on the subject, but they did shake hands one more time. "Take your boat on over and let's get your catch into the plant."

"Fair enough."

They unloaded the catch and then went to work cleaning the boxes once they returned to the dock. By the time they were done, Arty was exhausted and hungry. He and Jamie said good night to Lyle and Katherine in the parking lot, and lugged their things back toward the house.

"Hey, Dad, I'm back," Arty called as soon as he stepped inside.

"In here," his dad called, and Arty found him with his leg up. "I fell the other day. I'm okay, but I...." Arty barely heard the rest of it. The plans Arty had for being able to go back to his life sprouted wings and flew out the damned window. Hell, and damn.... This was so not what he'd been expecting, and he did his best not to let the anger that welled up inside him show. His dad was still laid up, and actually looked worse than when Arty had left on his second fishing run. It looked like he wasn't going to be able to work for at least another few weeks.

Arty dropped his bag by the door and went back outside to pace the yard, swearing under his breath. He knew what he had to do, but still wanted to yell at the top of his damned lungs. Not that it was going to do a fucking bit of good at all. He was stuck here, and that was all there was to it. His dad needed to eat, and he had to work the boat to make sure he didn't lose everything. Hell, for a second, he wondered if his dad might have done it on purpose. He clenched his hands, shaking them until the feeling passed. Finally, once he'd gained some control, Arty went back inside and picked up his bag, returning to where his dad and Jamie waited.

He closed his eyes and tried not to think about it too much. He'd have to make some calls to New York to make sure his job would be waiting for him and to tell Ryan what was happening. He'd been looking forward to calling Margaret to ask her to set up as many auditions as she possibly could. After these four, almost five weeks, he was ready to throw himself back into his career. "It will be fine, Dad. Just get better." He patted his dad's shoulder and went to take care of his things, needing to put some distance between the two of them.

"I'm sorry," Jamie said, and Arty hugged him just as soon as they were alone. Arty buried his face in Jamie's neck, inhaling and then groaning softly. He felt so vulnerable right now and Jamie felt like his rock, holding and supporting him. Arty knew he had to be strong most of the time, but with Jamie, he could let go of some of that and be vulnerable. He closed his eyes and relished the support that Jamie offered, and then he gave it right back to him. Inhaling and releasing his breath, he held Jamie even tighter.

"I was hoping we could leave soon." And now he was nearly back where he started, at least as far as his dad's health was concerned. The two successful trips would pay off much of his dad's business debt and get the bills current, thank God. But it basically meant he had been working for nothing for weeks. Arty got a load of laundry going and then closed the washer lid and leaned against Jamie. He was so tired.

"It will be okay. I can wait a little longer." Jamie stroked his hair, and Arty was grateful for the comfort. Then Jamie's phone rang and broke the silence. He moved away and pulled out the phone, shivering before answering it. Arty knew it was his dad on the line, just by Jamie's pained expression.

"Yes, I'm back. We got in this morning." Jamie's eyes grew wider. "No, Dad. That isn't going to make a difference. I told you when I left that I wanted to try something different…. Can't you just accept that?" Jamie sighed. "No, Dad. I'm going up north, and by the time you get here, I'll be gone. I promise I'll call you when I get there. I'll be staying with a friend…." Jamie rocked his weight from foot to foot. "Well, thanks for the warning." He ended the call, and his fearful eyes lifted to Arty's.

"I take it he's coming here?" Arty said, and Jamie nodded harshly.

"He says he knows where I am. How he did it is beyond me, but he said he was going to come to Longboat Key to get me."

"Then the easiest thing is for you to not be here. Before you go, though, I'd call your cell company to make sure he doesn't have access. Maybe change the password to your online account."

"Shit," Jamie swore. "I gave him access a while ago so he could pay my bill for me one month."

"That's all it takes," Arty said and let Jamie use his computer in the bedroom. He tried to think of how they could make this work, but Arty didn't relish Jamie's father coming here to make a huge scene. Neither of them needed that.

"Got it," Jamie said as he closed the application. "He can't see my stuff any longer, and I changed passwords on all my other accounts as well. But the damage is done. And I don't want to have a huge fight with my father. He won't listen, no matter what."

"You should talk to your aunt. You don't have to tell her exactly where you are, but she might be able to convince him that coming here isn't going to help his cause." If nothing else, he'd hear a second person telling him not to come. It might help defuse the situation. Though Arty was wondering if anything would. He had dealt with headstrong stubborn men before…. He actually looked into the living room, where his dad had fallen asleep. "See what she says, and we'll go from there."

Jamie nodded, and Arty left him alone to make his call. He got some water for his dad and set the glass on the table next to him, along with the pill he was supposed to take. Arty tried not to think of how these walls seemed to be closing in around him. This was where he had grown up, but it wasn't his home, not any longer. Yet there was a certain level of comfort here… if he was honest with himself. He had almost instantly become some sort of leader among the local fishermen. They asked his opinion, specifically on selling their catches, which was unusual and rewarding.

Jamie joined him in the kitchen and pulled out a chair. "Aunt Livvy said she'd call him and tell him to give me a little space. I don't know if it will do any good."

Arty nodded and snagged a tablet from near the phone. "I've been thinking. Maybe you should go on to New York, if that's what you really want." God, he didn't want to pressure him, but the thought of Jamie with him in New York, maybe the two of them building some kind of life together, got his blood racing. "I'll have to be here a few more weeks. We can arrange for a plane ticket and to get you to the airport in Tampa. You can stay in my room. Ryan has already said it's okay. I can call and tell him, and he'll pick you up from the airport. Ryan is a great guy, and he loves New York and showing it to people. You can get a job and start to get settled, and I'll join you as soon as I can get Dad back on his feet." It wasn't ideal, but it was better than Jamie's father bullying him into going back to Iowa. "What do you think? You'll get paid in a day or two and should have the money for a ticket. They aren't that expensive, and Southwest flies from Tampa into all the New York airports."

"It's a lot to think about," Jamie said with a slight smile.

"Think about it. I can call Ryan and let him know about the change of plans. You can talk to him as well, so you won't be total strangers, at least. And like I said, I'll join you as soon as I'm able." This could really work out.

Jamie didn't really respond. "I better change the laundry around and get the next load washing." He pushed back the chair, and Arty watched him go. Excitement warred with the thought that they'd be apart. Part of him worried that he and Jamie hadn't really known each other all that long. What if he found someone else once he got to New York? Arty was well aware of the fact that there was always someone around the corner… someone better looking, richer, on the way up…. Arty didn't really think that Jamie was that kind of guy, but temptation was definitely there. He'd be much happier if he was going with him, but Arty had no other option. He would follow when he could. Hopefully everything would still be good, and the two of them could figure out a way to be together for good.

"Aunt Livvy called. She said that Dad was completely unreasonable and determined to bring me back one way or another." Jamie sighed. "I'd better try to talk to him again." That was clearly an unhappy notion, but Arty nodded and pushed out the chair next to him. If Jamie wanted privacy, he could have it. But if he wanted support, Arty wanted him to know he had that as well.

"Why is he so insistent? I understand wanting to leave you a legacy, but forcing it on you...."

Jamie sighed. "I didn't get it for a long time. I think that after Mom died, he was determined to control everything and everyone, so nobody else could ever leave. She was his life... and he never figured out how to build another one without her."

Jamie sat down and made the call. "Have you come to your senses?" his dad said loudly enough that Arty heard it clearly through the phone.

"I'm not coming back. I want to see some of the world, and you coming out here isn't going to change my mind. Stay there and run your farm. Let me be to have my own life." Jamie wasn't taking his dad's anger bait, which impressed Arty a lot. Jamie put the call on speaker and lowered the volume.

"I built this farm and it's all I have, my whole life's work. And you want to just throw it away."

Jamie paled and looked like he'd been beaten. "Why do I have to be saddled with your life's work when I don't want it?"

"Do you think I wanted to be a farmer? I wanted to go galivanting off to the city, but my father got this land from his father, and it was passed on to me for you, and your son after that. It's your legacy. I built it up and made it a thriving and going concern and...." Jamie's father seemed to be running out of steam, which was a good thing.

"I'm done with farming, Dad... at least for now. I'm going to New York. If you want to come get me, then you can go there. Good luck finding me among nine million people. And you can't track me anymore either," Jamie said. "I want to live my own life. This is what kids grow up and do, Dad. I promise to call when I get there in a few days to let you know I'm okay, but I'm not coming home." Jamie pressed End on the phone and sat back. He seemed winded, and yet there was a gleam in his eyes. "I think I just decided."

"You definitely did."

Arty used Jamie's phone to call Ryan. "Hey, Ryan, this is Arty."

"How's Florida, and why are you on a strange phone?"

"Well, things have gotten complicated here. Dad isn't doing as well as I'd hoped, so I'm going to have to stay for a bit longer, but Jamie is going to come to New York. He can stay in my room. But I wanted him to meet you... sort of.... Jamie, this is Ryan."

"Hey, Jamie," Ryan said. "Are you ready to take New York by storm?" Leave it to Ryan to be welcoming and open.

"Yeah. I appreciate you letting me stay for a little while. I'll find a job as soon as I can, and I won't be a nuisance. I promise." Jamie seemed as excited as Ryan usually was. Those two were probably going to make the apartment combust. "I grew up on a farm in Iowa, and I know how to cook."

"A roomie after my own heart. You let me know when you're arriving, preferably from Newark, and I'll pick you up and get you to the apartment. I've seen a number of places that are looking for help, so I'll make a note of them and hopefully you can find something pretty quickly. I'll show you the town and help you navigate so you don't get into any trouble."

"Thanks, Ryan. Arty said you were a good friend," Jamie said with a grin. "We'll forward you everything. Thank you so much." Jamie looked up, and Arty took the phone off speaker and thanked Ryan.

"Is he as cute as he sounds?" Ryan asked. "Don't worry. I'll take care of him until you can get up here to join him."

"Thank you." Arty wasn't sure what to say. "I appreciate everything. You are a good friend." He was ready to end the call.

"I just hope you know what you're doing. I don't want you to get hurt, and I can already tell you're in over your head on this. Please be careful." Ryan could be so damned insightful sometimes.

"I'll do my best." It was the best answer he had. "I'll talk to you soon." Ryan ended the call, and Arty handed the phone back to Jamie. "It looks like we just need to get you an airline ticket and you'll be on your way."

Jamie nodded. "I'd feel better if we were going together."

"I know you would, and so would I. But unless you want to stay here for another three or four weeks arguing with your father… you should go and start building the life you want." Arty wished he could get back to his, but it was only a matter of weeks.

Jamie put his arms around Arty's neck. "I can't tell you how grateful I am for what you're doing. I never would have been able to do this if I hadn't met you. I don't know anyone there, and it's such a big city...." He sighed.

"You'll be fine. And you can call and talk to me whenever you want, unless I'm out fishing. Ryan will be there, and he'll answer any questions and make sure you know where the basic things are." Arty leaned closer. "And when I get there, I'll take you around to all the fun places to see. We can go to the park, see the zoo, take a boat ride on one of the ponds." He ached to go with him, but Arty couldn't leave his dad.

"Arty," his dad called, and he closed his eyes, taking a quick kiss before moving away to see what his dad wanted.

"Go ahead and use my computer to check flights. I can put the ticket on my credit card." He turned and left to look after his dad. "Did you take your pill?" he asked him.

"Yes," his dad said, growling as Arty helped him get up, and he hobbled his way down to the bathroom. The wheelchair seemed to be history... at least for now. Arty waited for him to get back and then checked the wounded leg. It was finally healing well, which was a relief. The infection seemed to be a thing of the past, and now it was just a matter of waiting for his broken leg to mend. Arty made a note to ask the doctor about physical therapy for him. "Is Jamie leaving?" his father asked.

"In a few days," Arty answered softly.

"That's too bad. I really like him." He turned on the television, searching until he found basketball, and sure enough, it wasn't long before Jamie came out to watch along with him.

"Did you find a ticket?" Arty asked.

"They were really expensive, so...."

Arty left him and went into the bedroom, grabbed his laptop, and brought it into the living room. He went to a couple of sites that offered last-minute deals to see what was possible to New York. "I got one for two hundred out of Tampa. The plane goes through Baltimore, but you don't need to get off." He continued searching and then showed what he'd found to Jamie. "Does that look good?"

Jamie nodded. "Lots better than anything I could find."

"Good." Arty reluctantly helped Jamie buy the ticket. He made sure Jamie had a license and ID and then sent the information to his phone. Once he was done, Arty closed the laptop and set it aside. Fatigue quickly caught up with him, and soon enough, he put his head back and dozed off. He probably should have gone into his room to sleep, but he wanted to spend as much time with Jamie as he could.

When he woke, he went to the kitchen to make some lunch. He took in sandwiches, and they ate and watched the end of the game. "What a basket," Jamie said, leaping to his feet and nearly sending his lunch flying. Where he got all his energy from was a mystery, but Jamie seemed to keep going and going.

Once the game was over, another came on, but Arty had had enough. He took care of the dishes and went to his room to lie on the bed, staring up at the ceiling. "Arty," Jamie said, cracking the door open.

"It's okay," Arty said. "You can watch sports if you like." He wasn't going to be a jerk about it. Basketball wasn't his thing, but Jamie really seemed to love it, and he wasn't going to expect him to deny himself what he liked. "Did you play back home?"

"When I was a kid, I like to think I was pretty good. But as I got older, it took up more and more time, and Dad put an end to it. There was work to be done on the farm." Jamie sighed. "So now I enjoy watching."

"That's cool. I was more into the arts, myself." Arty hated that Jamie had been forced to give up something he loved. That seemed to be a real pattern for him.

"Maybe we could go for a walk later," Jamie said, and smiled. "And I thought I'd make dinner tonight if that's okay."

"That would be great," Arty agreed, and Jamie leaned over the bed. Some time alone, just the two of them, would be nice. They shared a kiss, and then Jamie left the room, closing the door after him. Arty closed his eyes, wondering again what it would be like to have Jamie to look at each night and first thing in the morning. The last few weeks had been amazing, but he was well aware that good things didn't last forever—at least they didn't for him. His romantic past was a shambles. His career had been up and down like a deep-drop roller coaster. Hell, he was scared to make plans at all because they were only blowing up in his face. He sighed and pushed all that out of his head and tried to sleep. Maybe rest would give him a better perspective.

Arty eventually fell asleep and woke with Jamie lying next to him, an arm around his waist, draped over his belly. He closed his eyes again, and Jamie drew closer, as if he was cold. "I should check on Dad," Arty said softly, but Jamie held him tighter, and Arty really didn't want to move. He had no idea what time it was, but his body forced him out of bed and over to the bathroom. When he returned, Jamie had gotten up.

"I'd better start dinner, or we'll be eating at midnight." He left the room, and Arty followed, figuring he would help.

Jamie didn't make anything too fancy, but burgers with onions and cheese sure smelled good, and his dad joined them in the kitchen. It was pretty plain that his foot was hurting, but Arty was pleased that he came in to eat with them. And while they waited for Jamie to finish, he went over the catch details and the proceeds of the last run with his dad.

"You sold it locally," his dad said.

"Yes. I spoke with Gerald, and I think he learned his lesson. I don't want the plant to go under. It's important to the local economy. But I don't want people cheated either. I think we understand one another." At least he hoped that was true. "And look at the difference. Overall, there was a thousand dollars more for the trip because we got a better price. That's pretty big."

Even his dad had to admit that it was. "What's next?"

"Jamie is going to New York in a few days, and I'm going to find someone to replace him on the crew and go out next week again. I have to fish if we're going to make a living, though if our luck holds, we could reach our quota well before the season ends with fewer runs and less expense." All he wanted was to make enough that his father could return to his job on an even footing, both literally and financially.

His dad nodded and seemed to withdraw. Arty wondered if it was because he might be doing better at fishing than his dad had been. He hadn't meant to hurt his dad, just help him. Jamie brought over the burgers, and Arty left the figures with his dad, getting plates and drinks. By the time he was done, Jamie had the food on the table, and they sat down to eat.

His dad turned on the small television off to the side and found an old western, watching it as he ate. Arty wanted to turn the damn thing off, but he didn't want to start a fight. He didn't understand why his father wouldn't just talk with him. It didn't matter what the conversation was. But his dad would rather watch TV.

"Tomorrow we can get ready for your trip," Arty said to Jamie. Arty also planned to tell Jamie as much about his new city as he could. He wanted Jamie to be ready for the changes ahead, even though he would have given anything to be able to take Jamie around New York himself.

Chapter 10

HE AND Arty took a walk and talked after dinner, with Arty trying to tell him absolutely everything about the Big Apple. Jamie was afraid his head was going to explode... but he couldn't wait to get there. Only this wasn't how he had planned to go—alone. Arty's friend Ryan would be there to meet him and all, but it wasn't going to be the same. And he'd be lying if he said he wasn't nervous about it.

But lying in bed with Arty softly snoring next to him took away some of the jitters, especially when Arty rolled over and hugged him close. He'd spent the last few hours staring at the ceiling thinking about his father. Lately, his dad had become a tyrant, trying to force him to do what he wanted. It was as if he thought that his way was the only way and that Jamie should just toe the line. Things hadn't always been that way. He closed his eyes and let his mind go back to the times when his mom and dad had taken him swimming. He and his dad used to race to the swim platform, and his dad usually let him win. Jamie knew that man was part of his father as well. He only wished his dad would let him out sometimes. But people changed, and maybe that part of his dad was truly gone and probably only existed in Jamie's memories. The father he had now would never willingly let Jamie live the life he wanted, so Jamie's only option was to do it without his support. He had already come this far. He wasn't going to turn back now.

Jamie sighed quietly, hoping he was making the right decision.

"You have nothing to be worried about. The way I see it, you're going to take New York by storm. They aren't going to know what hit them." Arty chuckled, and Jamie slowly rolled over, drawing nearer until his lips pressed to Arty's.

He loved how Arty seemed to have more confidence in him than Jamie did in himself. It was like there was someone behind him, rooting for him—his own personal cheering section. Jamie had never had that before. "Come here," Jamie whispered, tugging Arty on top of him. He ran his fingers down Arty's side, and Arty writhed and laughed out loud.

"Ticklish," Arty warned, and Jamie did it again, only to have Arty retaliate, and soon they were giggling and squirming, tossing the covers onto the floor. "We need to be quiet. Dad's asleep."

Jamie settled down. "I think it's too late for that. If your dad is a light sleeper, I'm pretty sure the fact that the bed banged the wall is going to wake him up."

Jamie felt heat rising to his cheeks. "Maybe he'll just think you're fucking me and it's a head-banger." He covered his mouth with his hand as he snickered.

"A head-banger?"

"Yeah. You know, fucking someone with enough force that they bang their head on the headboard over and over again. You've never heard of that?" Jamie teased.

"Have you ever done it?" Arty stalked up the bed toward him. "It sounds hotter than it really is. By the time you're done, the headache lasts for days and all the fun's over... at least, so I hear." Arty grinned as he came closer. "Ryan is a real fan, so if you hear banging in the night, just close your eyes and try not to think about it. Ryan can go for hours, so...." Arty came even closer, and as soon as he got near his lips, Arty lost it and started laughing. "Dang, I almost had it."

Jamie smacked him on the shoulder. "That was a mean thing to say about your friend."

"Mean? You just wait till you hear all the kinky stuff he gets up to." Arty held him down on the bed, still chuckling for a few seconds before growing serious. Arty captured his lips, and the mirth disappeared, replaced with instant passion. Damn, the way Arty could make him want and think of only one thing with just a kiss.... Jamie wound his arms around his neck, pulling him nearer, wanting more and determined to get it, even if it was three in the morning.

Jamie settled on the mattress, getting comfortable, wrapping his legs around Arty's waist. He was so hot, and the warmth increased by the second. "We can't be like we were on Katherine's boat, where you scared the fish," Arty whispered.

"Me? I seem to remember a certain person yelling at the top of his lungs," Jamie countered. "You frightened everything in the eastern Gulf." Jamie cut off the argument with another kiss. Comfort, warmth, heat, passion, ecstasy…. One quickly followed the other, and soon Jamie lay still, both of them bathed in a sheen of sweat, satiated and quiet, the only sound in the room their ragged breathing.

Arty got one of his secret towels, wiping them both up before adding it to the laundry, and then sleep washed over Jamie after a few minutes of wondering how he was going to manage without Arty.

Jamie had quickly grown to count on Arty being there for him… and it was amazing going to sleep next to him. But now he was headed to New York, alone. Their separation would only be for a few weeks, and Jamie was going to have plenty to keep him busy when he got there, but still, it was going to be a huge adjustment. Jamie wondered if he should wait for Arty here, and take whatever his father had to dish out. But Arty and his dad didn't need the drama that would come with a visit from Jamie's dad. Besides, the ticket had already been bought, and Jamie was on his way toward a dream he had never really thought would come true.

"Just go to sleep. We can sort out everything else in the morning." Arty pulled him closer. "You're going to do great, I know it. New York is just like any other city, only bigger, and Ryan will be there to help you stay out of trouble."

"Trouble? Me?" Jamie asked.

"Yeah. I can tell you're a real wild man. I can see it now. You'll be out until all hours, getting drunk, coming home with a different guy every night…." Arty chuckled. "Just as long as the guy each night is me."

Jamie closed his eyes. "You're the only one I want." He let sleep overtake him as Arty gently kissed his shoulder. They didn't talk any more, and Jamie sighed as he drifted off. He still had plenty to be nervous about, but he felt better. If Arty thought he could do it, then he wasn't going to let him down.

THE NEXT day, his last in Florida, Jamie helped Arty get the boat ready for the next fishing run. They went for a walk, and Katherine took them both out on her boat to watch the dolphins play in the bay. They spent all their time together, and Jamie didn't want to let Arty out of his sight. It seemed like they'd had so little time to actually be together, and now Jamie was going to be leaving.

His father had called one more time, and this time he'd seemed more reasonable, even plaintive, until Jamie had told him yet again that his ticket was purchased and that he was leaving. Then his dad got angry in his usual way, even threatening to come to New York to find him. All Jamie had done was wish him good luck. "New York isn't Iowa, where you know everyone and there are no secrets. People disappear in New York, absorbed by the masses." He'd paused. "Dad, are you really trying to make me hate you? Is that it? Do you want me to be miserable? To come home so you can treat me badly?" That was received with stony silence. "I need to make my own way, Dad." He didn't give his father a chance to pick up steam once again. "I'll call once I'm there to let you know that I made it okay." He had ended the call and felt somewhat better. He had finally said his piece, and his dad might have listened this time.

Arty got him checked in for his flight and made sure he was packed. He had no idea it could be so hard to say goodbye to someone he had known only a matter of weeks, but Jamie didn't want to go. He had found someone who seemed to not only understand him, but who encouraged him and saw that he was worthwhile. And not just because he was strong or worked hard. Arty liked him for who he was, warts, short temper, and all. That was hard to let go of, even for a little while.

His flight was early in the morning, and Arty got him up and drove him the hour across the bridges to the Tampa airport. He pulled into the departure area under the overhang, and Jamie sat in the passenger seat, tempted to ask Arty to take him back. But he reached for the car door and paused. "You'll be out as soon as you can, right?" Jamie asked, biting his lower lip.

"Yes. I have to see my dad through this, and then I'll be back. It shouldn't be more than a few weeks. I'm going to make a call today to my agent and ask her to meet with you. I can't guarantee anything, and she might only give you five minutes, but it's something. Margaret is tough as nails, but she knows talent and a great look when she sees it." Arty leaned over the seat, and Jamie kissed him. "Just go and have fun. I'll be up as soon as I can get there. Remember to put on the sweater and heavy coat before leaving the airport. You're going to need it."

"I'm from Iowa; I understand cold." He smiled and kissed Arty one more time before leaving the car and getting his suitcase and small backpack out of the back seat. It was everything he had in the world. When he closed the door, Arty waved and then pulled away. Jamie stood outside the terminal doors and sighed. He was off on another adventure. He just wished he was doing it with Arty. Taking a deep breath, he took a step toward the terminal and went inside, checked in at the airline counter, then dropped off his suitcase and got in line for security.

It was too late now to turn back. He had already left Iowa to try to find a better life, and now, because of Arty—well, in part, anyway—he was on to the next stop in his dream.

"Ryan?" Jamie asked as he stepped out of the terminal at Newark and into the frigid wind.

"Yes." The small, agile-looking man in a thick coat that almost dwarfed him hugged him and then tugged Jamie back inside. "I don't have a car. We need to get to the train station so we can get into the city."

"Oh. I feel sort of dumb for suggesting we meet by the doors, then." It was obvious he had quite a bit to learn.

"Don't worry about it. This time of year, I try to stay inside as much as I can. Not that it's going to matter. The subway is going to be cold anyway." Ryan led him through the airport and then down to the train station. He bought two tickets and carried Jamie's backpack for him. "This will take a few minutes, then we're going to have to change trains, but we'll get close to the building." He stopped on the platform. "How was your flight?"

"Pretty smooth," Jamie answered. "Is everything here always so… busy?"

"Yes. It's all rush, rush, rush around here most of the time. You'll get used to it." The lights near the track began to flash, and then a train pulled in. Ryan said it was the one they wanted, and Jamie hurried on board after him. He ended up standing with his suitcase on the floor between his legs, clutching handhold as the train doors closed and they pulled forward. "Don't let this stuff overwhelm you or anything. Once we get to the apartment, you can settle in. And since I don't have to work tomorrow, I can show you around the neighborhood, and you can learn where to get what you need."

Jamie nodded, watching everyone around him, keeping hold of his suitcase as the train rumbled along, sometimes squeaking and groaning its way along the tracks. The section of what Ryan said was a tunnel under the river took a while and was smooth, long, and stuffy. Once they began to climb again, Jamie breathed a sigh of relief. When they pulled into the next station, Ryan had them get off and climb upward to another track, where they got on another train. Stop after stop passed, and then Ryan signaled that they were next.

By the time they got back up to street level, the sound of the city was deafening. At least, that's the way it seemed to Jamie. He had never been anywhere so noisy.

"We're just over here. This part of town is the East Village. Well, sort of. Our building is just on the edge."

Jamie nodded, looking around at the buildings near him. "I thought they were all skyscrapers."

"Downtown is, and so is Midtown. This part of the city doesn't have the bedrock that those areas have, so they don't build as tall. I think it makes it nicer." Ryan unlocked the front door of a four-story building and led the way up to the top floor.

"Wow, you do this all the time?" Jamie asked.

"Yeah. Arty and I have gotten used to the steps. It's an older building, so it doesn't have an elevator." Ryan unlocked the door, and Jamie went inside.

The apartment was small, with a single room that served as dining, kitchen, and living space. "Arty's room is right here and you can go right on in. It's not very big, but nothing is, here in the city. The bathroom is right there." Ryan pulled off his coat and took it to his room. Jamie went into Arty's room, and there was barely enough space to get around the bed. He set his bag on the single, small chair in the corner and wondered where he was going to put his things. Jamie figured he could live pretty much out of his suitcase until Arty got here and told him where things went.

Jamie sat on the edge of the bed and called Arty. "I made it and I'm sitting in your room."

"Awesome. There's a closet just outside. It's small, but you can put anything you want to hang up in there. I wasn't expecting company when I left, so the dresser is pretty full."

"It's okay." He'd figure things out.

"I called Margaret, and she said that she would meet you at her office tomorrow at three. I'm going to text you the address. Be there at least ten minutes early, and she'll probably give you five minutes, no more."

"Do I talk about what I've done or—"

"Hit her with your best shot. Play a character and do it to the hilt. Don't talk about yourself and where you grew up... all that stuff will come out if she's interested," Arty said.

"Did she have anything for you?" Jamie asked.

"She said she might have in a few weeks, so I need to get Dad better so I can get home again," Arty explained. "Just knock her socks off and smile. For God's sake, let her see that smile." Arty made him feel so good.

"Ryan said he wasn't working and would show me around tomorrow."

"Then tell him where her office is, and he'll make sure you get to the right place. I'm glad you made it okay. Enjoy your first days in New York. I wish I could be there to take you around, but have fun."

"I will. And you tell your dad that I'll miss my basketball buddy." Jamie smiled, and they talked for a few minutes more before hanging up. Jamie was already missing the quiet times he and Arty had shared, like their evening walks or their time on the water.

A knock pulled him out of his wishful thoughts. "Are you hungry? I have some eggs, if you'd like."

He lifted his gaze and left the room, joining Ryan in the kitchen/dining area. "Thank you." He looked around what seemed like a miniature living space. "Are apartments this small all over?"

"Yes. Some people live in a single room that's no bigger than this one. This apartment is rent-controlled, at least to a degree, and I was lucky to get it. Really lucky. It belonged to a friend who left the city, and he put in a good word for me. Then Arty came to live with me, and he took that space. It might have been a closet at one time, but it's a bedroom now."

"I don't want to sound like I'm being picky or anything. It's just very different."

Ryan nodded, added onions and some vegetables to a pan on the stove, then cracked a couple of eggs into a bowl. "You get used to a very different level of personal space here. Privacy is often simply a matter of not looking. Just mind your business, even when you're on the street. People sort of keep to their own zone. I don't know how to describe it. Arty said you were from Iowa. I suppose they have lots of fields and wide-open spaces there? The houses are bigger, and you probably had your own bedroom?"

"Yeah, I did, and we lived in a big old farmhouse that was my grandparents'," Jamie said.

"Here we live lives of efficiency. We shop several times a week, and only get what we're going to need for a few days because that's all the space we have." Ryan put the eggs in the pan with the vegetables, then got out plates while it cooked. "So… you and Arty."

Jamie blushed.

"I see," Ryan continued.

"Is that bad?" Jamie asked.

Ryan shook his head. "Not at all. It's about time that Arty got back out there again. It's been two years since he's dated. I was starting to think he had been revirginized." Ryan put his hand over his mouth. "I say things like that sometimes. Don't let it shock you. I forget that I shouldn't be out in nonqueeny company." He barely paused before continuing. "Not that I blame him. The last few guys hurt him badly—they didn't treat him well. A few cheated on him and used him as arm candy to boost their own images. It was disgusting."

Jamie laughed. It felt good. "I'm not offended. Arty said you work for a clothes designer."

"Yes. I love it, and someday I want to have my own line. But that will take a miracle and a half. I'm really good at my job, but I think my designs lack a particular spark. Chanel, Gaultier, Lagerfeld—they all had a vision and a way of making a design their own. Each of them could make a little black dress, and yet, you'd know it was theirs." Ryan put the plates on the table and sat down, then jumped up again. "I forgot drinks. I think I have a beer and some diet soda. Though I should probably just drink water. They say the diet soda is bad for you, but I like the bubbles and don't want all the sugar."

Jamie tried not to snicker. "Water is great."

Ryan got two glasses and returned to the table. "Anyway… I was saying…. Oh yeah. I need a way to freshen up my designs and somehow make them mine."

"Are you making dresses?" Jamie asked. He knew little about clothing designers, and the names Ryan had mentioned didn't mean much to him, but they seemed to get Ryan excited.

"Yes, and some people love my stuff, but I don't think my pieces have that pizzazz yet. I hope it shows up soon or I'm going to be sunk and stuck in the work-rooms for the rest of my life doing someone else's designs."

Jamie nodded. "Is that your passion? Women's fashion?" Jamie asked. He didn't understand it. "I mean, you're gay… right?"

"Yeah…," Ryan said.

"So why aren't you doing stuff for guys? You like guys and you think they're hot, right?" Jamie asked, and Ryan gave him a "duh" look as he ate. "So make clothes that will make the hottest guy even hotter." Jamie lowered his gaze. "Back home, there was nothing provocative. One of the stores outside of town had copies of Playboy and magazines like that. I never went in there except to buy a Coke when I was out that way, and I stayed away from that part of the store because I didn't want anyone telling my dad they saw me. So I used to look at the ads in the regular magazines."

"You mean like Calvin Klein and things like that?"

Jamie nodded. "They were hot, like on TV, when that guy jumps off the cliff in the white bathing suit to get to the woman down below. At first I thought they were selling swimsuits, not cologne. I mean, please, splash some of that stuff on and not only will you not suddenly look like them, but you'll probably stink to high heaven too. But if you could make a normal schlub look really good, then that would be worth something."

"But the money is in women's fashion."

Jamie sighed. "Follow your passion and the money will follow." Jamie scratched his head. "I wish I could remember where I heard that. Lord knows it wasn't from my dad."

"Now that sounds like Arty. He's always telling me to do what makes me happy." Ryan finished his eggs, and Jamie did the same. He'd been hungry, and they tasted good.

"Great minds think alike," Jamie quipped and took care of the dishes. It was the least he could do to help. "I talked to Arty earlier. He said that I have an appointment with his agent at three tomorrow. Can you tell me how to get there?"

"I can take you there when we're out. Don't worry." Ryan pushed his chair back. "You're an actor?"

"I want to be. I was decent in high school and got some really good parts. I think she's doing it for Arty."

Ryan scoffed. "I swear that woman does nothing for anyone except herself. In the beginning she got Arty some good jobs, but she hasn't done crap for him since. Who knows, maybe the old broad feels guilty… that is, if she can feel anything at all." Ryan clearly didn't like her.

"Have you met his agent?"

"No. But I don't like her on principle because she isn't helping Arty all that much." Jamie had to give Ryan credit. He must be a good friend if he could hate someone he had never met on someone else's behalf. "Still, if she's willing to see you this way, then maybe…."

"He said I'd get five minutes."

"Then make the most of it. Do you know what you're going to do?"

"I have to think about it. Last year I did a community production of *Streetcar* and I played Stanley. I could do something from that. There are some very powerful scenes," Jamie said. "Though I suspect she has heard them all." He sighed. "How do I blow her away?"

"Do your best. In this town, the trick is to fake it till you make it. So walk into that office like a star. Act as though you're on top of the world. Then deliver whatever you're going to do with your whole being, and see what she has to say."

"Fake it till you make it. Does that really work?"

"As long as there's something to back it up, why not? Someone like Margaret can spot a no-talent hack a mile away. But if you have talent… and confidence, along with drive, you might just get a chance."

Jamie hoped he was right. And he really wished he was having this conversation with Arty.

"THAT'S THE office," Ryan said the following afternoon, and Jamie nodded. The building looked like something out of a movie, and he was trying to figure out which kind. Horror came to mind, but that was probably just the way his stomach was still contemplating giving up the lunch he'd had earlier. "You have a few minutes. Call Arty."

The wind blew off the water, chilling everything, so he stepped closer to the building and pulled out his phone. "I'm here, right outside the building."

"Then take a deep breath. You can do this," Arty said.

Jamie swallowed, wanting to curl into himself. "How do you know? You never saw me act. I could be a no-talent hack, like Ryan said."

"You aren't. Remember, I saw you on the boat, and you can dance and sing. You have talent. Just give it everything you have. No one can ask for anything more than that. Don't be cocky. Just be confident, and don't suck up to her. Just be respectful, like you are, and knock her dead. I wish I could be there with you."

"I wish you were here too." It felt as though his big break was more of a baptism by fire. Jamie closed his eyes and let Arty's voice wrap around him and give him strength. The butterflies quieted and he stood up straighter.

Ryan tapped his wrist, probably to tell him that he had to go. "I'll let you know how it goes."

"You do that." Arty paused, and Jamie waited because he seemed to want to say more. "Just be yourself," he said after a moment. "Remember the day on the boat when you danced for me? Be happy and as carefree as you were then." The warmth in Arty's tone took away the wind and the cold from the air.

"I will." Jamie said goodbye and motioned to Ryan, who led him into the building and up to the second-floor office. Jamie told the lady at the desk, whose phone was ringing off the hook, who he was, and she motioned to a chair with one hand, holding the phone with her chin. Ryan sat next to him, and Jamie sighed as he waited for the woman to get off the phone.

"She'll be with you in a minute," the woman said and went back to talking, shuffling through things on her desk to find what she wanted. Jamie could imagine her as one of those octopus-dinosaurs on the *Flintstones*. Finally the phone stopped ringing, and she looked up from her desk. "You can go in now. Margaret will see you."

Jamie stood, walked over to where she pointed, knocked on the closed door, and stepped into a meticulously neat office to find a woman in her fifties, wearing a plain gray suit, her hair in a bun, with eyes that seemed to see into his soul, staring up at him. "I'm Jamie Wilson."

"Yes. What do you have for me?" She sat back in her chair. "I don't have all day. Just do what you're going to do for me, and we'll see what we have to work with." At least she wasn't rude or bitchy.

Jamie hurriedly took off his coat and tossed it into the chair in the corner, remembered that time was ticking, and went into his song and dance from *Oklahoma!* Jamie could hear the music in his head and let his feet tap out the beat as he moved. There was limited space, but he did his best to show that he could do both. He only did a short piece before quieting and presenting a scene with Stanley from *Streetcar*, pretending the agent was Blanche. Margaret blinked at him, but said nothing, and Jamie filled in Blanche's lines in his head and continued. He had no idea if she liked or hated what he did. She gave no reaction at all. Jamie supposed he should be grateful she didn't look at her watch or tell him to get the hell out of the office.

Out of desperation, he ended the scene, took three deep breaths, and collapsed to the wood floor, lifting himself as though he were being held by two invisible people, holding himself as though he were a small woman rather than the guy he was. He knew he must have looked out of his mind, but he held her gaze, which was a feat in itself, and gave his single line. "I have always depended on the kindness of strangers."

He hung his head demurely and stayed still, waiting as his character was carried off to the asylum.

Slowly he moved out of position to stand back up again. He hadn't narrated what he had been doing; he'd just done it and hoped that Margaret would understand the characters he was portraying. Jamie felt like he'd just run a sprint, and when she said nothing more, he turned to the chair to gather up his coat. He'd tried, and he was grateful to Arty for setting it up. He'd just have to do better next time.

But when he turned back around, Margaret finally reacted. "Holy shit."

Chapter 11

"MARGARET SAID what exactly?" Arty asked as he stood on the edge of the dock, looking out at the water.

"She said that she thinks I have something special, and she's going to take me on as a client. I'm supposed to get pictures taken, and she wants me to get a haircut and all kinds of things. She gave me a list." Jamie sounded overwhelmed. "I don't know where to get all this done here. Heck, I couldn't get some of this done in Iowa at all."

"Did she offer to help you?" Arty asked. He should have known that if things worked out, Margaret would move quickly. But he hadn't really expected Jamie to have this kind of initial success.

"I don't know. Everything was said so fast, and the receptionist never got off the phone, so I couldn't ask questions. I can't afford to have all this done. It's going to take all the money I have to be able to eat until I can get a job and get paid for it."

"Okay. You should have gotten a card from her. Call the office, you'll get the receptionist, and tell her what's going on. She can probably help you. Anne is pretty nice once you get to know her, and she knows everything about who does what. I also suggest that you ask if Margaret is going to help with the initial set-up. She does that sometimes." It could be a lot. Lord, he remembered how Margaret had peppered him with questions when she'd first taken him on.

"Okay." Jamie seemed so unsure. "I got another call, so I have to go, but I'll talk to you later." Jamie hung up, and Arty put his phone away, wishing he was there. He sighed as the sun beat on his back.

"Is everything ready?" Katherine asked. "We leave on Monday."

"Yes. I have the boat fueled and the tanks are full of water. I have some systems that I want to check, but we'll be ready to go." His head was thousands of miles away, and he wished he was home.

"How is your dad?" she questioned.

"Better. The pain seems to be less, and the infection has cleared up. The doctor said Dad pulled some muscles when he fell, but he didn't do any damage to the bone, so that was good. But he'll be laid up for another four weeks." He tried to keep the disappointment out of his voice and probably failed. His time in Florida just kept getting longer and longer, and Arty wanted to get to Jamie in the worst way. His feet tingled just thinking about it. He turned as Gerald strode over to where they were talking. "Morning," Arty said.

"Another run?" Gerald came to a stop a few feet away, his face as red as a snapper.

"We're getting ready to go next week. Is there a problem?"

Katherine excused herself and walked down the dock and out toward the parking lot.

"You and your dad are going to need to find another place to dock." He looked as smug as shit. "You know I just manage the plant. It's my father who owns the land, and this is written notice that you can no longer use our land to access your dock." He thrust the sheet of paper forward, and Arty stared at it, shaking his head. "I know your dad has been accessing your dock across our land for years, but that is going to end. See, you only own the piece of land your dock connects to the shore. You don't own any of the land around it." He grinned.

Arty sighed, and damned if he didn't need a cup of coffee. It was too early in the morning for this shit, and he had been up late equipping the boat. Arty turned away, headed for the Pelican, took one of the empty seats, and asked Milton if he could get a coffee. He motioned, and Gerald sat down.

"Do you really think we're that stupid? If you look at the deed to the land our dock occupies, you'll see that your grandfather, who sold the land to my dad years ago, added a clause to the deed that states that we get access to the land across your property… *in perpetuity*. So, your sheet of paper doesn't mean squat. See, our deed and the provision in it is recognized and registered by the state." He turned to Milton and thanked him. "I appreciate this so much."

"No problem," Milton said and sent a glare Gerald's way before leaving the table.

"You know this little stunt is going to be all over in about five minutes," Arty continued. He was really starting to hate this guy. Not that he'd ever thought much of him to begin with. "And I dare say that this will get back to your father." He stared hard at Gerald and saw him flinch. Just as Arty thought, Gerald's father probably knew nothing about this. God, this guy was stupid. He leaned over the table, lowering his voice. "You'd better drop this whole thing, or I will start telling stories about high school... and some of the things you used to like back then."

Gerald paled. "No one would believe you," he growled, soft enough to make sure no one heard. But there was fear in his eyes as he glanced from side to side. "And so help me, once you leave...."

"You sure about that? I have no reason to lie, and you aren't very popular right now. I suggest you drop whatever move you think you have cooked up, be nice, and walk away, or else I'll find a way to call on your wife and tell her some of the things I know that happen to turn you on." Of course, Arty had no intention of doing that, but the fear in Gerald's eyes was enough to assure Arty that he held the upper hand. "All I've ever asked is that you treat the people around here fairly. Nothing more. And this sort of thing...." He took the piece of paper and tore it to shreds, then put the pieces back in Gerald's shirt pocket. He definitely knew how to make a point.

"And after you go back to New York?"

The ass figured he could bide his time. "Information can be delivered in a lot of different ways. I can make sure my father knows...." That seemed to send

another shot of fear through Gerald. "I can write let-
ters, tell all my friends here, put it on Facebook. You
let your imagination run wild." He was tired of playing
this game. "I'm not asking for anything from you other
than to treat the people here well. Be a part of the community instead of an asshat. This is a good place, with
wonderful people who pull together when things get
rough. And believe it or not, things will get tough for
you eventually, and you're going to want them to have
your back." He sipped his coffee and tried not to think
how spread thin he felt. He was trying to hold on to a
budding relationship at a distance, keep the wolves at
bay for his dad, and protect the community from going under if the plant closed. Jamie needed him in New
York, and Arty wanted to go home. But he had a run to
make for his father and probably another one after that,
so he wasn't going to get to New York as soon as he
had hoped. On top of it all, he just plain missed Jamie.

He hadn't felt right since dropping Jamie off at
the airport, and he didn't understand why. At first he
thought it was because he was worried for him and had
gotten used to having him around, but that wasn't it.
Last night he had stood on the docks, and a pod of dolphins had frolicked just in front of him. He had turned
to point it out to Jamie, but of course he was alone.
Maybe this was how his father had felt... and maybe
still did, about his mom. One thing was for sure, Arty
didn't want to talk about it with anyone. Hell, maybe
in some way he was starting to understand his father.

"Arty," Gerald said, pulling him back to the
present.

"Sorry."

"I was saying that I need to get back to the plant."
He stood. "You won't say anything...?" he whispered,

and Arty nodded. If he had to use a little fear and even blackmail to get Gerald to behave like a human being, then so be it. The guy had been a real shit back in high school, and it didn't look like he'd changed very much at all.

Arty finished his coffee and figured it was time to go back to work. He had things he wanted to get done that morning, and they weren't going to get finished if he sat on his butt.

"HOW ARE things going now?" Arty asked Jamie that evening.

"I have an appointment for pictures, and Margaret has someone giving me a haircut tomorrow. She also wants me to get some new clothes, but Ryan is going to help me out there. We talked about him designing clothes for men instead of women, and he's come up with some wonderful designs, so he's making me some things to wear." He sounded a little more in control than he had been the last time they talked.

"That's really good."

"How are things there? Did you get a good crew?"

"Lyle and Katherine are going out with me again, and I found a fourth person. Everything is going to be fine on this end. I just need Dad to get better." This was taking longer than he'd ever hoped. "Maybe I'll be ready to come back in a few weeks." Three, maybe four, was reasonable. "Will you be okay until then?" He only hoped he would be.

"Yes. I asked about a job today at Chico's. They wanted a server to work evenings, so I applied. They seemed interested when I told them I had waited tables before. The man asked me a bunch of questions, and

I answered them all, so maybe I'll get lucky." Things seemed to be happening for Jamie, but Arty just felt like he was spinning his wheels… and doing a lot of waiting.

"That's really good and…." Arty's voice broke. "I really miss you, Jamie." He held his head and tried to keep his headache and heartache at bay, but nothing worked. With his dad's reinjury and Jamie being gone, he felt alone and his world looked flat. "When you were here, everything was bearable. I looked forward to getting up in the morning because I got to see you. Now… there's nothing." He knew he was in love with Jamie, but he wasn't going to tell him that over the phone. That seemed like a cop-out and wasn't fair… to either of them.

"I miss you too." He heard the same loneliness in Jamie's voice coming back to him. "Arty… I more than miss you. This is so new and nothing at all like where I grew up. And Ryan is helpful and nice… but he isn't you." He grew quiet, and Arty clutched his phone, wishing he could make Jamie feel better. Hell, he wanted to feel better… he wanted to be there. Arty closed his eyes, and he could almost imagine himself there, holding Jamie in his arms and telling him all the things he wanted him to know. Maybe he could get up the courage to tell Jamie that he loved him. "But you'll be here soon… right?"

The longing in Jamie's voice tore at him. Arty knew just how far New York was from Iowa, and the culture shock had to be bone jarring. "As soon as I can. I promise. Coming back to New York and seeing you is what's keeping me going right now." He took a deep breath.

"Me too. You do what you have to for your dad and then come here. I have things I want to tell you, but I can't say them over the phone." Jamie sniffed, and then the line was quiet. "I'm going to be better once you get here."

Arty pulled himself together and stopped the phone from shaking against his ear.

"Are you getting used to the city?" He needed to talk about something else, just to keep himself together.

Jamie didn't answer right away. "It's so loud all the time. Even at night with the windows closed and the curtains pulled, I can still hear everything outside. It's strange, but I think I'm getting used to it. I don't hear as much as I did at first. Ryan showed me around the neighborhood. He's really nice." Arty was grateful to Ryan, but he was also a little jealous. He wanted to be the one to help Jamie over these bumps and worries.

"Ryan is a special person with a kind soul. He'd be mad if I told you this, but he needs someone to take care of him too. So watch out for him a little."

"I see that. Ryan watches out for everyone else." He should have known that Jamie would understand right away.

"Yup, but not himself so much. Anyway, have you figured out the subway yet? It's the easiest way to get around that isn't going to cost you a fortune." Arty wiped his eyes and took a deep breath, going through the list of things he'd come up with to try to help Jamie. "For your appointments, make sure you leave early and give yourself plenty of time to get there. The people that Margaret set up to help you will report back to her if things don't work out." God, he remembered being late for an appointment and having Margaret chew him out big-time over it. She could be helpful as well as the dragon lady when she wanted to be.

"I think I'm all set. I know the route, and Ryan told me what time to leave." Jamie cleared his throat, and his voice sounded more like he had things under control, with little of the nerves from their previous call.

"Is that his sewing machine in the background?" Arty asked.

"Yeah. He's been working to make me something special, and he brought home some designer samples for me to take to the photo session. I know this is important, and I hope it will all work out."

Arty hoped so. "What I think is that you'll take really good pictures and that you'll also be able to let people see Ryan's designs whenever you show them your book. There are a lot of people out there with talent, and half the time, it's simply a matter of you having... or not having, the look the director or casting coordinator is looking for." He smiled. "Just relax, and try to take things one step at a time. There's a lot of activity at first, but then it's plenty of waiting—waiting for auditions, then waiting for callbacks. You wait even longer to find out if you actually got the part." God, he remembered those calls to say he had gotten the job. Well, as soon as he got back, Arty was going to be back pounding the pavement for auditions. Maybe after some time away things would improve for him.

"Of course. I'll do my best," Jamie said.

"I know you will. I have faith in you." Arty smiled and carried the phone into the kitchen with him, getting out the dishes that Mrs. Marshall had brought over. He peeked inside and then slid them into the oven. He and his dad were lucky that Mrs. Marshall was an amazing cook. He warmed up the potatoes and the sliced pork.

"I better go so I can get Dad some dinner." He was already tired. "I… miss you." Once again it was as close to the words in his heart as he dared say.

"I miss you too," Jamie said and grew quiet. Arty wiped his eyes with his fingers and tried not to sigh. "You have a good night and I'll talk to you soon," Jamie added hurriedly, then hung up. Arty felt the loss as soon as his voice was gone. If he was talking to Jamie, then he could pretend that he was still here, at least for a little while. Arty made a small salad for himself and dinner for his dad, then set the table. Once the food was hot, he called his dad, who came in using one crutch and sat down, immediately turning on the television. It was becoming a ritual, and with nothing else to do, Arty found himself watching whatever was on as they ate in near silence. As soon as he was done, he took care of his dishes and put the rest of the food away, leaving his father alone to finish his dinner and watch television.

He went out the front door to the road, walking toward the water and the docks. Maybe one of these nights he should borrow his dad's car and take a drive out onto Longboat Key just for something different to do. But tonight he climbed on the boat and sat in the back, looking at the dark expanse of water.

"Sort of intoxicating, isn't it?" Katherine said from the dock, and Arty waved her onto the boat. "I don't think I could live anywhere else. Once that gets in your soul…."

"It's only water, and sometimes it smells like dead shit," Arty retorted.

"What crawled up your butt and died?" Katherine asked. Arty shook his head and sighed. "Where's Jamie?"

"In New York. His father was determined to come here and get him. We were going to go to New York together anyway, so I sent him on ahead. Now I'm wondering if that was such a good idea."

"Because he's unhappy there?" Katherine asked, and Arty shrugged. "Or are you the one who's unhappy because Jamie's gone?" He nodded. "I see. You aren't going to be here forever, you know. You'll go home soon enough."

"I know. But with him here, I could bear this place. There was someone to show around and do things with. Someone…." He didn't want to go too far into what he said. "I didn't want to come here in the first place. I visit Dad sometimes, but now it feels like I've stepped into his life so I can keep him going, and put my own life on hold. I know I'm doing the right thing." He stood, went down below, and returned with a couple of beers from the refrigerator, then handed her one. "Is it wrong to want my life back?"

"You could just go and be done with it."

"No, I can't. Dad needs me. Not that he would ever tell me that he appreciates what I'm doing." He popped open the beer and took a swig.

"Are you doing all this for the accolades? That doesn't seem like you."

"No, I'm not. But my dad talked with Jamie more than he did with me. I have no idea what he thinks about anything. If something's wrong, he gets upset, but otherwise, he says nothing at all."

She opened her beer, but didn't drink. "Maybe he doesn't know what to say to you." She held his gaze and then drank from the bottle. "He could also be one of those people who, when things are fine, feels that there's nothing to say. My dad was like that. He would tell you when you were wrong, but otherwise he was happy just to leave me be."

"I don't know. Dad's getting older, and I don't know what he plans to do. Is he going to fish for the rest of his life? Jamie left because his dad is hell-bent on him taking over the farm in Iowa. Dad says nothing about me taking over the boat and his quota."

Katherine shook her head. "Are you dumb? My guess is that your dad wants a better life for you than this. Fishing today is one of the last vestiges of subsistence. Fishermen are almost like the peasants of old. That may be extreme, but they're dependent on the weather and the whims of the market, and beholden to someone to finance what they do. And they go down when there's no catch, like your dad almost did."

"He gave me a good life," Arty said.

"But you left," Katherine countered. "Not that I blame you, but maybe that's what your dad wanted. Not for you to leave, but to go out and find your own place. God, I don't know. I'm only grateful I date women and don't have to deal with this shit." She flashed a smile, and Arty rolled his eyes. "If you want my advice—which is free, so you get what you pay for—let your dad be. You can't teach old dogs like him any new tricks, and he is the person he is. Expecting him to be someone else is only going to give you an ulcer." She took another drink of the beer. "God, I love it out here on the water."

"Is that why you never moved too far away?" Arty asked.

"Pretty much. I like it here and I have a good life. After a couple more runs and when you leave and my sabbatical is over, I'll go back to teaching." She smiled and lightly patted the table.

"How did I never know that was what you did?" Arty asked, setting his bottle aside as he sat up.

"You didn't ask, and I didn't volunteer. Not that it mattered. I needed some time to get away from books and students and get in touch with my roots once again. I have a book that I'm working on and it hasn't been going well, so I thought a change of scenery would help. It turned out to be awesome. The words are flowing again." She tipped back the bottle.

"What do you teach?"

"Medieval history." She grinned. "So I know what I'm talking about."

"I guess you do." Arty sat back once again and relaxed. Katherine was right—it was nice out here near the water.

ARTY CALLED Jamie that evening before bed, and they talked again. He did the same each day, right up until he was scheduled to set sail. Then, with the boat ready and a good crew, he pulled away from the dock in the early hours of the morning, quickly passing out of cell signal range and away from most communication. Life on the boat required plenty of work, and Arty was grateful for it. It kept his mind on the task at hand and off of Jamie and what he was doing.

The days were easy because they were all busy. The nights were a completely different matter. The boat was quiet, and Arty lay in his bed, thinking of Jamie and wondering what he was doing and if things were going well for him. The days passed slowly, with some days of great fishing and others where they couldn't catch anything to save their lives. It only added to the frustration that built inside Arty each day they were out.

Finally, after long hours and some luck, they filled the boxes and headed back to port.

"Are we in a rush?" Katherine asked once Arty had set the course.

"It's been nearly two weeks, and some of the fish have been on ice for nine days. I think we had better make sure everything is well packed and get back as quickly as we can. Thankfully, it hasn't been too hot, but the heat is starting to build." He powered up the boat and sped along the water. It didn't matter that he was so tired he could barely stand up. He hadn't slept well for much of the trip.

"Fine. I can follow the course. You go down and get some rest before you get sick." She glared at him, and Lyle echoed her sentiment. Arty didn't fight them and climbed down into the cabin. The small area was already muggy, so he cracked open one of the small windows to create a breeze and climbed into bed. To his surprise, he fell asleep almost instantly.

Arty woke hot and sweaty. The engines still hummed and it was dark. His shorts and T-shirt were soaked, and his mouth was bone-dry. He got out of bed intending to change, but every muscle in his body protested. Still, Arty drank some water and took a couple of Tylenol from his kit and went up on deck.

His legs were unsteady, and he held on as he climbed. Katherine was behind the wheel, and the other two hands were nearby. "Is everything okay?" he asked and started to cough. Great, getting sick was the last thing he needed.

"We're fine. Drink something and go back to bed." Katherine pressed a bottle of water into his hands and shooed him back into the cabin. He changed his clothes and removed the blanket that was damp, then climbed onto the bed again and closed his eyes. It wasn't long before he went from hot to shivering cold, and he pulled the blanket over him, curling under it as he shivered. Eventually he warmed up again and the medication kicked in. Arty slept restlessly for a while, waking as the others came in and left.

He didn't want to move and felt somewhat better after sleeping. Katherine brought him some juice at some point. He drank it and went back to sleep, trusting that she was able to bring the boat in.

Arty was completely wrung out by the time they made port the following afternoon. He tried to get up to unload their catch, but he was too weak, and Katherine didn't let him anywhere near their cargo. He did sign for what was delivered, and then Katherine maneuvered the boat to the dock. Arty managed to muster enough strength to get off the boat with his things and down to the house. He dropped his bag on the floor of his room before crashing in his own bed with a soft sigh.

He lost track of time as he slept. "Drink. You need to drink." It was his dad's voice, but one he hadn't heard in a long time. Arty didn't have a chance to think about it. That took too much energy. Instead he drank, swallowed, and then coughed before drinking again. He probably should have been grateful he wasn't throwing up, because he didn't have the energy to get out of bed. "Have some more. You need to finish the glass." Arty did and then lay back down.

"Thanks, Dad," Arty whispered hoarsely as a hand pressed to his forehead.

"You feel cooler." His dad left the room and returned with a cool towel and some pills. Arty took them and groaned at the cool towel, which felt wonderful. "Just rest, and I'll get you up in a few hours for some soup." Arty closed his eyes, falling back into his disjointed dreams of Jamie lost in New York and Arty unable to find him, no matter what he did. Finally, after thrashing for a while, Arty was able to locate him, and his mind settled into a deep sleep that felt restful.

He woke with a start to a banging. "He isn't here," he heard his father say. Arty swung his legs over the side of the bed and lifted himself up. He didn't inhale too deeply because the entire room smelled stale and sickly. Arty pulled on a robe and opened the door, letting fresh air inside. He needed a shower and then maybe some food.

"I know you know where he is," a deep voice growled.

"Jamie isn't here," his dad said again, and Arty padded out toward the living room.

"You must be Mr. Wilson," Arty said softly. "I'm sorry, but Jamie isn't here. He left for New York more than two weeks ago, and I honestly haven't heard from him in a while." Not that he hadn't wanted to—he'd been out and then sick. But Jamie's dad didn't need to know that. "I'm sorry you came all this way for nothing, but can I offer you some tea or something?" Arty was planning to make some for himself and he figured he'd kill the guy with good manners and kindness.

"I don't want any tea. But I do want to know where Jamie is." He stormed across the room, and Arty stood as still as he could, rocking a little on his legs.

"You need to leave now. Jamie is in New York. I drove him to the airport myself. I'm sorry if you came all this way for nothing, but I believe he already told you that. Maybe you should listen for a change." Arty sat down, and his dad stood near him, leaning on his crutches.

"But I need him to come home."

Arty sighed. "Do you ever listen to yourself?" he asked, too tired to censor his thoughts. "This is Jamie's life, not yours. He gets to make his own decisions. He went to New York on his own accord, and I doubt you're going to get anything out of him by acting this way." Man, the guy was as stubborn as anyone Arty had ever met.

"Our farm is a family legacy. I can't just let it end," Mr. Wilson said. "Jamie knows that. It's something I've taught him since he was a child." He seemed so frustrated.

"Sometimes things are about what our children want instead of the things we want as parents. It's our job to support them and in the end let them make their own decisions. Not force them to do what we want." His dad turned and sat down. "Arty hasn't been feeling well, and you busting in here isn't helping him. I think it's time for you to leave."

Arty yawned, went over to the front door, and pulled it open. "I can't help you. But I will tell Jamie that you were here when I talk to him next." Arty was tired and, to his surprise, hungry.

"So, you do know where he is." The menace in Mr. Wilson's voice was unmistakable.

"I never said I didn't." Arty had had enough, and he stepped closer to Mr. Wilson, pulling his robe tighter around him. "What kind of friend would I be if I told you when he asked me not to? Like I said, I will tell him you were here the next time I talk to him, and I will say that you really want to see him. But…." Arty held up his hand. "I will also tell him how rude you were." He took a deep breath. "You know you can't make him do what he doesn't want to do." It sounded like the man was so wrapped up in what he wanted that he never stopped to think about Jamie... or anyone else.

Mr. Wilson's shoulders slumped, and he paused a few seconds and then turned to Arty's dad, as though he might understand. "But the farm is all I have to give him. I want Jamie to have things better than I did. When I inherited the farm, it was in debt and barely making it. Now it's doing well. I want him to have that kind of stability and a better chance than I did. Surely you can understand that."

His dad sat quietly. "What if Jamie doesn't want to be a farmer?" That was his dad. No explanations and as few words as possible. And yet, it told Arty more about how his father felt about him than if he'd written a thousand words in verse.

Mr. Wilson stared at both of them as though his world had just been rocked and he wasn't sure what to do. He opened his mouth and then closed it again, then turned and left the house. Arty almost felt sorry for him as he closed the door. He also felt for Jamie. Arty and his dad didn't talk, and his dad was still a mystery to him, but at least he and his dad weren't on completely different planes of existence. His dad was just in a box that Arty had never quite figured out how to unwrap. Still, he went over to his dad and leaned over the chair, hugging him before straightening up again to go make some tea.

While he had the water on, he returned to his room and rummaged through his bag until he found his phone, which was dead. He plugged it in and waited for it to power up. He had sixteen messages from Jamie, one each day asking how he was. And there was one from his boss at the restaurant, asking when he would be back. Arty called right away and explained the situation. His manager was understanding and asked to be kept in the loop. The last six were from Jamie, asking if he was okay, each sounding a little more worried than the last.

Arty called Jamie back and it went to voicemail, so he called Ryan. "My God, you are alive. We were going to call out the Coast Guard."

"I just called Jamie and it went to voicemail, so I thought I would let you know. I got back and then spent the last two days in bed. I was really sick and out of it." Thankfully he was feeling better. "The phone was dead, too, and—"

"I'll be sure to tell Jamie that you called. He's at a callback right now." It took a second for that to sink in.

"A callback… already?" God, that was shocking, and Arty blinked. Holy crap.

"Yeah. Jamie is at home in front of the camera, and he wears clothes like nobody I have ever seen. I have to let him tell you all about it, but this is the second callback in two days." Ryan seemed blown away, and Arty reached for a chair in order to sit down.

Arty's phone buzzed. "I have a call from Jamie."

"Take it. I'll talk to you later. Glad you're feeling better." Ryan hung up, and Arty answered.

"You're there." Jamie sounded breathless.

"Yes. Sorry. I got back and I was really sick. Katherine had to bring the boat in for me, and I've been sleeping. Dad has been taking care of me." Arty could already feel fatigue catching up with him. "I finally had enough strength to wake up and call. How is it going there?"

Jamie hesitated. "I got a job! Margaret has had me on lots of auditions. The first ones she said were just for practice, but the director of this play, Off Broadway—"

Jamie breathed hard, he was so excited. "Anyway, he said I had a great look, and his assistant gave me the script for *Fathers and Sons*. I read over the scene they wanted while I was waiting and thought about how to play it, because my character is me in so many ways. And when I went back out, I handed the assistant back the script and did the scene."

Arty was flabbergasted, and a million questions popped in his head. But he went with the one that was really important at the moment. "You did the audition off script?"

"Sure." Jamie acted as though it were nothing. "I was good, too, and they asked me to come back, and I did, and they gave me the job. Margaret called and told me. It's in six weeks, and I get paid scale. She says that a lot of people will see it."

"Was that what you were doing today?" Arty asked.

"Oh, no. That was a callback for a print thing. They wanted me to play basketball for a cologne commercial. That was a lot of fun, and they seemed to like me for that too." In his mind, Arty could see Jamie jumping up and down. "But I don't know. Ryan says that you never get too excited until they call, and I suppose he's right." Jamie seemed to calm down a little. "Oh, and I got a job… a real job at a restaurant just down the street. I started that last week. So I can pay my own way."

The kettle whistled, and Arty turned it off, got the tea bags into two mugs, and poured the water. "That's great. I knew you could do it."

"I guess I did too. Margaret says I have some kind of magic touch, but I don't know. Maybe I've been lucky so far and it isn't going to last."

Arty smiled and sat back down while the tea steeped. "You have talent, and people can see that."

"Yeah. But I know that most people have worked hard for a lot of years to get the breaks I got in just the last few weeks. I mean, I got an agent right away and even auditions and a job."

Arty could hardly believe it himself, but he refused to be jealous. It didn't take anything away from him and his efforts that Jamie was having some early success. It was unlikely, like lightning striking twice, but it did happen, and he needed to be pleased for Jamie. But, damn, it was hard. Of course, it didn't help that he wasn't feeling well. "That's true. But just be careful and work as hard as you can. Sometimes what comes today is gone tomorrow." Arty knew that pretty damned well. "Is everything else all right?"

"Yes, I know the subway now, and I can get around and find just about anything. Ryan has been great." Jamie paused. "When are you coming?"

"Hopefully in a few weeks." His dad had to be healed by then. "I have to take Dad to the doctor this week, and I'll know more then. Hopefully he can take over the boat soon."

"I understand. I just want you here with me," Jamie said, and Arty smiled, getting his cup of tea and sitting back down.

"I want to be with you too." He sighed. "I need to go and get Dad his tea, and then I'm going to lie down and rest again. You have a good night, and I'll call you again tomorrow." Arty hung up the phone and took his dad his tea before trudging to his room. Arty finished his tea, got some fresh clothes, then went to the bathroom to clean up before climbing back into bed. Maybe the best thing for him would be to just stay in bed. His career had stalled, and Jamie was doing well enough on his own.

Chapter 12

"I ALREADY have several jobs. Do I need to go on more auditions already?" Jamie asked Margaret as he sat on the edge of the bed in Arty's tiny room. He had been here long enough that Arty's scent had faded from the space and it smelled like him now. Even the clothes in the room had lost their Arty-ness.

"Yes. These are auditions for jobs that will happen once the others are done. Word about you has gotten around. Do you remember the photographer you worked with for the basketball ad? He was thrilled with you, and he told some friends. That company might want you for a follow-up. You're a hot commodity, an instant success of sorts, and I'm trying to line up enough work to keep you busy. Do you have the rehearsal schedule for your play? Send me copies so I don't overbook you."

Jamie nodded. "I will email it over right away." This was all happening so fast, it was hard for him to get his head around it.

"Very good. I'll use that to have Anne put together a calendar for you so you know where you have to be. Okay? Just do your best to relax and take things one step at a time."

"I will," he agreed, even though Jamie felt like he was going to fly apart. This hadn't been the deal at all. Arty was supposed to be here with him, and things were supposed to take much more time. He was supposed to suffer and go through rough patches, go to audition after audition with very little to show for it. He'd been prepared for that because that was what they always showed on television. He and Arty were to spend their time curled up in their little room away from the rest of the world and be happy. Instead, all this activity swirled around him, and Arty wasn't here. "Thank you," he said rather quietly, and when she hung up, he tossed the phone on the bed and held his head. Maybe his dad was right—maybe he should have stayed on the fucking farm.

He was a success—that should have made Jamie happy. But all it did was fill him with fear. The shoot for the basketball ad had been a blast, and he'd loved it. The photographer had been fun, and he'd even approached Jamie after they were done to ask about getting some coffee and maybe dinner. Jamie had thought he was being nice. He'd called Ryan to tell him that he wasn't going to be home.

"He asked you what?" Ryan had said. "No, no, no. That isn't professional or usual. Photographers don't ask their subjects for coffee or dinner unless… well, he's thinking of it as a date, or maybe a hookup." Then Ryan had paused. "Is that what you want to do?"

Of course, Jamie had thought of Arty and shook his head. He also knew what Ryan was thinking. Jamie had just wanted to make a few friends and thought this might be the chance. "I'll ask him what his intentions are."

Ryan had laughed at that. "Just don't get yourself into situations you aren't comfortable with. You can always call me, and I'll come get you if you want."

"Thanks." What Jamie wanted was for Arty to be the one he could call and the one to come get him, and maybe put an arm around his shoulder and explain to the photographer that Jamie had a boyfriend. Hell, Jamie just wanted someone to have his back. Jamie had explained that he could go out as a friend, but that he was seeing someone. Rodney had nodded and then sighed and remembered an appointment that he had forgotten. At least it didn't seem that Rodney was angry about it, because he'd recommended Jamie to others. So that was okay.

Jamie left the room and stepped out into the tiny central area of the apartment, where Ryan was making some dinner. "Margaret has some more auditions for me, and she's going to have Anne make a calendar." He hurried back, snatched up his phone, and forwarded the rehearsal schedule to Margaret before he forgot about it.

"You can share my mac and cheese and tell me about what's going on," Ryan said, "and then I can tell you my good news." He finished up and sat on the sofa, handing Jamie a bowl. It was the box kind—comfort food at its finest.

"What's your news?"

"I got a call from your photographer's assistant. Remember, I made you the outfit in your photo book, and you must have told him about me." Ryan seemed about ready to jump out of his skin.

"Yeah, he asked when he was looking through it. Why?"

"He's putting together a spread for a magazine, and he loved the work I did and wants to use the outfit I made for you. He and I are going to meet to discuss what he wants." He grinned. "This could be my big break." Jamie set the bowl on the table and gave Ryan a hug. Then he picked up his food again and took another bite, growing quiet once more. "You should be happy about what's happening," Ryan said, studying him.

"I know, and I am...." It was hard to put his finger on why he had the blues. Guys would kill for the luck he was having. Movies had been written about people who came to New York to find fame and fortune and spent years chasing it. And yet here, things seemed to have found him instead. Maybe it was his dad's voice in the back of his head telling him he didn't belong here. That his place was on the farm. Jamie had heard that refrain almost since he'd started walking.

"Yeah. I should be too." Ryan looked out the small window. "It isn't the same without Arty. He and I used to celebrate our successes with a pizza and beer."

Jamie pulled his feet up on the sofa and turned to Ryan. "Am I being supremely stupid?" Somehow he needed to get his father's message out of his head, and he couldn't replace it with Arty. Hell, that's what he'd been doing. Jamie had been holding on to Arty as a way of gathering his strength to fight his father.

"Okay…." Ryan paused with a fork on the way to his mouth, and the pasta glopped back into the bowl. "What brought that on?"

"I've been here almost a month now, and I've got all this good stuff happening. I should be jumping out of my skin with excitement. But it seems wrong, somehow." Jamie tried to get a handle on it. "I knew Arty for a little over three weeks, and I can't stop thinking about him. This was supposed to be our next adventure together."

"Next?"

"Oh, yeah. That first fishing trip was one hell of an adventure—the weather, Reginald falling overboard, the huge grouper, and when the engine stopped dead." He smiled as he remembered all of it. "The hours we sat on deck, just the two of us, talking. The nights I lay in bed with him so close, but not able to do anything about it, wondering if he felt the same way I did. It was one hell of an adventure."

"You always remember when you fell in love," Ryan said, batting his eyes, and Jamie snickered. Sometimes Ryan could make him forget the crap that swirled in his mind. He also knew Ryan was right.

"What I don't understand…. I only knew Arty for three weeks or so. I've been here longer than that now, and I'm starting to wonder if he's going to be coming at all. Or if what we had was just a figment of my imagination."

Ryan set his bowl aside and returned the hug Jamie had given him earlier. "He'll be here. I know he will. Think about this. If this is a new adventure, then it's possible that you need to take the first steps of it on your own." There was something in the way that Ryan spoke, a steel rod under his words. "Now finish eating, and you check that calendar when it comes in. And don't you have lines to learn for your play?"

"I already know the whole thing, and my first rehearsal is in three days. I'm pretty sure how I want to play my character, but I'll talk it over with the director as well. I don't want to be a dick or anything." Even though parts of the play mirrored his life so closely it was almost spooky. Reading through the play and learning his lines had made him think about his own father. In the play, his father was filled with so many expectations for his son that he refused to let go of him. The two men struggled for almost the entire first two acts, fighting each other, and in the end, parted ways forever. The more he read it, the more Jamie realized that while that outcome was a possibility for him and his dad, it wasn't the one he wanted. But he hadn't quite figured out how to change the ending for them. And maybe it wasn't even possible. But Jamie could see through his character in the play that he needed to make the effort. Still, the end result would ultimately hang on whether his own dad would be willing to change in the way his father in the play wouldn't.

Jamie finished his snack and figured he might as well get ready to go to work. He was due for his shift in the restaurant in an hour. Jamie took care of the dishes and went in to change.

When he came out wearing his black pants and crisp white shirt, Ryan was on the phone. "I didn't mean to disturb you, Mr. Reynolds, but I was calling Arty." He huffed slightly. "I see… I need to speak with him. Could you tell him I called, or I can just leave him a voicemail…?" Ryan listened, and Jamie got his things ready for work. "Thank you." Ryan hung up and shrugged as Jamie went to put on his coat and got ready to brave the short walk to work.

Chapter 13

ARTY RETURNED from his walk. He had gotten back from another fishing trip, this one shorter than the last one, and thankfully he hadn't gotten sick this time. He pulled open the back door to find his dad sitting at the kitchen table. "Arty…." He lifted his gaze, his eyes deadly serious as he held up his phone.

"Yeah, Dad." Arty sat down across from him. "Is something wrong?"

"Arty, you're fired." Then his dad stood up and slowly left the room. The chair creaked in the living room as his father sat down.

"What do you mean?" Arty asked, pushing back his chair. "You can't fire me. I never worked for you." He stood in the doorway, seething.

"I mean that you're fired. Your fishing days are over. My leg is feeling better, and I'll take the boat out next week." He reclined in his chair and turned on the television as though he had just explained that tomorrow was going to be hot… in Florida.

"Excuse me?" Arty was shocked as hell, and anger threatened, but he did his best to control it and stay calm. "What do you think you're doing? You were going to lose the house and the boat when I came down here. I got a better price for the catch, financed four fishing runs that were some of the best we've ever had, got the bills caught up, and actually have the family business humming, and you tell me I'm fired? I don't fucking understand you at all."

"Don't use that language with me." He lowered his feet and sat up. "You're hiding. I don't know exactly what from, but you are. This isn't what you want out of your life, and it isn't what I want for you." Jesus, his dad was actually talking to him. Arty sat down before his legs collapsed out from under him in supreme shock.

"I'm making sure you have something to return to once you're on your feet," Arty explained feebly, a little shocked at how dead-on his father was. Maybe he was hiding, but life was easier here and more predictable. It seemed he was good at fishing and could make a success of it. What if he wasn't good enough to make it in New York? What if his career truly was over?

His dad stood up without a cane or cast on his foot. "I'm back on my feet, and I'm taking the boat out for our next run. You need to stop this moping that you've been doing. You're driving me crazy."

"Me? I'm driving you crazy? I'm here with you for weeks, and you never say a word. You watch television, eat, and that's it. Your friends come over and you talk to them, but I spend hours with you in the same damned house and you say nothing until it's 'You're fired, Arty, I don't need you anymore. Get the fuck out.'" He was working up to a good tantrum.

His dad just looked at him like he had two heads. "You helped me when I needed it. And I'm grateful. But it's time you went back to your life. The one where you show up on my television every once in a while. The life that you made and tell me about whenever you call. I like hearing about your friends and the auditions you go to." He smiled. Fucking hell, his father actually smiled. And he'd been listening. All this time, he had thought his dad just sort of zoned out on their calls. He never said much on the phone; Arty had always done most of the talking.

"But, Dad, are you…?" He trailed off at the look in his father's eyes, the same one he'd gotten as a kid and knew he was treading on thin ice.

"I'm fine, and I will be fine. Thanks to you. I'm proud of the way you came down here, determined to help an old fool who thought he was still a kid."

Arty blinked. "You're proud of me?" Those were words Arty had never thought he'd ever hear from his dad.

"Of course I'm proud of you. You left this place to make something of yourself. You wanted to be more than what I was, and I want that for you too." He paused. "I remember you and your mother talking about your dreams, and you were on your way to making them come true. And that's what I want for you… so much more than this." His dad had just said more to him than he had in a year.

"But don't you still need my help?" Arty asked.

"No. In a week, after I get the boat cleaned and equipped again, I'll be ready to go out. With three crew members, I'll be just fine. And honestly, it will be good to get back out on the water again. I've been feeling a little trapped lately," his dad said with a slight smile, nodding at his leg. Then he narrowed his gaze. "What is it you're hiding from?"

Arty shook his head. "You never ask me about my life. Are you sure you want to hear all this?"

"I never ask because most of the time you just tell me. Now you're being secretive and sulky. It isn't like you." His dad knew him better than Arty would ever have thought. The older man stayed quiet, watching him.

"Jamie doesn't really need me. He's doing great in New York, and everything has been going to shit for me. I figured at least here, I was needed."

His dad clapped his hand on Arty's knee. It was a much more intimate gesture than Arty could remember from him in quite a while. "Your career there isn't going to change until you get your ass back to it and work hard. As for Jamie doing well, he's struggling and he needs you. That's what your friend Ryan said." His dad sat back in his chair and put his feet up. "You need to go to New York and back to the young man who made you so happy. He needs you, and you need him. I'll be just fine." His dad grabbed the remote and turned on the television. Arty sat still, not even hearing the television as he wondered what the hell had just happened. Hell, his dad understood that he was gay after all. That blew his mind just a little, because he never really acknowledged it. Maybe his quiet father knew him better than he thought.

Arty didn't waste time. He left the room and got his laptop, booking a flight to New York as soon as he could. He made some other calls about his job to say he was going to be returning, and left a message for Margaret to let her know that he was coming back.

"Line up as many auditions as you can. I'm ready to take New York by storm." Once everything was booked, he sighed, and the fatigue that had plagued him for days fell away. This was the right thing to do. He knew it in his bones.

ARTY DROVE his dad's truck to the airport with his luggage behind the seat and his dad in the passenger seat. "You know, Dad, you could come to New York sometime to visit."

His dad shook his head. "What would I do there?" He continued watching out the windows. After the conversation a few days earlier, things had returned to the same sort of short bursts of words that Arty knew his father preferred. "You come home when you can."

"I will." He retraced the drive he had done with Jamie weeks before and pulled into the airport. He got out and grabbed his things from the back, saying goodbye to his father, who stood at the curb. Arty took a few steps away and then turned, letting go of his suitcases, and hugged his father. Damn, he might not say much, but still Arty felt closer to him than he had in a very long time.

When he stepped back, his dad turned and got to the driver's side of the truck, stopping to look at him across the bed. Arty took his suitcases, nodded, and turned away and headed into the terminal. He had spent weeks ready to go home, and now that he was on his way, he was reluctant to say goodbye to his dad. Maybe that was truly the mark of a good visit, and one he'd needed to have.

THE FLIGHT to Newark was fine, and he got his luggage and waited for the train to take him into the city. There was some issue on the line, and Arty ended up taking a bus into the city, where he transferred to the subway line and then rode to his apartment. By the time he got there, he was grungy and exhausted. The flight hadn't been that long, though everything around it had been hellacious. But now he was home.

The street outside the building had gray snow piled along the curb. Thankfully, it was melting in the afternoon sun. The cold was bracing, but it felt good. Who would have thought he would miss the smell of the city? But he had. One thing he hadn't missed was the flights of stairs to the fourth floor carrying all his danged luggage, but he made it and opened the door.

"Well, look what the cat dragged in," Ryan said quietly, even as he got up from his sewing machine and rushed over before engulfing him in a hug. "Jamie is in the bedroom. His first rehearsal was yesterday, and then he had a late shift at the restaurant. He decided to take a nap when he got home today, and needs to be to work in an hour. The kid is a trooper."

"Jamie is that," Arty said. Ryan stepped back and thumped him on the side of the head. "What was that for?" Arty rubbed the now sore spot.

"He's been working and worrying, and over-whelmed. You were supposed to have come back weeks ago. Everything is moving so fast, and it's damned near overwhelmed him. Then you go on those damned fishing trips and don't call. That man in there jumps every time the phone rings because he hopes it's you." His lips drew a hard line. "He's had to learn a great deal about the city, as well as the fact that he's had success, and that's damned overwhelming as well. So, you deserved a smack." Ryan turned him around. "Now you go in there and talk to Jamie. He's convinced you're never coming back and that he's here all alone."

"But I texted that I was coming and tried to call."

"His phone was stolen yesterday and they cloned it, so he had to get a new one, but he didn't have the money, so I found someone to loan him one, and he had to get a new number. Don't worry about that shit now. Just go on in there and see him. He's had a very busy couple of days, and the city has been a little rough on a trusting guy from Iowa."

Arty sighed and left his bags where they were. Ryan went back to his sewing machine, and Arty quietly opened the bedroom door and went into the darkened room. Jamie was asleep on his side, and Arty closed the door and sat on the edge of the bed.

"I'm getting up, Ryan," Jamie said and rolled over. Then he shot to a seated position, and Arty tugged him into a hug. "You're here! My God, I thought you were going to stay down there forever."

Arty felt so stupid. "Dad is doing better and he can take over now, so I came home." God, he hated the way he'd made Jamie feel. "I wasn't going to stay away, and I got here as soon as I could." He inhaled deeply, reveling in Jamie's scent. He closed his eyes as a sense of rightness settled over him. How things could feel so right so fast….

"So much has happened. I have to tell you all about it," Jamie said.

"I know. Ryan told me that you've been running yourself ragged and working really hard all the time."

"Yeah. I have this play and another photo job. I heard the photographer say he was looking for another guy. So now that you're back, maybe I can call Margaret and she can see if you can do it with me." Jamie rested his head on Arty's shoulder, and Arty closed his eyes one more time. He knew that wasn't likely, but Jamie was Jamie—open, friendly, caring, trusting, and so full of hope... even for him.

"You have to work tonight, don't you?"

"Yeah." Jamie yawned. "Until eleven." He lifted his head, and Arty leaned closer, capturing Jamie's lips. The heat became an explosion, and Arty pushed Jamie back on the bed, tugging at his shirt while Jamie got to his clothes. They thrashed and writhed as their clothes hit the floor. Jamie laughed when Arty accidentally tickled him, the sound drawing out to a soft moan. "I don't want Ryan to hear."

"I'm fairly sure Ryan has a pretty good idea what's going on in here." Arty ran his hands over Jamie's smooth skin, sending his desire through the roof. It had been weeks of thinking, wondering, and lying awake at night wishing Jamie had been there.

God, he was so stupid to have stayed away. Somehow, he should have figured out a way to come back to Jamie sooner. He was happier and felt so much better. Of course, holding Jamie in his arms was reward enough for anything. Arty kissed Jamie once again, needing to taste him.

A sharp knock sounded on the door. "If you two are about done getting reacquainted, Jamie needs to get ready for work, and Arty has to take care of his bags and things, because if I trip over them again, there's going to be hell to pay all over his ass."

Arty held still and waited for Ryan to leave and then buried his face in Jamie's back, laughing.

"You did say he would know what we were doing."

"Yeah, I did. I just didn't think he'd cockblock me like that."

Jamie stroked his cheek. "I'll be back after my shift, and he'll be asleep. Then you and I can have the rest of the night. I have a rehearsal at nine tomorrow, and…."

Arty closed his arms around Jamie, holding him and just breathing him in. "That sounds perfect." He stayed where he was, letting some of the excitement fade. He was just happy to be here. "You should change for work."

Jamie squirmed out from under him and padded bareassed to his suitcase, where he pulled out his neatly folded clothes. "I need to hurry or I'll be late." He dressed quickly and left the room.

"That was mean, you know," Jamie told Ryan, his voice drifting through the door.

"Yeah, yeah," Ryan said and then the sewing machine hummed. "You know, I'm working to make clothes for you, and you're in there fooling around while I'm love-starved and working out here like a dog."

Arty pulled on his clothes and left the room. "Yeah, yeah." He joined Jamie, able to kiss him goodbye before he left the apartment. Ryan settled down to work, and Arty took his bags into the room to put his things away.

ARTY WAITED up for Jamie, even though it was nearly midnight before he got back. He turned off the television as soon as Jamie came inside, and got up from the sofa. "How was your shift?"

"Great. I got really good tips, and I called Margaret and told her what Andre had said about needing another guy. She said she'd call him in the morning." He came right into Arty's arms.

"Things don't work like that," Arty said. "But thank you. It's likely he's found someone else already."

Jamie stepped back. "Maybe he did." He turned away and sat on the futon. "I think you and I need to talk." He patted the seat beside him.

"It's late, and—"

Jamie shook his head, so Arty sat down. "I've had a lot of time to think about things while I was here and you were still in Florida. I came here because I thought it would be an adventure and you would be here to help me. But instead, I ended up coming alone, and—"

"I'm so sorry about that," Arty added. "I wanted to come with you."

"I know. But then you were gone so long...."

Arty nodded. He had a pretty good idea what Jamie was leading up to. "You met someone else and I missed my chance."

Jamie laughed. "No...." He rolled his eyes. "But Ryan made me see that I needed to do things on my own. I was overwhelmed and I still am, but I'm learning to navigate things by myself. I know a few people now, and every day, I meet a few more."

"What is it that you're trying to tell me?" Arty asked.

"That when I first met you in Florida, I was scared and trying to just set my foot on a path to independence. You've been here and made it, so I wanted to follow you. I had this dream that I might be able to act, and since that's what you did, I jumped at the chance to follow you. I figured that I could come here, and you would be there to help me in case things didn't work out." Jamie shook his head. "I was a fool."

"Why is that foolish? I came here and struggled to figure things out too. I was lucky that I had Ryan to help point me in the right direction so I didn't end up living behind a dumpster somewhere. And I wanted to be there for you, the way Ryan was for me. Is that so bad?" Arty was really confused by this conversation. His heart raced, and he wondered what Jamie was getting at.

"I'm not saying this very well. I needed to get away from my father and the farm to see if I could have a life of my own. Because if I didn't, I'd never know if I could stand on my own two feet. The farm was there, and I could have just stepped into that life."

"I think I understand," Arty told him.

"How can you?"

Arty smiled. "You think I was always independent? The easy path is always alluring. The last few weeks, until my dad fired me, I'd been tempted to do the same thing. New York had become hard and nothing had been going my way before I left, so staying on the boat and fishing had become my own means of escape, like the farm is for you."

"Your dad fired you?" Jamie asked, his eyes widening.

"Yeah. He told me that he was going to go back to fishing, and that I needed to get back to my life and you." Arty leaned closer. "He told me that he wanted me to be happy and that he knew that you were what makes me happy." Arty put up his hand. "Honest to God. He actually said that much to me, and I think I understand him a lot better now. Fathers. Sometimes they're a pain in the butt, but then again, maybe we just need to take the time to understand them."

"I'll never understand my dad," Jamie said.

"I think we're getting a little off the topic of what you were saying," Arty said.

Jamie shrugged. "I think it's all wrapped together. I had to be independent and stand on my own two feet while you were gone, and I think I liked it. Dad wasn't there to look out for me, or yell if I didn't do something, and you weren't there to make me get up and fish so we could get home. I had to do all that."

Arty turned toward the door. "So do you want me to leave?"

Jamie snickered and put his arms around his neck. "No. But it means I have to be able to stand on my own and make my own decisions. The other day, I got offered another job… and I turned it down." Arty's eyebrows shifted upward. "They wanted me to pose naked, and I wasn't going to do that. I talked it over with Margaret, and she didn't think it was right either."

"Margaret has good instincts most of the time," Arty agreed with a relieved sigh, grateful that he wouldn't open a random magazine and see his boyfriend's nakedness splashed over the pages.

"True. But I made the decision myself, and I can continue to make them for myself going forward."

Arty leaned back. "Of course you can. You already made the hardest decision—you left home in search of your own life." Arty smiled. "Did I tell you that your dad showed up in Florida after all? Yeah, I'm sure I did."

"And you didn't tell him where I was. I called my dad, and he was furious, stewing in a hotel room near the airport, waiting for the flight home. God, he was so angry with me. He blamed me for the fact that he came to Florida and I wasn't there, even though I had told him not to come. Apparently he thought that I'd said I was going to New York just to put him off." Jamie shook his head slowly.

"I wish I could have been there for you," Arty said.

"Well, I had to be there for myself, and I told my father that I wasn't coming back to the farm. I told him about my play here and that I was going to be in a magazine ad for cologne and one other, maybe. It seems the cologne people really like me and are negotiating with Margaret for me to be exclusive with them." He shrugged. "I'm not holding my breath on that one." It seemed Jamie was too excited to stay on his train of thought. Not that Arty minded. He didn't particularly want to talk about the drama with Jamie's father right now anyway.

Arty groaned. "I'm gone for a few weeks, and you become a cynic. What the heck have I done?" He fanned himself with his hand, and Jamie pushed him back on the cushion, his weight pressing wonderfully down on top of him.

"I sort of figured things out. If they want me to be exclusive with them for a period of time, then they have to pay me to compensate for the other work I might get. It's that simple. Just like on the farm, when you choose to plant corn and then the price of sorghum goes through the roof. It's all about weighing one thing against the other, because you can't do both."

Arty grinned. "Damn… just damn."

"What?"

"Here I thought you were a country kid, and I was afraid the city might chew you up and spit you out.

But damn it all if you aren't playing the game better than I did."

"It isn't a game. It's making your choices and sticking with them. I had to do that on the farm. I had Dad to help me there, and here I have Margaret and Ryan. And now you." He laid his head on Arty's shoulder with a soft sigh. Arty wound his arms around him, and Jamie relaxed into him.

"I hope we have each other, because I'm going to need you just as much as you're going to need me. I somehow have to kick-start my own career, and I don't quite know how I'm going to do that." Still, he would figure it out.

Jamie lifted his head, meeting his gaze. "Are you going to be jealous if things take off for me and not for you?" Sometimes Jamie knew exactly how to get to the heart of things. "You know stuff is happening for me, and I could just not tell you about it. But I should be able to share good news when it happens, and I don't want to feel bad about it."

That was the heart of what Arty had been fearing, and Jamie had just brought it out into the open. "You should never feel bad about anything good or exciting that happens for you." He held his breath. "I can't say I won't be jealous sometimes, but I'll also be happy for you even if the green-eyed monster kicks in." Sometimes things weren't fair, and that was how it was. Arty was going to need to fully understand that. "As long as you aren't jealous when I land a big movie role."

Jamie shivered. "I don't know if I want to do that kind of work. I really love the stage, and it feels so amazing to be working in that theater. There's an energy there that I think I want to have in my life forever.

Maybe Broadway is in my future and maybe it isn't, but I do love doing live performances. They feed my soul."

Arty tugged Jamie down into a kiss. He had an amazing soul, and Arty was lucky to have him in his life. "Just never sell it."

"Sell what?" Jamie asked.

"Your soul. People do that all the time in this business, and I don't want you to ever do anything that makes you uncomfortable or unhappy. You and I can work as waiters and eat mac and cheese every day for a year, and I'll be happy as long as we can look ourselves in the mirror."

"I can't sell my soul any more than I could sell my heart, because they don't belong to me anymore." Jamie kissed him once again, and Arty felt his own heart warm and his pulse race.

"Are you two still up?" Ryan asked as he padded out of his room and over to the kitchen. "For goodness sake, go to your room, and please keep the screaming to a minimum. Some of us haven't had a date in weeks and have to get up in the morning to go to work." He opened the small refrigerator and pulled out some juice.

Jamie stood, blushing. "We're going to bed now." He took Arty's hand, tugging him toward the bedroom. "Night, Ryan." He closed the door and pushed Arty down onto the bed. "I think it's time that you and I get reacquainted, and I don't mean by talking the entire night." He crawled toward him on the bed. "Sometimes talk is cheap, and tonight I have much better ideas about things we can do." He took possession of Arty's lips, energy radiating off him like a heater, surrounding Arty in a bubble.

"When did you get so bossy?"

Jamie's eyes darkened as he reached for the light next to the bed. "I've been waiting for you to come for weeks. What do you think I did here night after night? I stared up at that ceiling, imagining what I was going to do to you once I had you again."

Arty shivered as Jamie tugged off his U of Florida T-shirt, tossing it over his shoulder. He clearly wasn't wasting any time—something Arty was more than grateful for. His hands shook as he reached for Jamie, trying to get at his skin as Jamie bared Arty's.

Between the two of them, it didn't take long until they were naked, heat to heat, Jamie pressing Arty against the mattress. It may have been cold outside, but the small room was warm and growing hotter by the second. "I'm not going to be slow," Jamie warned, and Arty understood. There was plenty of time for slow and tender later. Right now, the attraction and need were too great. Jamie grabbed a condom out of the single bedside stand and rolled it onto himself before getting into position. "Tell me if this is too fast...." He gave Arty about three seconds before pressing into him.

The burn was exquisite and nearly overwhelming as they joined together once again. This was the intimacy and intensity Arty craved. Arty gasped, his muscles tensing.

"Did I—?"

"Don't you dare stop," Arty told him before Jamie could finish whatever he was saying.

"I won't for as long as you'll have me." Arty arched his back as Jamie proceeded to send him on a trip to heaven that he hoped lasted for hours. It sure as hell felt like it. Time finally seemed to stand still. After weeks of wanting, hoping, and even his own idiocy, he was here with Jamie.

"Is it too much?" Jamie asked.

Arty cupped his cheeks in his hands, drawing him down into a sloppily deep kiss. "It will never be too much. You are all I could ever want." He groaned as Jamie continued moving, rolling his hips, driving deep until Arty could hardly breathe and then pulling back to give him a respite, only to drive him forward once again.

"You know we're going to wake Ryan."

"Then he's going to have to get himself a set of earplugs," Jamie countered, moving faster. Arty's eyes rolled to the back of his head and he reached for himself, but Jamie batted his hand away, stroking him in time, keeping Arty on the edge until he quivered from the depths of his toes. This was intense control, and he wasn't going to be able to hold off much longer. The heat from inside intensified and bubbled toward the surface.

Arty held his breath as pressure built more and more until he could hold it no longer and tumbled into release, with Jamie following right behind him. Arty held Jamie close, gently stroking up and down his back, content and damned happy. "I love you, Jamie," Arty whispered. Yes, he still had the postsex floaties, but that had nothing to do with it.

"How can you?" Jamie asked, and Arty paused, slowly angling his head until he could see Jamie's eyes. "I mean…." He smiled. "I love you too, and I missed you like I'd miss a limb. But are we jumping into this too soon?"

"Says the man who's been sleeping in my bed for the last month."

"Alone," Jamie retorted.

"Yeah, and I missed you every second of the time I stayed away. I know what it's like to be in love, because it felt like some part of me was missing and now, right now, it feels right once again." Arty cleared his throat. "The longer I was in Florida after you left, the more I kept thinking how easy it would be to stay there." He wanted to say this right. "I haven't had any good parts in months, and I figured that maybe my career was over… is over. I don't know. Maybe what I've gotten is all I'm going to get and staying there was the best I could do." He had to be honest.

"Why didn't you stay? Because your dad fired you?" Jamie slowly sat up, his eyes filling with doubt and hurt that Arty knew he'd put there by not being clearer.

"No. As soon as he fired me, he freed me. I didn't have to worry about him anymore because my dad, the fisherman, was back. I think that maybe this was one of those 'life coming full circle' sorts of things. In order to appreciate my father, I had to spend some time in his shoes. And he had to stay out of them, in order to appreciate what he had and what he wanted. God, I don't know. I don't write plays or shows—I act in them… when I can get the work." Arty shook his head as his heart sped up. He'd been rambling, and he needed to get to the point. "I came back… hell, I couldn't get on a plane fast enough, because of you. I don't know if my career is going to stay in the toilet forever. I have no idea if I'll ever work again, but I pictured myself in five years, and I don't know what my job was or much of anything else. But I was happy and I was standing right next to you. That much I knew." He held Jamie's gaze. It was frightening to say those words, but he was more afraid that if he didn't, he'd regret Jamie not knowing exactly what was in his heart.

Jamie swallowed and nodded. "Damn, you sure know how to sweep a guy off his feet." Jamie pounced, kissing Arty as he pressed him against the mattress again. "God, I missed you. Don't worry so much. Nobody knows what the future is going to bring. We never really have a clue."

"True." Arty closed his eyes, holding on to Jamie tightly. It was time to face whatever the future held. But at least he wasn't going to have to do it alone.

Chapter 14

JAMIE PACED the living room of the apartment, staring at his borrowed phone. He needed to get a new one, but he hadn't had time. Still, he wasn't sure what to do.

The key sounded in the lock, and Arty strode into the apartment, closing the door after him. "How did the audition go?" Jamie asked.

"Really well. I think I have a chance at this job." Arty put his bag down on the futon and hurried over, wrapping his arms around Jamie's waist. "I got a call from Margaret, and it seems that you and I have a job next week." He grinned, and Jamie hugged him in return. "Andre apparently liked my look as well, and when Margaret told him that you and I were together, she said he was thrilled."

"See? Sometimes things do go right." Jamie grinned. He had indeed called Margaret, and things looked like they were going to work out. The shoot was for another fragrance print ad.

Jamie had asked if this was a good idea with the other company still in negotiation for exclusive representation. "Honey, you can't turn down work because they can't seem to make up their minds," she had said. Margaret had something up her sleeve, and Jamie had booked the job.

"That's excellent. Maybe my dry spell is over." He flashed a smile, but Jamie saw the strain in Arty's eyes. He had been to so many auditions and calls in the last few days. Jamie wondered how there could be that many in the entire city, but apparently there were. When Arty wasn't sleeping or working, he was coming or going from an audition.

"What does Margaret say?" Jamie asked.

"That it's just a matter of time before everything lines up and things come together. It's what she always says, but I'm holding on to that anyway because it makes me feel better than the voice in my head that tells me I'm a worthless hack who just got lucky before." Arty smiled, but Jamie knew it was forced.

"You know that isn't true, so let that crap go." He hugged Arty. "I could talk to some of the people I'm working with to see—"

Arty's eyes became hard as granite. "I'll find my own jobs. I'm really grateful for the one we have together, but you don't need to be the one to find me jobs. Your career is your own, and I'm happy for your success. If my fortunes turn, then that's wonderful, but I

need to know any success I get will be because of me.
Not because you did something, okay? You're a rising
star; I know that. Don't worry about me. I'll make it on
my own, or I won't. I don't want to be an anchor around
your neck. It's your time to shine, so make it happen."
He sighed. "What were you pacing about when I came
in?" Arty asked as he stepped away, took off his coat,
and hung it up in his closet.

Jamie held up the phone. "I need to call my dad
and I don't want to. But I have to explain things to him
one more time. I can't leave them the way they are."

"I see." Arty patted the seat next to him. "If you
feel you have to do this, then make the call and get it
over with."

"That's just it. I don't know what to say to him.
I've been running through things in my head, but nothing sounds right."

Arty chuckled. "That's because this isn't a play
and you don't have a script to work from. Just tell him
the truth and let it come from your heart." He pulled out
his phone and handed it to him. "Does your dad have
FaceTime?"

"Yeah…," Jamie answered.

"Then call him that way. Let him see your face,
and you can see his. I know it isn't the same as being
in the same room, but it could help." He slipped an arm
around Jamie's waist, and Jamie took the phone. Maybe Arty was right… well, right and wrong at the same
time. This wasn't a play and there wasn't a script, but
Jamie had to play to his audience. That was something
he'd learned the first time he was onstage. With live
theater, every performance was different because the
audience was different. They laughed at different times,
and the energy was different, so you gave a different

performance. He needed to try something else, give a different kind of performance with his dad—take a different tack if he wanted to get different results.

He dialed the number he knew by heart and waited as it rang. Jamie expected his father to decline the call, but instead, he was surprised when his dad answered.

"Jamie," his dad said, rather happily.

"Yeah, Dad." He tilted the phone so Arty was in the frame. "Arty's here with me." He turned the phone again, so it was just him on the screen. "You and I didn't exactly leave things very well the last time we talked. In fact, you and I haven't talked in a long time. We either yell at each other or tune the other out." His breathing shuddered, but he held it together.

"I take it you're in an apartment in New York," his father said.

"Yes. I'm living with Arty and Ryan. The three of us share the place. It's small, but it's nice." He slowly turned the phone so his dad could see it. "The entire place would probably fit in our living room and kitchen, but it's ours, and we live differently here."

"I see," his dad said.

"Mr. Wilson," Arty said from next to him, and Jamie shifted the phone. "I know you want the best for Jamie."

"Yes. I always have. I'm his father." It sounded more like a royal pronouncement than a tender expression of love, but Jamie hadn't expected anything different.

"Dad, I didn't call to fight with you. I really didn't. You're my dad, and nothing is going to change that. Not the fact that I live in New York or that I don't want to farm. I'm still your son, the one you held in those pictures that hang on the wall as you go up the stairs.

And I'm still the kid that you got a pony for when I was five years old. I remember you walking me around the farmyard for an hour after I got her. She was the best gift ever."

"That was your mother's idea," his dad grumbled.

"Maybe. But you were the one who walked me around the yard on her back. That wasn't Mom. You did, every night after you came in from your chores." Jamie could feel a lump forming in his throat. "We've been fighting and at odds with each other for so long, I was beginning to think there was no way you and I could communicate any other way." His hand shook, and Jamie transferred the phone to the other hand to steady the video.

"I suppose so." His dad's voice held none of its usual fight.

"Dad, I don't want to spend the rest of my life on the farm. I really don't. I love being onstage. And I think I'm good. I told you I was in a play here in New York, and the director really likes my work. The play is called *Fathers and Sons*, and it's about two dads and two sons and neither set can talk to each other. But the sons can talk to their friend's father about just about anything. It seems weird until you realize that the fathers and sons have all these expectations about each other that the others don't. I play one of the sons, and it's a huge role."

"And you think you and I are like that?" his dad asked really skeptically.

"In a way. You have a bunch of expectations about what I should be and how I should act, and I don't meet them. I want to be someone different from what you want me to be." Jamie paused because he needed a second to get his thoughts together. "Let me ask you this.

Do you want me to be happy?" It was a loaded question, and Jamie knew it.

His dad seemed taken aback by the question. "Of course I do."

"Then, Dad, you have to let me go out and find what makes me happy. You can't make that decision for me. Things would be great if I wanted to be a farmer, but I don't." He had to go for broke and push his point. "Did you want to be a farmer? Was this the life you had pictured for yourself when you were my age?" His dad didn't answer, and Jamie saw the conflict behind his eyes, as well as the anger that was about to explode to cover up what his dad didn't want to say. "Then sell the farm and go do what makes you happy."

The stunned expression on his father's face was almost priceless. His dad had always talked about how the land had been in the family for three generations and that Jamie was to be the fourth. "But—" Jamie knew he'd hit the nail on the head.

"Good farmland in Iowa, especially what we have, which is perfect for raising corn, is selling for ten thousand or more an acre. The farm is worth millions, Dad. Why continue to do something you don't want to do when you can do something else? Lease out the land if you want, sell the livestock and travel maybe. Meet someone who makes you happy. You're still young—you can do whatever you want." It occurred to him as they were talking that his dad wasn't happy either, and it probably had been quite some time since he had been.

"Jamie, I don't think that's…."

"The thing is, Dad, just do what you want. I just want you to be happy… as much as I want to be happy." Finally, they seemed to be listening to one another. "See, I want the man who walked me around that yard on the pony to smile the way he did back then. I always remember the times you were happy. They were fun, and you used to play with me." God, those times flashed through his head like a magic slideshow. "Go out and decide what you want to do. But all I ask is that when you're out there getting your mojo back, you let me find my own."

His dad did something Jamie hadn't seen him do in quite some time: he smiled. The lines around his eyes deepened and then, as the smile faded, some of the worry and care that his dad always seemed to carry with him slipped away. His dad looked younger. "I don't know what to say about all this."

"You don't have to say anything. But maybe once you've figured out what you want to do, you can come to New York for a visit. We'll show you all the sights." Never in a million years had Jamie expected to be inviting his father for a visit, but it seemed right. And when Arty put his arm around his waist and leaned closer, staying out of the picture but there in case Jamie needed him, that felt right too.

Jamie watched for the very first time in his life— that he could remember anyway—as his father wiped his eyes. He said nothing about it, but knew his dad had teared up. "I think I'd like that. Though you know, it's hard to get away from the farm."

"Maybe you could come for one of the holidays." Jamie liked the thought of having his father come for Thanksgiving or Christmas. "You don't have to make plans now, but think on it." Jamie swallowed hard and wanted to visibly relax, but things could go downhill pretty quickly. "I'll let you go, Dad, but I'll talk to you in a few days."

"And you have to let me know when that play of yours opens."

Arty smiled up at him, and Jamie tried to keep his voice steady. "I'll send you a ticket if you want to come." He ended the call and handed the phone back to Arty. "Well, Jesus, Mary, and Joseph, I had not expected that at all."

Arty set the phone on the table and nestled right in. "You found a way to speak to him that he understood. And someday I want to see those pictures of you on the pony."

"That just might be possible now." God, he felt like the knot in his gut had started to unwind. His phone rang and he snatched it up. "It's Margaret."

"Huh?" Arty said, checking the time on his phone.

"This is Jamie." He tried to sound as happy as possible whenever he talked to her. He figured she had to deliver enough bad news that she needed someone happy to talk to sometimes. "How are you, Margaret?"

"I'm exhausted, and it's all your fault. I have spent the last two hours going back and forth among cranky creative types, but I have things sorted." She shuffled papers on her end. "Are you ready? I'm forwarding the images that will be used in the Uomo Elegante cologne ads to you. They are stunning and they plan to use them on a billboard in Times Square. They want you as their spokesperson."

"Does that mean I shouldn't do the other job with Arty?"

"That's what I've been on the phone to work out. They have agreed to extend an exclusive contract for two years. You will only appear in their ads, and they are going to pay you handsomely for it. The fact that you already have this other job allowed me to ask for more." She was clearly happy. "Everyone had agreed to the stipulations, so you and Arty are going to do the shoot. It's for a literacy campaign, and they are going to step in as a sponsor, as well. So everyone wins. I'll have more details once I get the contracts, but brace yourself for these images. They are amazing and some of the sexiest I have ever seen with clothes on." She was nearly laughing.

"Thank you. Arty is right here with me, so I can tell him that we'll be doing the photo shoot together."

She paused. "I need to talk to him as well."

"Is it good news?" Jamie asked.

"Naughty boy. He deserves to know before you do."

Jamie snickered and handed the phone to Arty. "Hey, Margaret," Arty said, and Jamie let them talk, getting up to get himself a beer. Hell, he was wondering if it was too late to go out to celebrate. He didn't have a shift tonight, and Jamie was pretty sure Arty was off as well. They usually got one night during the week when neither of them worked. Though it looked like he wasn't going to need to wait tables much longer. Jamie pulled open the refrigerator.

"You have to be kidding me!" Arty said with absolute delight. "No way!" He listened some more as Ryan closed the door, looking to where Arty stood, his eyes alight, practically dancing in the middle of the floor. "I'll be looking for the information tomorrow. Thank you. I take back every nasty thing I ever said about you." Arty laughed and then ended the call, whooping and racing over to Jamie, practically lifting him off the ground in his excitement.

"What's going on? I could hear you in the hall," Ryan said.

"Well," Arty said, "both of you get changed, we're going out for dinner. I did it. Broadway!" He could barely stand still. "A producer, one of the best, is mounting a production of a new play by Harold Meyer. It's not a starring role, and Margaret is going to send the script over, but she says it's a prime supporting role and they want me. She says a huge star has been contracted for the lead. She can't say who it is, and the run is limited to three months, though there is an option for three more. But it's Broadway, the big theaters."

Jamie hugged Arty tightly, both of them jumping up and down, with Arty pulling in Ryan and the three of them shaking the entire floor. "We definitely need to celebrate," Ryan said, and then Jamie explained his news. "I need to go change." Ryan hurried to his room, and Arty tugged Jamie into theirs, closing the door.

"We're both on our way," Jamie said, and Arty nodded. "I know, don't count on anything."

"Exactly," Arty said as he tugged Jamie into a hug. "But this is a red-letter day, one of the best of my life."

"Not the best?" Jamie asked, because both of them signing for deals that could make their careers was pretty auspicious.

"Nope, not even close. The best day of my life will always be the day I was at the Pelican, when this adorable man in jeans and a T-shirt came up to me, mashing his hat in his fist, to ask for a fishing job."

"That was some trip," Jamie said, remembering how nervous he'd been.

"Yes, it was." Arty pushed his fingers through Jamie's hair. "Who could have possibly known then that you, Jamie Wilson, would turn out to be the catch of a lifetime?"

Epilogue

SOMETIMES ARTY never knew what was going to happen. Who could have known that Jamie's Off-Broadway play would be a big enough success that a larger production would be mounted and Jamie asked to reprise his role, with Arty being given the role of the other son? And who would ever have thought that both of their fathers would come to New York to sit in the front row, opening night? In a way, it was life imitating art, the healing of old wounds… resulting in happiness and joy. Standing on that stage was a dream come true, and Arty tried to see beyond the lights and the roar of the crowd to the people out front. It was nearly impossible. So much light came at the stage that it was impossible to see through. Arty took his bow and held out his hand. On his left was their leading lady, looking radiant, her eyes sparkling with excitement as adulation came their way and only intensified as the audience cheered.

A stagehand in black moved closer, placing red roses in her hand, and she beamed, holding the flowers close to her as she took another bow. She took Arty's extended his hand, and Jamie took his other. He couldn't help looking over at him. After a roller coaster year of career ups and downs, learning to live together, and actually... somehow, finding the time to love and maybe have a few minutes to talk, they had arrived at this spot—together—in a stunning opening night.

Jamie squeezed his hand as the entire cast stepped forward, took a bow, and then stepped back. They did the same as the applause continued, and then the curtain lowered and Arty held his breath. The curtain rose again, and this time the lighting was different so he could see beyond the lights and out to the first row of seats.

The cast stepped back, and Arty went to the center of the stage. He'd arranged to be the one to speak briefly. "All of us want to thank you for coming here tonight. This show is about fathers and sons." He held out his hand, and Jamie came forward to take it. "It's particularly meaningful tonight because both of our fathers are here, right in the front row." The audience applauded, and Arty smiled out at the crowd. "We're so happy that both of them could be here." He looked at his father sitting next to Jamie's, and applauded for them. "Having you all join us is amazing, and we want to leave you with this thought.... If we all listen a little more and talk a little less, we can do anything." That had been true in the show and in their real lives. It continued to guide his and Jamie's relationship.

The audience rose to their feet with thunderous applause, and the cast stepped forward for one last curtain call before the red velvet fell and Arty drew Jamie into a kiss.

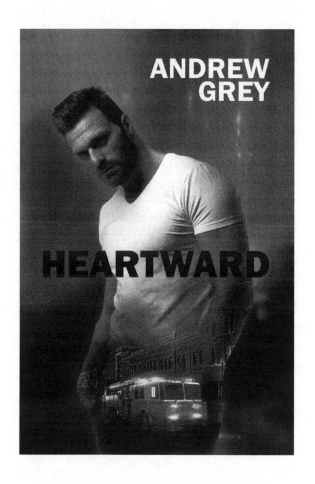

He doesn't know that home is where his heart will be....

Firefighter Tyler Banik has seen his share of adventure while working disaster relief with the Red Cross. But now that he's adopted Abey, he's ready to leave the danger behind and put down roots. That means returning to his hometown—where the last thing he anticipates is falling for his high school nemesis.

Alan Pettaprin isn't the boy he used to be. As a business owner and council member, he's working hard to improve life in Scottville for everyone. Nobody is more surprised than Alan when Tyler returns, but he's glad. For him, it's a chance to set things right. Little does he guess he and Tyler will find the missing pieces of themselves in each other. Old rivalries are left in the ashes, passion burns bright, and the possibility for a future together stretches in front of them....

But not everyone in town is glad to see Tyler return....

TYLER BANIK sighed as he drove the rental car down the freeway. He probably should have just gotten a hotel, but he was tired of traveling, and after being delayed and diverted, he had figured it was better to drive than to try to fly. His parents were expecting them, and all Tyler wanted was to get where he was supposed to be.

Abey, short for Abraham, stretched in his car seat, and Tyler was afraid he was going to wake up, but he settled once again. Tyler pulled his attention out of the rearview mirror and back to the road ahead. At least he was settled and not fussing the way he had for much of the journey across the Atlantic. Not that Tyler could blame him. The flight wasn't the most comfortable, and Tyler could understand why Abey hadn't been at all interested in the food.

"Papa," Abey said groggily, and Tyler slowed and pulled off to the side of the road. This had been one hell of a long trip.

"Are you thirsty?" Tyler asked, already fishing through the bag on the passenger seat for the cooler with the sippy cup.

"Potty," Abey said, and Tyler pulled back into traffic, never so grateful to see one of those supertall McDonald's signs shining over the trees ahead.

"Okay. There's one just ahead. We'll be there in a minute." Tyler wasn't sure how much of what he had just said Abey comprehended with his language barrier and age, but he got off the freeway, parked, and helped Abey out of the seat before taking him inside and rushing to the bathroom. Abey hurried into the stall and used the toilet like the big boy he was, or at least wanted to be. When he was done, Tyler helped him get his pants pulled up and flushed. "Are you hungry?"

Abey thought a second and nodded, so Tyler took him to the sink, held him while he washed his hands, and then put him down. He took his hand as they stepped out and up to the counter. Tyler ordered some chicken nuggets, fries, and some apple slices for Abey, along with some milk, and then took the dinner to the table. Abey climbed right up and tucked into the food as though he hadn't seen any in days. Whatever Tyler put in front of him, Abey shoveled into his mouth as fast as he could chew and swallow. It broke his heart to see it, even after six months, but he let Abey eat and didn't try to sneak one of his french fries. Tyler had come to realize that Abey wouldn't understand and would become very upset.

Once he was done, Tyler lifted Abey into his arms, his son curling in for warmth and almost immediately falling to sleep. Tyler took care of the trash and went to the counter, quietly placed a to-go order for himself, and once it was ready, left the restaurant. He got Abey buckled in, slid in the driver's seat, and returned to the highway before eating his own food one-handed.

His phone rang as he finished the last of his fries. "Hey, Mom," Tyler said, answering the phone and putting it on speaker. "We're just getting past Grand Rapids, so we're a couple of hours out yet."

"Okay." She sounded tired. "The man with the house called and asked when you wanted the keys. You know the two of you could just stay here."

"It's okay, Mom. I'll call and leave him a message." Not that they had a great deal of things to worry about. After three years of travel from one relief location to another, and living out of suitcases and what he could carry, Tyler was looking forward to having a place of his own. Besides, he and his dad didn't exactly see eye to eye on things, and his mom…. Tyler loved her, but after too much time under the same roof, they would stomp each other's last nerves. "You go on to bed. I have Abey's things in the car, and I can set them up in my old room with me."

"Don't be silly," his mother said. "I'll see you when you get here." She hung up, and Tyler continued driving.

Abey slept the rest of the trip, and Tyler was never so grateful to see the freeway exit to Scottville in his life. He took it and navigated to his parents' home on the edge of town. He pulled into the drive and turned off the engine, staring at the ranch house he'd grown up in and suppressing a sigh. He had made it. Six hours from Cleveland, after God knows how many hours from Venice. At least Abey was still asleep, and Tyler didn't want to wake him.

He got out of the car, and his mom came out, pulling her robe tighter around her against the spring chill in the air. Tyler hugged her. "Where's my grandson?"

That single question nearly brought tears to his eyes. "Abey is asleep, Mom. We've been traveling for so long that he's just worn out." Tyler popped open the trunk and pulled out their suitcases. His mom took the small one as his dad came out.

The greeting was tense. His father hugged him, but there was no warmth in it, like his dad thought it's what he should do, so he did it. He took the bags and went right back inside. Tyler opened the car door, unbuckled Abey, and lifted him out of the seat. Abey barely stirred, and closing the car door and leaving everything else until morning, Tyler followed his mother inside.

He carried his son through the familiar house, which hadn't really changed in twenty years, and down the hall to his old room. It hadn't changed much either. Well, it was clean and neat, and his mother had cleared out a lot of his things, but the pictures of exotic cars and the bedspread were the same. Tyler got Abey's jacket and clothes off and pulled a pair of pajamas on him. Then he turned down the bed and put Abey in it. Thankfully, he settled right back down and was slumbering within seconds.

Tyler sat on the side of the bed, watching Abey, his heart sighing with relief. They had gotten home, overcoming all the months of challenges and roadblocks.

"Tyler," his mother whispered when she cracked the door open.

"I'll be right there." He adjusted Abey's covers and then slowly stood and left the room, cracking the door in case Abey woke. Tyler found his mother in the kitchen, sitting at the table with a cup of tea. "Is Dad in bed?"

"He has to work in the morning." There was little else she needed to say.

Tyler pulled out a chair and sat down, his head drooping forward.

"Are you all done with disaster relief now?"

"Yes. Abey pretty much saw to that." He was a fireman and EMT by trade, and after finishing school, went to work for the St. Louis Fire Department. When his life completely fell off the rails, he needed a change and took a job with Red Cross Disaster Relief because he thought it would be a great way to help people and see the world.

"Why didn't you go back to St. Louis?" she asked as she slid over a mug.

Tyler took it absently and sipped the hot brew. "There's nothing for me there now, and it's for the best. I left to start over and ended up taking a three-year detour. Now it's time I built a life, and the department here offered a job." He took another sip. "I thought that maybe it was time to come home." Lord knows he had done a shit job with his life on his own. "And I have Abey now."

"I still don't understand how that came to be." She finished her tea, stood, and pushed in the chair. Tyler was well aware of how his mom and dad felt about the entire situation, though it was completely irrelevant as far as he was concerned.

"I'll tell you all about it eventually." He drank the now-cooled tea and took both mugs to the sink. "I'm going to go to bed. I don't have to do anything tomorrow before noon, so don't wake either of us, please." He left the room and went to where Abey was still asleep. Tyler changed into a T-shirt and shorts and climbed into bed with Abey. There would be time tomorrow to get all the things they needed so Abey could have his own bed. Right now, Tyler was too tired to think about it. He rolled onto his side and closed his eyes.

For good or bad, he was home, and that carried with it issues but also a sense of peace. His hope was that the little town would be slower-paced and make things easier for Abey, in contrast to the big city. Only time would tell if this was a good decision or the worst one of his life.

A SOFT poke on the shoulder woke him, followed by another. Then a giggle and footsteps on the floor. Tyler kept his eyes closed, listening for another giggle and waiting for a pounce. When it came, Tyler held Abey as he tugged him up onto the bed, to much laughter. It had taken months to hear that expression of joy, and it rang in Tyler's ears as the most wonderful sound on earth.

"I heard you," his mother said as she cracked the door open.

Abey immediately stilled, grew silent, and then buried his face in the covers.

"That's your grandma. She's really nice. I promise." Tyler held Abey closer and waited for him to lift his face out of the blankets. "It's okay." He sat up and lifted Abey along with him. He went right to him, burying his face in Tyler's neck.

"I'm making you something to eat," his mom said quietly.

"Thanks. I'm going to get him cleaned up, and then we'll be out." He held Abey tightly and grabbed some of their stuff. He had gotten used to doing a lot of tasks one-handed, and once his mom had gone and closed the door, Abey let Tyler put him down. Tyler grabbed some fresh clothes and things, then headed to the bathroom with Abey.

Tyler got Abey washed up and helped him dress. Abey wanted to do it himself, which took three times as long, but Tyler could be patient and was relieved that Abey was acting a little more like a normal three-year-old. "Are you hungry?"

Abey nodded.

"Grandma is making us something to eat." Tyler knelt down right in front of him. "Your grandma is very nice, and she is going to love you a lot. I promise." God, he wished he knew if Abey understood him at all. Most of the time, he talked but thought all of it went right over Abey's head. Not that he could blame him. This entire situation was difficult for both of them, but all the change for Abey had to be overwhelming his young mind.

Abey hugged him around the neck, and Tyler lifted him up. Few things in the world were as rewarding as those hugs. He carried Abey out of the bathroom and back to the bedroom, where Tyler changed quickly and took Abey into the kitchen.

It was nearly eleven and his mom had made pancakes. Tyler got Abey in a chair and placed a plate of cut-up pancake and a few pieces of bacon in front of him. Abey tasted the pancake and must have liked it, because he started shoveling in the food like crazy.

"Slow down, honey. No one is going to take your food away," Tyler's mother scolded, and Tyler shook his head.

"That's exactly what he thinks, Mom. Abey has been without food before. He was undernourished and probably starving when I found him, so he eats every meal as though it's his last."

The pieces of pancake disappeared into his little mouth, and he only slowed down when the first pancake was gone and Tyler added some more to his plate. Then he settled in to eat more slowly.

"Here," his mom said, flipping three pancakes off the griddle and onto a plate for him.

Tyler sat down, and Abey watched him until Tyler began to eat. She brought over a plate of bacon, and Tyler took a few pieces and added one more to Abey's plate. He fisted it in his left hand, eating pancakes with his right.

"My God."

"It will be okay, Mom. Things are getting better, but it will take some time for the memories to fade." At least he hoped to God they would.

"Does he talk?"

"Some. But he was learning another language up until six months ago, so he says things I don't understand. I am teaching him English, and he's picking it up pretty well. He's like a sponge, Mom, but there's a lot going on with him right now."

Abey finished the last of his food, and Tyler got up for some paper towels, washed him up, and followed Abey out of the room. In the bedroom, Tyler fished in the bags until he found Abey's toys, then handed him the worn stuffed monkey. Abey cradled it to him, and Tyler grabbed the rest of the toys and carried Abey to the living room. He set Abey down with the toys, intending to let him play, when his mom came in. She sat down and leaned forward, trying to get Abey's attention.

"Let him come to you. He will eventually, just out of curiosity." He settled to watch, and Abey played with the cars.

"You didn't tell me what happened," his mom said, and Tyler sat back. She seemed… not older than the last time he'd seen her so much as more tired.

"It's a long story." And one he really didn't have the energy to talk about right now. "You'll find out soon enough."

Abey stood and hurried over to him, holding out his monkey. Tyler took it and placed the floppy stuffy on the sofa next to him. Abey went back to playing, and then after a few minutes, took the monkey back and ran it around in the back of the truck.

"I got him some toys when you called to say you were coming. I wasn't sure what he needed, so…."

"Mom, Abey's things fit in the little blue suitcase that you carried in last night. That's all there is, and everything I have is in the ones I brought. There's nothing else. I've gone from the site of one humanitarian disaster to another over the last three years, and Abey—" Tyler's throat clenched and he shook his head. "I'm sure what you got is perfect. I want to go to the store, and once we get into the house, I'll need to get furniture and things. I also need to return the car to the rental place." There was one in Ludington, so he had made sure to use the rental place that he could return there. "And I need to buy one."

"Where did you get the car seat?" his mother asked.

"The Red Cross provided it for Abey, and I brought it with us on the plane." They had been so supportive for months.

Abey got up off the floor with his monkey and carried it to Tyler's mom. He held it, watching his mom, and then set it on the arm of her chair. Abey turned around and went back to playing. His mom reached for the toy, and Tyler shook his head.

"Leave it right there, Mom. He knows where it is and he trusted you with it."

She narrowed her eyes. "It's just a stuffy, and a beaten-up one at that. I should take him to the store so he can pick out a new one."

"No."

"Where did it come from?" she asked, lifting it off the arm.

Abey hurried over and practically jumped up on her lap, snatched back the monkey, tucking it under his arm, and went back to his trucks.

"I told you. It's his favorite toy, and he trusted you with it. Next time, just leave it. The doctors I talked with said that they think he uses the toy as a surrogate, putting it out there first to see if it's okay. If the toy is good, then he might follow. But if something happens to Simeon, then Abey stays away. I've seen it time and time again."

His mom smiled when Abey looked at her again, and he came over to her. This time he held Simeon, but let her ruffle his hair. "Do you want some juice?" she asked, and Abey turned to him. Tyler nodded, and his mom slowly got up and left the room.

"I have sippy cups for him."

"I washed the one from last night." She returned with his cup, and Abey took it, then hurried over to stand by Tyler, Simeon tucked under his arm, his free hand clutching his pant leg as he drank.

"Can you say thank you?" Tyler prompted.

Abey pulled the cup out of his mouth, looking at his mom, but didn't say anything.

"You need to be nice and say thank you." Tyler was trying to teach him to be polite.

"Fank you," Abey said, and put the cup back in his mouth.

Tyler leaned down, praising him softly and ruffling his hair. He loved it when Abey looked at him, smiling from behind the cup.

"When do you start your new job?"

"Monday, though I want to stop in to the station so I can meet some of the other guys before I start. There's also some paperwork and background information that they asked for, and I wanted to get that to them." He was looking forward to starting something new.

"All right. Do you want me to follow you to drop off the car, and then I can take you where you need to go?" She checked her watch. "I'm supposed to work at four."

"It's all right. I don't want to put you out. The agency will give me a ride after I drop off the rental, and I thought I'd buy a car." Lord knew he had the money. For years his salary had been deposited in the bank each month, and since most of the time he'd ended up living in camps alongside the people he was trying to help, his expenses had been limited.

"Do you want to go for a car ride?" Tyler asked Abey, who handed him his empty cup and nodded.

"Potty?" Another nod, so Tyler took Abey down to the bathroom. He used it, and Tyler got them ready to go.

"Will you be home for dinner? I work until eight, so I can tell your father to bring home enough of whatever he gets for dinner." Obviously with his mom working, his dad hadn't bothered to learn to cook.

"That would be good." Tyler had hoped to be able to talk to his dad alone, and maybe he'd get the chance tonight.

Abey pulled on his pant leg, and Tyler said goodbye to his mom, scooped Abey up, and flew him toward the door. The sound of his son's laughter rang like a well-tuned bell that touched the soul. He got him out to the car and into the car seat. Then he remembered all the stuff they'd left inside and hurriedly emptied the car of trash and the debris of their trip before pulling out of the drive to make the once-familiar drive to Ludington, the next town over by the lake.

Turning the car in wasn't a problem, and the agent had someone drive them to the local Ford dealership, where he got them out of the car, held Abey's hand, and received permission to put Abey's car seat in the salesman's office. Then he and his son went to look at cars.

Abey only wanted to look at the red ones, and in the end, Tyler picked out a red Escape, signed all the paperwork, and after making a few calls to wire the money, was able to drive it off the lot, with Abey in his car seat in back. Tyler was thirty-four, and this was his first brand-new car.

It was sunny, so he decided to drive through downtown to the park by the lake, actually finding a spot to park. He got Abey out, and Abey ran over to the fenced-in area with playground equipment, staring through to where the other kids played.

"You can go play." Tyler took his hand to lead him around to the gate, and Abey raced inside. Tyler sat on one of the swings, put Abey on his lap, and slowly moved back and forth. Abey didn't much like it and hurried off to watch the other kids on the climbing fort. That he loved, and Tyler watched as he played, at first alone, but soon enough with the other small children.

"Tyler? Tyler Banik?" someone called, and he turned toward the voice. It took him a second to recognize him. "It's Joey Sutherland."

"I remember." Though the scars, now faded, that marred part of his face were different than in high school, he remembered the eyes and the smile. "How are you?" He went over to shake his hand.

"Good. I heard you were coming back to town. It doesn't take long to get people talking around here, and you returning has some of the ladies in town wondering if they should bring their daughters past the firehouse." He smiled, and Tyler shook his head.

"Barking up the wrong tree, I'm afraid," Tyler said, turning to watch where Abey played. "It's been a long time since high school." He'd left town after graduation, gone to college, and then on to firefighter and EMT training.

"Thank God for that. Some things around here never change, and other things…." Joey pointed to a table in the shade where a man sat with what looked like a tablet in front of him. "That's my husband, Robbie." Apparently quite a bit had changed for both of them.

Abey raced over, and Tyler picked him up. "Firstly," he whispered, and Tyler bounced him.

"Then we can go to the snack bar and get you something to drink." He smiled. "Abey, this is an old friend of your papa's. Joey, this is my son, Abey."

Of course, Abey chose that moment to be shy and hid his face against Tyler's shoulder.

"If you're headed that way, I'll walk with you," Joey volunteered. "Just let me tell Robbie." He jogged over to the table, then after a brief conversation, returned, checking his wallet. "It seems I have an order to get." They walked together, with Abey eventually getting over some of his shyness.

"What are you doing now?" Tyler asked.

"I manage crop production at Laughton Farms out on Stiles and Sugar Grove. Robbie and I have a house just up the road, and he manages the office for Geoff. It's turned into quite a big operation. Geoff has upward of four thousand head of cattle now, and we have thousands of acres under cultivation to support them." Joey seemed proud of what he did. "I hear you're joining the fire department. They've been looking for someone to fill that captain's position for a while."

"Yeah. I was in the department in St. Louis for seven years and worked my way up. I spent the last few years working for the Red Cross." Tyler held Abey a little tighter as the familiar jittery butterflies awakened in his belly. "Do you want french fries too?" Tyler asked Abey, who nodded. He ordered fries and two drinks. "You need to share with me. Okay?"

Abey didn't look like he thought too much of that.

"You should share with your papa, because he shares with you. Right?" Joey asked, and Abey seemed unsure but nodded. At least he didn't hide this time. Joey placed his order, and once the food came, they carried it back to the table.

"Robbie, this is Tyler and his son, Abey," Joey said as they approached. "I went to high school with Tyler—I think he was a year behind me then."

"It's good to meet you." Robbie held out his hand, and Tyler set Abey down to shake it.

"Abey, this is Robbie. He isn't able to see," Tyler explained, and put his hands over his eyes to demonstrate.

Tyler wasn't sure if he should say anything, but he wanted Abey to be aware. Abey turned to him, tilting his head slightly like he either didn't understand or was confused. Tyler nodded, and Abey turned to Robbie, watching him and then waving his hand. Okay, so Abey really did understand more than Tyler thought. He had to keep himself from chuckling, but Robbie just searched for his food with his hands and didn't say a word. Abey then turned away and dug into the french fries like he hadn't eaten in weeks.

"That wasn't very nice," Tyler scolded, though Abey ignored him in favor of the food.

"Is Abey your biological child?" Robbie asked.

"No. He's been with me for six months, and the adoption papers came through just two weeks ago." Tyler didn't go into all the palms that had to be greased to make it happen, but it didn't matter now. Abey was his, and of all the decisions he had made in his life, good or bad, this one was the one he was certain of. "We left Italy just yesterday and flew for hours. We were supposed to fly into Grand Rapids, but there was fog and they couldn't land, so we got diverted to Cleveland and drove the rest of the way.

So we're still getting acclimated to the time zone." He snagged a few of the fries, and that only made Abey try to eat faster.

"I understand. I hate plane travel. Every time I do it, I get really disoriented. The plane is noisy, and the change in pressure messes with my ears, so I can't hear very well. I've heard stories about deaf people who lose their sense of equilibrium in dark places because they orient themselves almost strictly by sight. Well, I do the same audibly, and with the engines and so much surrounding noise, it's hard to find anything to orient to. The last time we went to Natchez…."

"I held your hand the entire time, and you did amazingly well," Joey told him. "I got him noise-canceling headphones to see if they would help and then hooked them to my iPhone so he could listen to music." Joey guided Robbie the last way to his food without breaking the conversation at all.

"Are you in town to stay?" Robbie asked.

"I'm joining the fire company as a captain," Tyler answered, and Robbie patted Joey on the arm. "What is it?"

Robbie patted Joey again. "Tell him."

"What?" Tyler turned to Joey.

"The chief, Tillis Coburn… there have been rumors about him that go through town every few years. No one seems to know if they're true, but…."

"What sort of rumors?" Great, just what he needed. Tyler had come here to start over and have the chance to build a quiet life for Abey. He wasn't looking for a bunch of small-town drama.

"Okay. Here's the deal. About three years ago, a family out on Jebavy Road were cleaning out their grandmother's house to get it ready for sale, and they found a trunk in the attic. It was filled with robes and documents related to the KKK. I know you don't think of that sort of thing here, but they were everywhere apparently. And prejudice and intolerance may not wear white robes any longer, but they exist. Anyway, the family wanted to get rid of them, and when they had the auction, there was a huge amount of interest. Geoff and Eli went because there were things they wanted for the farm. But they said that most of the people there were interested in the KKK stuff. The police had to keep order with the number of people there. What I do know is that Chief Coburn was bidding on that stuff, and there were rumors about him before that."

Tyler gaped in disbelief. "You think that the fire chief in Scottville, Michigan, is a member of the KKK?" That idea didn't seem believable to him.

"I know it sounds ridiculous, but the rumors haven't died down, and frankly, he hasn't done anything to change them… if you know what I mean. He probably isn't a member, but he also isn't exactly the most tolerant person, especially when it comes to gay people or diversity of any kind. People just started equating the two things in their minds. Look at the department when you get there. It's lily white, and there are no women either. He keeps saying that there are no qualified applicants, but I don't believe that. Did he hire you? Because you're obviously white, but if there was any hint of the gay…."

"No. I applied to the council, and they hired me. I figured since it was a senior position, they had gotten involved."

"Maybe, and maybe it's because they wanted to make sure the screening process was done correctly and fairly." Joey seemed to believe the rumors. "Either way, be careful. If the rumors are true, then you aren't going to find favor with him because of how the council hired you, and if they're not, then something else seems to be going on."

"Joey, don't scare him. Yes, there have been rumors, but no one can prove anything. If they could, he'd be gone. Even out here, people aren't going to stand for that sort of thing as long as it can be proved. Coburn has been on the job for a while."

That didn't bode well either. If this was true, then it was possible that Coburn's ideas permeated the entire department. Tyler was going to need to be careful to check out the attitudes of the various firefighters. Shit, this was not at all the kind of thing he expected, though maybe he should have. Lord knows. "I'll be careful."

Abey had eaten the last of the food and drank his milk. He settled in Tyler's lap, resting against his chest, and would probably go to sleep.

"It looks like he's ready for a nap."

"Yeah." Tyler stood. "It was good seeing both of you."

"You should come out to the farm and bring Abey. Eli does therapy riding, and he has ponies and things. I bet Abey would love a ride," Robbie said, extending his hand.

Tyler shook it and said goodbye to both of them, then carefully carried Abey back to the SUV and got him in his seat.

The drive back to Scottville took about fifteen minutes, and he called along the way to arrange to get the keys to their house. He met the landlord at the small house a block off the main street. Abey woke as soon as he pulled to a stop, and Tyler got him out. "Mr. Wilson?"

"You must be Tyler." They shook hands, and he unlocked the house and handed Tyler the keys. The building had been well maintained. There was only a living and dining room, kitchen, a bath and a half, and two bedrooms, but it was enough for them.

"That's your room, Abey," Tyler said as he let him go inside the empty space. He had tried to find a furnished place, but there wasn't anything. "It looks great, thank you," Tyler said as he turned around in what would be their new home. He hadn't had a place of his own in quite a while.

"There's a second-time-around store just outside of town. You might look there for some furniture and things if you need it. At least it's a place to start."

"Thank you." The idea of starting over completely just hit him. He and Abey were going to need everything from a sofa to chairs, a table, and beds. He signed the paperwork he needed to in order to finalize the rental and handed the pen and papers back to the agent. "I appreciate your help."

"Here's my number if you need anything," Mr. Wilson said, and he left the house.

Tyler returned to where he left Abey and found him standing at the window in his room, looking out into the backyard. Tyler followed his gaze and smiled. "Yes. There's a swing set, and it's for you to play on." He lifted Abey into his arms and swung him around, to laughter. "This is where you and I are going to live." It was going to be their home. Now he just had to figure out how he was going to make it feel that way.

ANDREW GREY is the author of more than one hundred works of Contemporary Gay Romantic fiction. After twenty-seven years in corporate America, he has now settled down in Central Pennsylvania with his husband, Dominic, and his laptop. An interesting ménage. Andrew grew up in western Michigan with a father who loved to tell stories and a mother who loved to read them. Since then he has lived throughout the country and traveled throughout the world. He is a recipient of the RWA Centennial Award, has a master's degree from the University of Wisconsin–Milwaukee, and now writes full-time. Andrew's hobbies include collecting antiques, gardening, and leaving his dirty dishes anywhere but in the sink (particularly when writing). He considers himself blessed with an accepting family, fantastic friends, and the world's most supportive and loving partner. Andrew currently lives in beautiful, historic Carlisle, Pennsylvania.

Email: andrewgrey@comcast.net

Website: www.andrewgreybooks.com

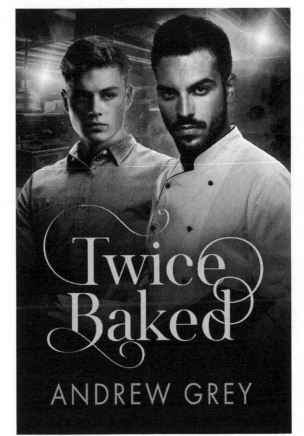

Twice
Baked

ANDREW GREY

When the pickiest eater in America is tapped to judge a cooking competition along with his chef ex-boyfriend, will it be a recipe for a second chance... or disaster?

Luke Walker's humor about foods he can't stand made him an internet celebrity and his blog, The Pickiest Eater in America, a huge hit. He plans to bring that same lighthearted comedy to the show—but he won't be the only host.

Meyer Thibodeaux might be a famous chef, but he's solemn, uptight, and closeted. He's also Luke's ex. As different as they are, the sparks between Luke and Meyer never really went out, and as they work together, each begins to see the other in a new light, and the passion between them reignites, hot as ever. But secrets, gossip, and rumors on the set could sour their reunion.

www.dreamspinnerpress.com